ELIOT BLISS

was born in Jamaica in 1903, the daughter of Eva
Lees and John Plomer Bliss. Her father, an English
army officer with the West India Regiment, was
stationed at the garrison there, and in Sierra Leone
on the Gold Coast. Eliot was educated at convents in
England, and on leaving school she lived for a year
with her grandmother in Strawberry Hill, Twicken-
ham. In 1923 she and her brother joined their
parents in Jamaica. She left for England in 1925,
never to return, and later her family emigrated to
South Africa.

It was at this time that she adopted the name
Eliot, from T. S. and George Eliot, whom she
admired, and because it was a family name. She took
a diploma in Journalism at University College
London, going on to work in publishing, for Faber
& Faber, and for the literary agents A. M. Heath.
She had begun writing as a child, stories and poetry.
Her first novel, *Saraband* was published in 1931 and
this was followed in 1934 by *Luminous Isle*, also
published by Virago. A part of literary life in
London of the 1930s, Eliot's friends included
Dorothy Richardson, Jean Rhys, Romer Wilson,
Vita Sackville-West and the poet Anna Wickham,
who had a great influence on her life.

At the outbreak of the Second World War Eliot
Bliss moved to the East Coast of Britain to escape the
Blitz. She now lives in Bishop's Stortford, Hert-
fordshire.

SARABAND

ELIOT BLISS

WITH A NEW INTRODUCTION BY
PAUL BAILEY

> *Down Time's quaint stream*
> *Without an oar,*
> *We are enforced to sail,*
> *Our Port—a secret——*
> *Our Perchance—a gale.*
> *What Skipper would*
> *Incur the risk,*
> *What Buccaneer would ride,*
> *Without a surety from the wind*
> *Or schedule of the tide?*
>
> EMILY DICKINSON.

PENGUIN BOOKS – VIRAGO PRESS

PENGUIN BOOKS
Viking Penguin Inc., 40 West 23rd Street,
New York, New York 10010, U.S.A.
Penguin Books Ltd, Harmondsworth,
Middlesex, England
Penguin Books Australia Ltd, Ringwood,
Victoria, Australia
Penguin Books Canada Limited, 2801 John Street,
Markham, Ontario, Canada L3R 1B4
Penguin Books (N.Z.) Ltd, 182-190 Wairau Road,
Auckland 10, New Zealand

First published in Great Britain by Peter Davies 1931
First published in the United States of America by
William Morrow & Co., Inc. 1931
This edition first published in Great Britain by
Virago Press Limited 1986
Published in Penguin Books 1987

Printed in Great Britain by
Anchor Brendon, Tiptree, Essex
set in Caslon

INTRODUCTION

When *Saraband* was published in 1931, a reviewer compared its young author to the then already mature Ivy Compton-Burnett, whose *Men and Wives* appeared that year. It's an odd comparison, for reason of its being so wildly inexact, since no two writers could have less in common. We know from Hilary Spurling's superb biography that Ivy Compton-Burnett had little patience with novelists who indulged in lengthy descriptions of places and people. 'It really is full of *very* good descriptions,' she once observed of a novel by Olivia Manning in the course of a conversation with Elizabeth Taylor. 'Quite excellent descriptions. I don't know if you care for descriptions? I don't.'

Saraband contains any number of 'quite excellent descriptions', for this is a book conceived and designed descriptively. Practically everything is seen through the eyes and felt through the sensibility of Louise Charlotte Mallord Burnett—Louie—as she grows slowly towards adulthood. Louie is a girl who notices birds and trees (a willow, in Leathley, Eliot Bliss's imaginary Berkshire village, has a 'Rabelaisian face' that is 'always laughing') and the subtle changes of the seasons. As a consequence, she tends to look at the men and women (relatives, mostly) with whom she comes into contact either in the forefront or in the background—in other words, in relation to objects and furnishings or to the weather. They are seldom just people talking—as they are, imposingly, in the fiction of Ivy Compton-Burnett.

There is no plot, in the conventional sense, in *Saraband*. The story, such as it is, is slow moving, like the dance of the title. Its characters, with one belligerent exception, behave with a certain decorousness, as the dancers of a saraband are required to do. They age, these characters, almost imperceptibly, in the manner of one's friends and acquaintances in the real world. Eliot Bliss knew from the start of her lamentably brief career as a novelist that it's the accidental that causes the most severe jolts to our sense of well-being, and there is one such telling jolt in *Saraband* when a young girl falls to her death down the lift shaft at Bengartens, the dingy college Louie is attending in order to learn shorthand and typing. It happens off-stage, as it were—but the reader is made to feel its effect on Louie. Her new friend, the outgoing, chatty Jonquil, sees the accident as just another aspect of life—an awful aspect to be cluck-clucked over and then put firmly out of mind. For Louie, who has thought about death and dying throughout her childhood, it has considerably more significance. It gives her a mental and physical jolt, in fact.

Ivy Compton-Burnett's novels are constructed on the principles of Aristotelian drama. Things happen in them, for all that those—usually terrible—things are recounted chorus-fashion. The family skeletons can be heard rattling in that unique dialogue, making a chilling and sombre music. The things that happen in *Saraband* are rarely dramatic and seldom mentioned. Past suffering is felt, of course, and occasionally summoned up when someone glances at an old photograph, but it is relegated to a place far beneath the surface of everyday discourse. Perhaps the most beautiful scene in the novel occurs when Louie's beloved cousin—the brilliant violinist, Tim—calls on her at her convent school, Mexican Gate, bearing the news that her father's ship has gone down at sea. The time is 1915, or thereabouts:

She took her hands away from him and went to the piano seat. She knelt with one knee on the hard upholstery and stared over the piano at the picture of the Vatican. In that moment she was swung out into space and the world seemed to cease to exist. She was leaning against iron-grey railings on the deck of a man-of-war in mid ocean. There was a high wind blowing and a grey swell on the sea and the ship pitched. There was nothing at all in sight but the sea, and a grey sea it was. Byng had told her to stay there and he would come to her in a minute, and so she would stay, although it was extremely cold. The wind seemed to scrape one's cheeks. She moved her knee against something and found it to be the hard, raised pattern of the piano seat, and that she was looking at the picture of the Vatican which hung inside its velvet frame over the piano. Tim came across the room to her and put his hands on her shoulders. The fog seemed to be lifting outside, because it was lighter. She leant her head against him and let her hand lie in those exceedingly beautiful fingers—fingers that hardly looked practical enough to belong to a musician, to the hand of a performer. The end of the world was in the parlour with the stiff-backed chairs. It had been brought to her by the most civilised of people.

That passage evokes something of the hallucinatory quality—the vague, numbing dullness—of the first stage of bereavement. Grief has a way of knocking one all but senseless, and it's that 'all but' Eliot Bliss captures here. This entire section of *Saraband* exhibits an astonishing maturity in the twenty-eight-year-old novelist, and it is dismaying to reflect that she was to produce only one other book—the extraordinary *Luminous Isle*—before lapsing into a lifelong silence.

It's dismaying on several counts, not the least of which is an ability to create young women in a state of subdued, but actual, rebellion. Like the slightly more extravagant Em in the second novel, Louie is on the verge of making great discoveries. She loves music, she writes poetry, she forms deep attachments to unusual and gifted people, the majority of whom are women. Both Em and Louie are unsure of what the future holds for them, but they are adamant in their denial of the lives their mothers led. These are girls who realise that the old world is collapsing: Louie, indeed, hears that it is from the lips of her reactionary and misogynistic Uncle Heston and can barely disguise her scorn for him. They are remarkable creatures, Em and Louie, because they are not flamboyant, not theatrical, not prominent—as yet—in the battle for the rights of their sex. They are both possessed of loving feelings—in Em's case, for the oppressed Blacks on the island of Jamaica; in Louie's, for her dreadfully sick friend, Barty, who is unable to escape from the clutches of a tyrant. With the awareness of those feelings is born a set of values—values, Eliot Bliss implies, that may not be so socially acceptable.

I can think of few novelists who have drawn so convincingly two such intelligent heroines. Em and Louie are nearly, but not quite, asexual. They are looking for a person, another free spirit, to release them—it might be a man, it could be a woman. Louie has Barty and Tim and Mark, alias Marcelle, to choose from—except that I feel, though I'm possibly wrong, that Tim has found his love in Mark's brother, Bernard. I know, because Eliot Bliss has made me know as a good novelist always does, that if Louie ever puts pen to paper seriously, she will come up with more substantial works than those accredited to the hysterical Stephen in Radclyffe Hall's *The Well of Loneliness*.

And it's really Radclyffe Hall to whom Eliot Bliss ought to be compared, so that a patent literary injustice can at last, I hope, be corrected. Hall's prose is earnest sludge; Bliss's is weighted, considered, and—at its best—properly lyrical. I say 'properly' because I don't think prose-poetry of the kind that draws attention to itself has a rightful place in a novel. Lyricism in Eliot Bliss's two books is part of her principal characters' natures, and thus earns its fictional keep. The relationships in *Saraband*—between Louie and her grandmother, Lulu; between Louie and the delicious Zara, her friend at Mexican Gate, and—especially—between Louie and Tim are sketched in with a subtlety quite beyond Hall's tub-thumping talent. The passion in Eliot Bliss's writing has been deliberately banked down, I suspect. It's there, though, unmistakably.

The slow-moving, delicately constructed *Saraband* contains one irritating stylistic device, I am compelled to say. How I wish that Eliot Bliss had substituted a necessary 'Louie' for the overworked pronoun 'she' at several key points in the narrative. But that's a tiny cavil. This is a lovely little book, as fresh and original today as it must have seemed to its discerning admirers fifty-five years ago.

Paul Bailey, London, 1986

I

ALL along the road from the river the frost made patterns on the ground, and how beautifully the air smelt . . . The sharp air hung over one's head like the blade of a knife, she imagined it saying 'Behold, you shall be cold, behold, you shall be cold . . .' Winter had a most exciting smell, it made one think of people whom one knew and yet had never met, places where at some time or other one felt sure one must have lived and yet could not remember. The frost hung on the trees, it made them look as if they had gone white during the night from fear, it gave them a very queer stark look.

Whenever she went out for a walk by herself, smelling the cold air all along the road, with the trees stark and white on either side, the exciting feeling took hold of her, the feeling that at any moment she was going to meet somebody or something. She had had it for years. Far away back when she was five years old she had had it; then she had believed in it, it had filled her with happiness, and each time, although it was only a repetition of the last, she had known the same disappointment. Once she remembered crying, but the days of crying over that at any rate, were over. It was a bad joke her brain played upon her, always at certain times of the year she had it. It did not matter what the season was; in spring when the leaves were coming and when the air had a kind of sparkling sweetness in it, in autumn when the air smelt of damp leaves and scented smoke, in summer too, though it was dim then—the shadows even seemed to be saying that the thing she had expected had come and gone, the flowers smelt heavy, the air was still, the thing had come but not to her. But in winter it was strongest of all; once outside the gate, and there it was, waiting in the cold air like the knife over one's head. Surely she must meet it this time, this time she would meet it, but she never did, and here she was returning along the road back to Linden.

She sighed, then she put the thought of it out of her mind because the frosty day reminded her of something else, the day of her first Communion. It had been December, so cold, just like this, with stinging air around one, the feast of the Immaculate Conception. She had worn a white velvet dress with a lace collar, a white veil and a crown of little wax roses. They had marched two and two into the convent chapel which had been decorated with flowers; a grand triumphant day like being married. The organ pealed and they went in, hands inside white silk gloves clasped together, singing 'Venez, Venez, Jésu'. The smell of new clothes, new prayer-books, the pealing, throbbing organ, the incense, the flowers, parents kneeling in rows, turning a little to glance as one came in and went to one's place in the benches set apart for the first communicants, lined with satin, hung with flowers and ferns. No, she would never forget that day; it was the only day in her life she felt she had really looked beautiful.

She arrived at the gate, it had *Linden* written on it in white letters. It was beginning to get dark, and the light was on in the dining-room. They always had tea in the dining-room because Lulu said she hated fussing about with cups on a small table, she had heard her say it to Aunt Gainy: 'The days of that sort of thing are over for me.' Perhaps they were already at tea and she would be scolded for being late; she hoped very much she wasn't late, on Lulu's birthday too. But Lulu wouldn't let her be scolded. Would she? No, of course she wouldn't. Ring the bell. Now, don't be nervous. How old are you? Eleven. Fancy that! One would never have thought it, my dear. She pressed her face against the cold glass in the upper part of the door, it was divided into red and green squares, and made the hall look from the outside by turns red and green, a strange interesting impression. But now the white frilled apron of Frances was appearing out of the green distance, the door was opened and the illusion destroyed.

'Hello, Frances, I've been for such a long walk by the river. Frances, am I late for tea?'

'No, Miss Louie, I was only just coming out to ring the gong.'

Thank goodness at least for that.

'Is mother in?'

'Yes, Miss Louie, she's in the drawing-room with the mistress, I think nearly everyone's in.' Frances paused, then she whispered: 'It's a cherry cake!'

'Oh, is it, Frances? How nice.'

She would go and take her things off. No, she wouldn't. She would just peep in and tell Lulu she was back. Frances stooped to ring the gong; what a tall woman she was. The thundering sound boomed through the hall and went up the stairs, she waited till it had died down, then she opened the door. She was hidden from them all by a black and gold screen which protected the piano from the draught caused by the door being constantly opened. She could see them through a crack in the screen. Lulu was sitting in her chair by the fireplace, her feet crossed on the footstool, she was knitting. Her mother and Aunt Gainy were sitting on the sofa, and in an arm-chair between them and Lulu was Aunt Elise, she was also knitting and she smoked while she knitted, she was always smoking.

'The gong's rung,' her mother said. Lulu's pince-nez dropped off her nose. 'Yes, I suppose we must be going in.'

'Oh, botheration!' said Aunt Gainy suddenly, slapping down the paper she had been reading on to her knee. 'I forgot to order those biscuits to-day. What a confounded nuisance!'

'Surely we won't want them to-day, dear,' said Lulu.

'Oh, probably not, but it only means I shall have to order them to-morrow, and ten to one I shall forget again.'

Aunt Elise laughed and shook her head; she had pert black eyes. Lulu got up, pulling her bag by its silver chain from the depths of her chair; she turned round and looked at them all, with her back to the mantelpiece.

'I wonder if my Louie's back yet,' she said.

It was strange to hear oneself talked about when one was not supposed to be there, it gave one the feeling of being invisible. She ran out from behind the screen.

'I'm back, Lulu, I'm back!'

Everybody looked up.

'Good heavens, child . . .' said Lulu, holding out her hands. 'Where have you come from? I never heard you come in.'

'I was hiding behind the screen.'

Lulu laughed. 'Have you had a nice walk?'

'Yes, lovely. I'll tell you about it afterwards. Going to take my things off now.'

She turned away and rushed out of the room. Upstairs, she threw her hat and coat on the bed and unbuttoned her gaiters; she stood before the wardrobe mirror to brush back her hair. Rats-tails her mother called it, and she was right. That was what it was, rats-tails. Uncle Heston had once told her that it was mouse-coloured, that meant no colour at all, it had hurt horribly for days, she had hardly been able to look at herself in the glass. What would happen? Would beauty come upon one suddenly when one was grown up? Would one's nose cease to spread, as it seemed to be threatening to do over one's face? Would one's hair change its colour and not hang in lank strands over one's shoulders? Or would people be a little more polite when one was grown-up and not make remarks?

The family were sitting round the table. She came in quietly and slipped into her place beside Lulu at the head of the table. She always sat there because Lulu liked to have her near.

'Where did you go, Louie?' asked her mother.

'Along by the river, down by the old houses where the big trees are.'

She loved watching Lulu pour the tea out of the huge pale blue Wedgwood teapot; the cups were handed round, her own small golden-rimmed cup was given to her.

'There,' said Lulu, smiling.

She smiled back. The great brass Indian tray spread itself out before them with the silver jugs and the slop basin and the marvellous teapot in the middle; she loved it because it was so fat, it was the fattest teapot she had ever seen. Uncle Philip came in and the door swung gently after him; he shuffled into his seat, next to Uncle Heston at the other end of the table.

'Well, how d'you feel to-day, Phil?' said Uncle Heston in his slow heavy voice which always sounded as if he was thinking over every word before he said it.

'Oh, much the same, you know, thanks, old chap. Heart's been playing me up again.'

Now that he had come, his large cup, which held half a pint easily with room to spare for more, had to be filled. It was a thick-rimmed cup with heavy yellow roses painted on it, and underneath the roses were the words:—*I am not greedy, but I like a lot*. It came on the table at breakfast and tea. He said the reason why he liked a large cup was that no cup of tea was like the first, every cup after the first was dish-wash. When she had asked him why, he said that he did not believe a good thing could ever be repeated. Aunt Elise and Aunt Gainy were talking about the cinema.

'Moving pictures will never replace the stage,'

Uncle Tony said, from the other side of the table.

'Ah, Tony, I'm not so sure,' said Aunt Elise. 'I shall never like them myself as much, but I rather think they're going to be the theatre of the future.'

Uncle Tony shook his head. 'No, the theatre of the future will not be moving pictures.'

He was in the theatre himself, though at the moment he was out of a job, that was why he had not liked her saying that about the cinematograph.

'Really, how can you tell, Tony?' said Aunt Gainy. She seemed to be annoyed with him.

'One can't tell, one can only speculate.'

And now he was rather cross too, and passed his cup up the table to Lulu.

'Well, I think the cinematograph is a marvellous invention,' her mother said emphatically.

'Yes, I enjoy the pictures very much,' said Lulu, pouring out Uncle Tony's second cup. 'It's so nice to be able to have a nap occasionally in the dark.'

For some reason everybody laughed. Then the birthday cake was cut, the cherry cake that Mary had made.

'That's your piece,' said Lulu, putting a slice on her plate.

'How silent our little Louie is to-day,' Aunt Elise said, smiling with those sharp black eyes. There was only one thing to do and she did it, she smiled politely back.

'She's dreaming,' her mother said, and there was a sigh in her voice. 'She's always dreaming. I think she lives in a world of her own.'

'Oh no, only brown studies,' said Aunt Elise pleasantly, but with a little sharpness. 'She'll grow out of it, Daisy was just the same at that age.'

She did not like Daisy and did not think that they were in the least alike, but she only picked a cherry out of the cake and ate it slowly so that she might enjoy every moment of its flavour. Tea was nearly over. The uncles and Aunt Elise lit up, nobody else smoked.

The dining-room was dark. The lights hanging over the table under the pink shade gave the things on the table, and even the pale yellow tea-cloth spread in three corner-wise fashion, a slightly rosy look. The fire was burning behind Lulu's chair under the tall black marble mantelpiece; now and then a streak of yellow light flared up on to the dark red walls and lit up the pictures hanging there, one on top of another so close together, nearly all of them oil paintings. Pictures of the sea in rough, squally, and calm weather. Pictures of fish. Pictures of houses where Lulu and the family had lived long before she was born, in Ireland, and in other parts of England. A picture of Linden with the garden looking a long way off —Lulu said it was out of drawing—West Indian palms blowing on a long stretch of beach, and the sun setting in a pale green sky as she remembered seeing it; these pictures had been painted by an uncle who was dead, but whom they had stayed with when Byng's ship had been cruising in the West Indies and they had gone out so as to be able to be with him now and again. She remembered so well Uncle Fielding's long brown moustaches, and how he used to twist them round and round when he was painting, and the huge canvases and the divine smell of the oils mixed with the dreamy scent of his cigars; she had often sat in the verandah and watched him. And tall Irish Aunt Mimi with her bright eyes and the thick silver bangles on her wrists which made a noise when she moved. As she had moved often and very quickly there had always been the tinkling of those bangles; and there had always been in Aunt Mimi's house a wonderful smell that she had never found anywhere else, a rich walnut smell. Thinking of it now she sometimes wondered if she had not imagined that smell. After Uncle Fielding's West Indian pictures there were two portraits. One of Lulu when she was young, beautiful, with black hair piled on her head as she still did it; and the other of the second Grandpa, who had had red hair and who was dead. She had been terrified of him when he was alive, because once he had shouted down the table at her: '*You* like a lot of butter on your bread, don't you, Louie?' She had never got over it. She had never even tried to like him afterwards. Now they were getting up and going into the drawing-room, Lulu got up first, taking her bag from the arm of her chair.

She went upstairs to get a book, paused on the landing and looked into the spare room where her mother slept with Max. Nurse's work-basket lay open on the sofa, but nurse had evidently gone downstairs for something. She went in. A blue and white cot stood by the side of the double bed where her mother slept. Max was asleep. A tuft of yellow hair had begun to grow out of his head; his appearance was changing, he was now less like a small pink pig and more like the beginnings of a person. He held a piece of blue-edged blanket in his small fat hand.

With the birth of Max something had happened; she had realized that she did not love her mother in the same way. She could not tell how it had happened, or what had happened, but she had simply realized it. One day something her mother had said or the way she had said it, and she had known. She was very sorry about it. Very sorry for her mother who was always asking her for love. At the same time she was always making terrible and indecent remarks, she said things no one ought ever to say; she seemed to wish to pierce through into one's soul as if she wished to see one's soul naked, and so she had withdrawn her soul. She was not altogether sure that she liked Max, he had come too late in her life, and he was a boy. She hated boys. Some years back at the day school, horrid little Philip Peel had broken the doll she had loved so much, he had taken it out of her desk in the lunch hour and had brought it to her showing the huge crack he had made down the middle of the china head. He had flung it on the path in front of her and waited with two or three others to see her cry; but she had not cried. She had found herself suddenly so angry with him that she had smacked his nose and banged his head till he had stopped staying 'Look at your poor little doll,' in what he thought was a mocking imitation of her own voice. After that he shouted his mockery from a safe distance, a long way behind her on the road from school. Since that day she had hated boys more than ever. If Max had turned out to be

a sister she would have liked him, but of course it
was not his fault that he had not. Sometimes she
felt sorry that she did not like him because of this,
and would lean over the cot and tell him not to be
hurt about it, but he was too young to understand.

The after-tea feeling was the best feeling of the
day; then one began to live. Life became toned. It
was the realized hour, the pause between day and
night. The powder-blue curtains were drawn in
the drawing-room, the lights were on under their
shades, and the fire was burning in the blue-tiled
fireplace. Lulu sat knitting in her chair with her
feet crossed on the footstool, her mother was
making clothes for Max, Aunt Elise was also doing
some needlework. Ulysses spread himself in front
of the fire. He looked as if he were trying to lose
himself inside his grey-blue fur; he had an uneven temper, and if anyone disturbed him from his
place he was quite likely to scratch and bite. He
looked at her uncertainly as she sat down on the
rug beside Lulu's chair, but decided that she was
not yet near enough to be dangerous to his comfort, and closed his eyes. She opened her book and
began to read.

'That's rather old for you, isn't it, Louie?' said
Aunt Gainy, sounding amused.

Her mother laughed. 'She adores that book.'

'What is it?' Lulu asked.

'Trilby.'

Aunt Elise made a queer sound in the roof of
her mouth. 'Daisy was just the same at that age,
and now it's Waddy, always reading grown-up
books. I believe in letting children read what they
like, within limits, of course.'

'I don't suppose they understand most of it,' said Aunt Gainy.

She wished they would be quiet, they were spoiling the after-tea feeling as they always did when they were in. Oh, for the days when they were up in town shopping, and she and Lulu were alone at this hour. This was not the first time she had read *Trilby*, she had read it several times; long before she had learnt to read she had looked at the pictures. She had made up her mind, standing on a chair to take it down from a bookshelf when a very small girl, that it would be the first book she would ever read. But it was a difficult book; there were many things in it which she would like to have been able to understand a good deal better. It was a very sad story, and Trilby had a very sad face.

'Trilby was a model, wasn't she?' Aunt Elise was saying. 'Of course it must be very difficult to keep straight in those circumstances. I wonder why artists always seem to lead such loose lives. I suppose they have so many temptations, poor things.'

What an extraordinary remark. Why should she think such a thing? And she had turned the page, and there was a picture of Mrs. Bagot, Little Billee's mother, and the Reverend Bagot, talking to Taffy about Little Billee's proposed marriage to Trilby, and they seemed to think something very like Aunt Elise's remark.

'Won't you play something, Gainy dear,' Lulu was asking, 'as it's my birthday?'

'Oh, do you want me to?' said Aunt Gainy, absently.

'Come on, Gainy, give us a tune, you never play nowadays.'

She also lifted her head. 'Oh yes, do, please, Auntie.'

Aunt Gainy laughed and flung down the paper. Ah, music. The highly polished, sweet smelling, mahogany Bechstein took up nearly the whole of one side of the drawing-room; it stood against the white wallpaper like a thing removed from the world of ordinary things. It was a beautiful instrument and had been a birthday present to Aunt Gainy from Lulu many years ago. At the very end of it on a pale blue Japanese silk embroidered cloth were some family photographs, one of Byng in full dress naval uniform, three carved ivory monkeys stood next to him, a set of Indian ornaments, and a tall turquoise vase with three sheaves of some white dried grass in it. Aunt Gainy lifted back the lid, sat down and sighed.

'What do you want me to play?'

'Oh, anything you like, my dear, anything you like.'

Aunt Gainy put her fingers on the white and black keys and went straight into a melody. It was Schumann. She had heard it before; a sweet mellow cake dipped in wine. Her soul was borne upwards on soft wings, caressed and comforted; the longing to be beautiful slipped off and got lost among a crowd of wine-coloured days falling, falling into eternity. Evening on mountains, blue mountains full of rain and smelling of sweet heavy smells, pale green twilight music. She leant back by Lulu's chair and her body left her; this was realizing the after-tea feeling to the fullest. All the time patterns kept forming themselves in her mind, made by the music. They flowed into one design and flowed out of it into another; at the same time there was a divine sensation like intoxication, there was the feeling, and the changing coloured patterns, the shapes growing, growing, gradually melting away. Aunt Gainy went from Schumann to Chopin, and some of these things she had heard her play before too, they were called 'nocturnes.' At the end of the second one Aunt Gainy stopped. Behind the black and gold screen someone was coming in. Although she knew it was hopeless before anyone could speak she cried:

'Oh, please, please, Aunt Gainy, play something by the man you call Bach.'

But it was too late; she knew that her wish would not be granted, she was in vain trying to hold back the happy moment. Aunt Gainy had already got up.

'I really can't play any more now, Louie, another day, to-morrow. I promise you I'll play some to-morrow.'

It was done. She went back to the sofa, and Aunt Margaret came into the room, a tall black figure in her out-door clothes. She had been paying the weekly tradesmen's accounts. Now she bent over Lulu's chair and explained something in a low voice, glancing round the room to see who was there. Aunt Margaret was cold, it was freezing outside, and she wanted her tea, she felt so sorry for Aunt Margaret. Lulu nodded.

'Yes, yes, thank you very much, Margaret.'

The parchment-like skin looked grey with cold. Aunt Margaret smiled down at her by Lulu's side, then she went out of the room without another word.

Aunt Elise shook her head several times, smiling that smile whose kindness was so killing.

'Poor Margaret, she's a very good soul, I'm very fond of her.'

'Oh yes, she's awfully kind,' said Aunt Gainy impatiently rustling her paper.

'She likes paying the bills,' said Lulu; 'she likes having a chat with the shop people.'

Her mother looked up over her sewing at them all.

'I can tell you this. I notice a great change in her within the last few years, she's much more eccentric than she used to be.'

Lulu moved in her chair as she did when she was annoyed, and frowned.

'Oh well, well, I believe in people doing as they like, and going their own way. I never interfere with anybody.' Her voice had a certain fierceness in it. 'And I don't expect anybody to interfere with me.'

'Well, I shall stick to my point, I think it's a pity to isolate oneself entirely from one's fellows,' said her mother.

There was a silence. Suddenly she felt she could not stand it any longer; the criticism of Aunt Margaret, the disappointment over the music were working something up inside her, she would have to get out of the room. She got up carefully. For a moment she stood in front of the china cabinet looking at Lulu's vast collection of china animals and birds which she had been getting together for years, she examined some old fans on the wall, all the time watching them through the gilt mirror which took up the whole of the wall opposite, she reached the screen, felt the door-rug under her feet, and opened the door.

Frances was polishing glasses in the pantry when she went down the dark passage to the kitchen. At this hour of the day she might expect a welcome from Mary, for it was nearing the six o'clock cup hour.

'Och, 'tis my Biddy, it is,' said Mary. 'Come and sit down in your chair, and tell me how 'tis with ye.'

As she had expected, Mary was rocking herself to and fro in the rocking chair and holding in her hand a breakfast cup full of tea the colour of a beautiful West Indian nigger. By the window the kitchen girl was cutting up onions; even now the smell of deep rich gravy and other savoury and spicy smells told one that the beginnings of dinner were in preparation. She loved Mary; her name was Mullins and she expressed her opinions freely on all subjects. She had been with Lulu for so many years that nobody was quite sure how long it was, and she said she had forgotten herself; but she disliked England, and was everlastingly threatening to pack up and return without further ado to County Kilkenny. She was a great and pretty fighter, she said so very often herself. Her red hair was always wildly straying over her head and getting into her pale green eyes, and her face was like a sunburnt apple. Every time she had a row with a maid, or a fight with the tradespeople, or a disagreement with anyone in the family, she would give notice. Lulu would go into the kitchen, sit down on the horse-hair chair and say: 'Well, Mary?' 'Faith, an' I think it's lavin' you I'll be this toime melady.' She had known Lulu in the days of her first marriage when she had been Lady Mallord, and never called her anything else. How often had she not been there during these con- versations when Mary was about to be leaving? She would curl herself into the rocking chair by the great range; and the glow from the fire, the singing of the kettle, the smell of baking pastry, the billowy motion of the rocking chair, would all seem to be part of the scene. She would lie back in rapture listening to the wonderful rising and fall- ing of that voice. It was not what she said, it was the way she said it; and it would always end up in the same way—she was getting old, her strength was going, and she was wanting to go back to old Ireland and the home of her fathers. Lulu would listen to it all, then she would get up. 'Mary,' she would say, 'you've always been free to do as you liked all the years you've been with me. Why, dear me, I don't like to think how many it is, I'm getting old myself, and all my old friends are gone. You must do whatever you think is best for your- self. You owe it to yourself to do this. After all, it's a good many years that you've been working, isn't it? When one is getting old, when all one's friends have left one, one looks forward to a time when one will be able to lay down one's bones.' Mary would hold the door open for Lulu to go out while she herself wiped her eyes with a corner of her apron. And that was the end of it, she never went. She had heard it so often that she sometimes wondered if Mary did not enjoy it, if she only gave notice in order to have this little talk with Lulu in which they would both say that they were getting old and looking forward to their graves, while both of them were the most active of people, and Lulu could not bear anybody to talk about death in front of her. Mary was most delightful when she was a little drunk, and she did drink quite openly; she made no secret about her drop, and her favourite drop was rum. After one or two or more drops she could tell the most marvellous stories in that rising and falling voice; sometimes she would fall into talking in another language, and would go on for quite a long time if one did not pull her up. She smoked a pipe, too, but only in her room; the strong smell of her tobacco used to come up in gusts from her window sometimes at night. Now she was rocking herself to and fro with one hand over her bosom which also rocked with the motion of her body.

'Well, avourneen, and what is it you'll be after askin' me now, for I can see you've something in your mind?'

'Tell me about Grandpa Mallord.' She could never get over the fact that Mary had known him; nobody ever talked about him in the family and she felt drawn to him by a sense of mystery.

'Faith, I've told ye all I can be telling ye. He was a foine-lookin' man was your grandfather, Biddy. Oh, he'd a pretty manner he had, of the old school, you know, of the old school; always so courteous. An' there he'd be, bowing out the ladies. Ah, an' there was many an eye on him; an' he led melady a dance he did—'twas meself that was there an' saw it all—for he was a hoigh flyer, an' he loved the ladies. Indade, if there were any women around at all, at all. Ah, there used to be great goin's on at old Cassel Dibden, and melady so young and beautiful, it was a shame it was. Many's the day when she'd go stormin' up to her room in a passion of tears, and faith, Sir Bryan would be a kissin' of somebody else round the back gate. Och, 'twas something chronic his lady loves and his blarney an' all, an' though 'twas a sad day, I didn't blame melady for divorcin' him. Ah, but these Protestant Oirishmen, ah! An' then, begorrah, what does she do but two years afterwards she goes and marries a second Oirish Protestant, would you be believin' it now? Of course, he was a nice gentleman, the master, but he'd not the stoile or the manner of Sir Bryan. An' oh, Biddy asthore, he wasn't good enough for her —he was slow where she was quick—thick where she was foine.'

She shook her head, put her cup on the table and got up. She took down a huge saucepan and began examining the inside of it. All at once, without any warning, she had worked herself into a towering rage and thrust it into the hands of the astonished kitchen girl.

'Will you be out an' clanin' this, if you plase,' she shouted. The kitchen girl took it away to the scullery. When she had gone Mary turned round and smiled very slowly over her burnt apple face.

'Those girls they listen and listen until you'd be askin' yourself why their ears don't drop off.'

She began to roll up her sleeves, showing her freckled arms, and Frances came into the kitchen. It was time to go; the sense of ease and comfort that she always knew sitting on her red cushion which Mary kept for her in the seat of her own chair was beginning to dwindle away. They were approaching the dark and barbarous hour of night.

THERE were two people standing over her, they were breathing hard upon her neck. Their breath hissed; it was black breath and came out of their mouths in hissing gusts; then they began to torture her. It was a delicate refined torture; it began by tickling the back of her neck, then her ribs, it became fiercer, fiercer, more unbearable. She would not let them see that she was afraid, she would hold out as long as she could. But now she couldn't bear it any longer, she ran, she ran, she ran. They were behind, always so near, always the noise of their hissing breaths, the sound of crackling laughter. They were devils, she knew them well, she had met them on other occasions. She found a dark room and locked herself in. There was silence. She had outwitted them; she crouched panting by the door. She looked round and recognized the room, it was her own room. She looked up at the ceiling and saw an enormous white hand coming slowly down to crush her into nothing. She shrieked and tried to flatten herself on the floor. Now outside the devils hammered at the door, hissing and kicking; probably they knew she was trapped. The hand descended, she felt it on her head pushing her down, down, it was deathly cold. She went down with a terrible aching weight on her head. Now she was going to die. Would it hurt much? Her heart clicked and she died. The door was burst open and the devils walked in over her, carrying torches and singing, 'Allelulia, allelulia!' They smiled down at her with the slits in their faces; they had no mouths. She was dead, and they had come to take her to Hell.

She woke up screaming in the dark. The night-light in the basin had gone out. She was sweating with fear; waves of heat and cold shot over her. It was humiliating and awful, but she would have to go downstairs, she would have to be near some-body. Even now perhaps the devils were waiting in the darkness, grinning, waiting for her as her feet touched the floor. She found her slippers, tore her dressing-gown from the end of the bed, and hurled herself across the darkness. The glare of the light on the landing sobered her a little, but she was still trembling. Then behind there was a sudden scuffle, the door of her room banged, she shrieked, and rushed down the stairs. They were finishing dinner; for a moment she felt quite mad. She stood screaming in the doorway, she could hear herself scream but could not stop it. People rose. Her mother from the other side of the table. Aunt Margaret. Somebody laughed. Frances, putting down a dish, stood with her hand sus-pended in the air. A long way off somebody said:

'Nervous child.'

It was Aunt Elise. She flung herself at Lulu's feet, her dressing-gown trailing behind her trip-ping her up, and cried into the folds of Lulu's dress.

'Save me, save me, Lulu!'

Lulu put her hand on her head and said: 'Oh, my little Louie, what is it?'

Somebody said: 'Nightmare.'

Aunt Margaret said loudly and angrily: 'It's a shame!'

And she heard her mother's voice saying: 'Shut up, Margaret.'

Her mother took her hand and wrapped her dressing-gown round her. As the door swung behind them she heard the uncles laughing. That was right, humiliation, shame, laugh, laugh. It was dreadful to be humiliated in front of them all. She began to sob.

'There, there, what were you dreaming about?'

'Dreamt I was going to Hell.'

Her mother laughed. 'Oh, darling, really, but you're awake now.'

She got into bed. A moth had fallen on to the wick of the night-light in the basin, that was what had put it out. Her mother got a new night-light and lit it. She suppressed her sobs and lay still. She did hope she wouldn't be kissed.

'Now are you going to be all right?'

'Yes, thank you, I'm all right now.'

'Poor little girl.' Her mother kissed her cheek, then she went. The small chaste glow of the night-light flared up from the large white basin. But she wasn't all right, she rubbed off the kiss with her handkerchief, and burst into a passion of sobs. She rocked herself to and fro sobbing. It was terrible, it was too awful, it was impossible, she could not go on living, life was too much for her. It was the second nightmare this week; always the same thing, waking up and having to go to people who never understood. 'But it was only a bad dream, you're awake now,' and behind their eyes they laughed. 'Nervous child.' Why was she made like this, lonely, unhappy, frightened? She knelt up in bed.

'O God, let me die, let me die, please, please let me die before I'm twelve. I can't bear it any more.'

She beat her head upon the pillows, her eyes ached, her head was heavy with pain. *'Holy Mary, mother of God, pray for us sinners, now, and at the hour of our death.* Beautiful, comforting death, come soon.'

There was a very quiet knock upon the door and Frances came in with a tray in her hand. On the tray was a wineglass half full of an amethyst-coloured wine, and a saucer with a piece of cake and two Marie biscuits.

'Mary says you're to have this,' said Frances.

'O Frances, Frances!' Here was a friend into whose neck she could sob; Frances sat on the bed and she sobbed into her neck.

'For goodness sake don't take on so, Miss Louie.'

Christ was forsaken by all his friends, but an angel visited him and ministered unto him. She sipped the Madeira, leaning against Frances. She ate the cake and dipped the biscuits one after another into the wine; she liked the taste of it, also it made her a little drunk. A sensation of rather holy peace seemed to come over her mind as the Madeira went inside.

'Mary sends you her love, and she says you're not to fret,' said Frances, rising with the tray in her hand.

She held on to the slippery white cuff.

'O Frances, thank Mary very much, but oh, I wish I could die.'

'O la, Miss Louie, what nonsense! You don't wish anything of the sort, you're just feeling a bit tired, that's all. I must go, I haven't cleared the table yet, fancy that! Sleep well,' she said at the door, her pale blue eyes smiling behind her thick spectacles.

She sank down under the bedclothes. If she was to die that night she would drift out of life very tranquilly and dreamily like this, they would say she had died in her sleep. As a preparation for death she made an act of contrition. She had not quite finished it before she began to float down a cool green river where trees bowed low on either side, dipping their long golden and green branches into the water. Of course it was the Thames, and she was floating down to Leathley, where once when she was much younger, Lulu had taken a house for the summer. She had loved Leathley from the first day she saw it; she had always wanted to go back again, and now she really was going back, floating down the river to it. She did not remember getting into the river at Wickhamstead, but she must have done so, how very brave; but one did not know until one had tried how easy it was to float, another time she would not be afraid. The river was getting more and more blue; so blue that she wondered if it was not the sea after all. But she did not want it to turn into the sea, that would be frightening, she would have to try and prevent it from turning into the sea; but she had passed the blue part and now the gold and green

trees had come back and the water was even a
deeper green than before.

SHE went up to Pomoroyal—her own secret
country—and shut the door. Outside it was a
wet day. The rain poured down from a sky which
looked as if it would be swathed forever in grey
clouds, while the trees, now quite bare of their
leaves, stood stiffly dripping. She had seen the
garden through the drawing-room windows, had
shuddered and come up to Pomoroyal. The wet
day made the top-storey room dark; at the best of
times it was not a bright room. One side of the
roof sloped—it was the side over the window—
and gave it an attic appearance. There was a
small stone balcony outside the window from
which one could look down on to the front gate,
but Aunt Margaret who slept next door, said she
did not think it was at all safe; she was always
coming in when one was playing and saying: 'You
won't go out on the balcony, will you, Louie?
Because you might fall over and kill yourself, you
know.' There were two iron bedsteads, side by
side, covered with flowered bed-covers. The floor
was covered with a cold, slippery oilcloth, good to
slide about on, and the wallpaper, a composition
of now very old yellow roses climbing up faded
green streamers, was fascinatingly hideous. She
took Omenatab out of the huge camphor-smelling
wardrobe. Omenatab had been a lay figure and
had once belonged to Uncle Ken, Aunt Elise's
husband, and Lulu's second eldest son now that
Uncle Bryan, whom she had never seen, was dead.

Uncle Ken had at one time thought he was going to be an artist. Remembering Aunt Elise's remark about artists, it was perhaps a good thing he had changed his mind. Omenatab was not quite two feet high, he was bald and had aquiline features. His body, a deep coffee colour, was made of wood, and she always thought there was an eastern look about him. His body did not tell one to which sex he belonged, he seemed to belong to a sex of his own. He had for some time been the Lord Chancellor of Pomoroyal. She had given him this position herself the first time she had discovered him in the top-storey room. She had been fascinated by him. He had given her the most peculiar sensation, for a few days she had been in love with him. But she had never felt sure that the love she had felt for him in those days was a very good love, there had been something uncanny about it from the beginning. But it was now over, the passion had died. She was still interested in him, but he did not give her the same feeling. She no longer wanted to arrange his jointed arms around her neck and feel his smooth wooden face against her cheek as she had done before, and when they had embraced she had always had a sensation of guilty pleasure. Although he came of a race of people who either had no feelings or thought it wiser to wear a blank expression, she suspected him of having had a curious life, and of having strange powers. He was distinctly evil; a suave, smooth-faced devil.

She put him in the doll's rocking chair, Pauline and Valentine, her favourite dolls, sat in their two white chairs on either side; they were the last she

had left out of a family of sixteen. She was really
glad that the family had gradually, during the last
five years of moving about, become less, because
there never had been enough underclothes or shoes
and socks to go round. She had once made a
resolution that she would never grow out of her
dolls as most people did. She had held Pauline and
Valentine to her breast and had promised them
that she never would, and that if a time came when
she could not have them with her she would put
them away in two little boxes, or in the same box
for company, and keep them forever. They had all
been much affected; the tears had rolled down her
cheeks on to theirs, so that they cried with her.
Now sitting on her cushion in front of them with
the doll's table between, she opened her notebook.
She had called a conference, as she always did on
serious occasions in the kingdom.

'My dear people, a most dreadful thing has
happened. A boy is coming to stay in this house.
He is my first cousin. His father was Uncle
Bryan, who, as you know, is dead. And now his
mother has died in Paris, which is, as you know,
the capital of France. And Lulu says he will have
to come and stay here until she can think of something to do with him. She does not like the idea
either. But that is not the worst. My darlings,
Lulu says he will have to have this room because
there is no other room in the house for him.' Tears
were now thickly flooding her eyes. 'We shall not
be able to have our meetings here any more. Dear
friends, Pomoroyal is a kingdom. It can never
cease to be. You know my hatred of boys, how I
dislike them above all things. I propose that you

and I shall have nothing to do with him. He shall
have no part in our country. I am now going to
pass a law forbidding him, under pain of death, to
enter Pomoroyal.' Like a dark cloud which had
been hovering uncertainly for some time over-
head, the full force of her own grief and anger
gathered itself together and rained upon her. She
put her head down on the dolls' table. 'Oh Dalius,
Dalius!'

'What is it, my dear?' said Dalius, the deputy-
prince, who was standing beside her.

'I can't bear it, I can't bear it.'

'Courage, my darling; remember that you are a
Queen.'

'How can I be a Queen without a kingdom?'

'A kingdom is not dependent upon a place, my
dear,' said the voice of the sage Dalius. But it was
too much. She had not realized till now how painful it would be to give up her kingdom.

'WHEN is he going to come?' she asked, standing
in the doorway of her mother's room, the next day.

'Who? Your cousin, Timothy? Oh, some time
within the next week or two. It'll be very nice for
you, you ought to be very pleased. Someone for
you to play with. There, there, my little sweetheart
baby-boysie.'

Her mother began to undress Max as it was
time for his bath. She could not stand seeing boy-
babies undressed; she backed out of the doorway.
The softer mood of this morning had left her. Now
she was very angry. She went into her own room
next to Lulu's. It had once been a dressing-room

and there was very little spare space in it. A large
wardrobe and dressing-table combined were built
into one side of the wall; on the other side was her
bed and the locked door between herself and Lulu.
The wash-hand stand stood in a little niche between
the end of the bed and the door. She climbed on
to the dressing-table and sat there swinging her
legs. On either side of her were her silver brushes
with her initials on their backs in smug letters,
L.C.M.B. That meant Louise Charlotte Mallord
Burnett. Why had they given her all those names?
She wished she had been able to speak when she
was christened, she would have shouted at them
from the font and told them that Louise Burnett
was quite enough. Suddenly a rising column of
passion rose higher and higher. She took hold of
the brushes by their handles, shook them, and
threw them with all her strength at the door behind
the bed, where they fell with a metallic peevish
noise. Outside the window, the apple tree growing
by the wall looked at her gravely. But she did not
care, she was now beyond reflection. She seized
the clothes-brush and threw it against the wash-
stand, hoping it would hit the jug. It caught the
water-bottle and there was a sound of smashing
glass then very sweet to her ears; the tumbler had
broken. Then she threw everything she could
think of except the hand-mirror because of the
seven years' bad luck. She threw the china toilet-
pots, the pin tray and the fat pin-cushion in its lace
petticoat. She took off her shoes and flung them
each at a different picture; one at *Our Darlings*,
and the other at *The Days of Youth*. She stood on
the bed and flung the books down from the shelf

C

above it; standing on the bed gave her another idea.
She tore off the bedclothes and threw them round
the room. She opened the wardrobe, took out her
clothes and tossed them one by one into the air.
She jumped back on the bed and began to sing a
kind of barbaric chant. As she sang, she went
round and round in circles waving her arms.

'I hate boys! I hate boys! Allelulia in the
Highest! I hate boys! I hate them, I hate them,
I hate them. I'll sell my soul to the devil, I swear
I will, but I'll never, never like them. Thank God
I'm not a boy and it's too late now to make me into
one. May the devil and all his angels take them to
Hell!' And she jumped in the air on the bed, filled
with a delirious sense of liberation.

'Louie, what are you doing?' said her mother at
the door. In a second she was over the carpet and
had turned the key in the lock.

'Let me in at once!' said her mother, her voice
gradually rising.

'I won't.' Drunk with her own anger, she went
on singing on the bed: 'I hate boys! I hate boys!
I hate boys!'

'You wouldn't do this if Byng was here. Louie,
if you don't unlock the door and let me in at once,
I'll give you the worst thrashing you've ever had
in your life. Come along now.'

The what? The worst thrashing. How dare
she, how dare she speak like that? She stopped
jumping on the bed. She drew herself up and
looked at herself in the wardrobe mirror. The
door handle was being rattled.

'Do you hear what I said?'

She went to the door and stood drawn up to

attention, every nerve taut, feeling her life-force, her pride, and an unconscious sense of her own personality separate and remote from her mother's, moulding itself together into a block of granite. At that moment she was confronting the enemy in her mother, long sensed, but never before accosted in the open. A rowdy, vulgar enemy clamouring at the gates of her soul.

'If you touch me, I shall kill you,' she said, coldly.

'Louie, how can you? You wicked little girl. To me your own mother.' The voice seemed about to break into tears.

'Well, you shouldn't have said it. I'm too old to be beaten, and I'm not going to be any more.'

On the other side of the door her mother was crying, but she remained standing with her shoulders thrown back, her teeth set together. There was a movement of skirts, and her mother went. She sat down and rolled herself in the down quilt on the floor. A lovely quiet was all around her, in spite of the chaos which she, ordinarily so tidy, had made. The pin-cushion floated on the top of the water in the ewer, its white lace flounces spread around it, and the coloured pins, once the property of Lulu, stuck up like a clump of trees on a desert island. It survived among the wreckage of the room, keeping its smug appearance. She felt now very tired; she looked into the glass and began half to laugh and half to cry.

A week later, in the spring twilight, they were waiting in the drawing-room for Timothy's

arrival. The bell rang; there was a noise in the
hall, then silence. She heard Uncle Heston's voice.
Lulu got up with a sigh from her chair and went
out of the room. She continued to crouch by the
fireplace while Ulysses glared from the footstool.
The door opened behind the screen, and she heard
Lulu talking in French to somebody who was with
her. Her mother and Aunt Gainy both rose and
kissed the person. Then her mother said to her:

'Aren't you going to say how do you do to your
cousin?'

And she had to get up. She stood with her
hands behind her back. A person taller than herself, dressed entirely in black with a black overcoat
hanging open, put out his hand. His white collar
was the only relief against his dark clothes. He
had dark hair and dark eyes and his fine eyebrows
were like Lulu's. She put out her hand, but only
very slowly, partly to hide her surprise, and partly
because she had to abandon with some reluctance
her preconceived idea of the rosy-cheeked, shape-
less schoolboys of her acquaintance at the day-
school and other places. Instantaneous relief
mingled in her mind with a vague and quite un-
reasonable sense of annoyance with him for being
so different from what she had expected. He bowed
and smiled at her over their handshake.

'Is it Louie?' he asked.

She said 'Yes.'

In the background she was conscious of her
mother and Aunt Gainy watching them and being
amused.

Uncle Heston came in rubbing his hands
together.

'Tea is ready for you,' Lulu said. 'I expect you're tired.'

The person in the black clothes bowed and said, yes, he was a little tired. Uncle Heston clapped him on the shoulder and said: 'Tea, my boy, tea,' in his most pompous manner.

The door swung after them. She went over to the windows and looked out on to the lawn, listening, but not really attending to the conversation behind her in the room.

'What Frenchified manners the little thing has.'

'Very effeminate-looking, but I suppose French boys are like that.'

'Well,' Lulu was saying, 'I think manners for a change in a boy are rather agreeable. He speaks beautifully. Bryan always spoke French well, and I suppose living in Paris and all that——' She could hear in Lulu's voice that strange note of dismissal which meant that the subject was beginning to tire her.

'But Anita was Spanish, wasn't she?'

'Oh yes, but they always lived in France, she and Bryan. Poor thing, she died of cancer. I suppose I ought to have done something about it.' And Lulu sighed, because she was tired of the whole thing, tired of other people's troubles.

'Don't see how you could have done anything when you didn't even know she was ill. They never wrote, after all. They cut themselves off from everyone, didn't they?' said Aunt Gainy, faintly irritable.

She kept her eyes on the garden. A hedge-sparrow was singing in the fir tree near the house.

The dining-room chairs were difficult things to manage, but she drew one a little away from the table and wriggled herself in; she wanted to have another look at him. Uncle Heston turned on the light because it was getting dark; outside the sky was a deep spring-night blue. She did not like Uncle Heston and he did not like her, but she had come out of curiosity. Timothy was looking down at the white faces of two boiled eggs. Uncle Heston was talking in his heavy voice about the train service in South Africa; he had met Tim at Dover. If one remained in his company longer than ten minutes one might be sure of always being led round to the same subject, which began with: 'Now, in South Africa,' or, 'Of course, in South Africa'; the reason for this was that he had never expected to come into the baronetcy. There had been two uncles before him who had died, and until a few years ago he had been farming in South Africa, and he had not yet got out of the way of thinking about it. A silver pot of fern stood on the table between herself and Timothy. She watched him by stealth. Strictly speaking, she realized that this was not a boy at all. He had the face of a beautiful girl, yet it was not a girl's face; those small straight features and that line going through the middle of his mouth, where the lips closed, was not girlish. He had very beautiful long fingers with nicely shaped nails, not like Philip Peel's which had always been filthy. It was as if life said: 'Look at him well, this is my masterpiece, I shall not do this again in a hurry. Your Philip Peel was a stupid little animal compared to this. I haven't blown this together, I have taken a long time to make it.' 'How long, a hundred years?' Because the time things took always interested her a great deal; at the day school they had called her slowcoach because she could never do anything quickly. 'A hundred years?' Life was scornful. 'Two or three hundred is more like it.' Timothy, happening to look across the table, smiled at her; she smiled back and felt herself blushing, and Uncle Heston caught them and stopped himself in the middle of a sentence.

'Why have you honoured us with your company, Louie?'

She looked vacantly at him and said nothing.

'Your friend, Monsieur Bidaud, told me that you played the violin very well, Tim.'

'Oh, that was very kind of him, Uncle, he does it to encourage me, he plays so well himself.'

'Does he, indeed? Ah, it's very hard for people who have the artistic temperament to get on in this world, you know; you see there's so much that stops them from succeeding. Only do things when they want to and that sort of thing. Music isn't a paying concern now that we have gramophones and pianolas and things, you know. *They* don't only when they feel like it, they play when *we* feel like it. Heh?' He brought this out with great triumph.

'That is true, but a machine is only a machine, an artist is an artist. If there were no artists to make the records for the gramophone in the first place, there would be no music.'

Uncle Heston did not seem to like this, he looked at Timothy as if he was not quite certain about him.

'Well, perhaps you'll give us a performance one
night, eh? Your Aunt Gainy plays the piano.'

Timothy bent his head. 'I shall be pleased,
Uncle, when you wish it.'

So in addition to being beautiful he was a
musician. When he had finished tea she offered
to show him his room.

'I hope it will be all right for you. It used to be
my playroom.' She wanted to say something
gracious and polite, to make him feel that he was
welcome.

'Does that mean I have taken it from you?'

'Oh no, of course not. I mean I don't mind you
having it in the least.' She stumbled over her
words, remembering in her embarrassment, how
she had hated the idea of his having the room.
How dark it looked now, how solitary. And he
had blue rings under his eyes, he too looked dark
and sad.

'I am so sorry, I am afraid I have taken it from
you.' He stood before her holding his fiddle case
in his hand, fully realizing the situation, and
apologizing for his intrusion with his voice and his
eyes.

'It's quite all right. Please don't worry about it.
I'm very glad you're going to have it.' She paused,
then rushed into the only channel she could think
of to change the subject. 'You're older than me,
aren't you?'

'Perhaps a little. I am fourteen. Does that
matter?' She was startled, thinking it a strange
thing for him to say.

'No, of course not. I'm so glad you play, I love
music,' she said quickly. He looked pleased. She

turned away and left him to unpack. All the way
down the top-storey stairs she was trembling. To
be beautiful and a musician seemed the height of
human achievement. She looked upon him as a
work of art, he was something marvellous and
holy, he was the thing she could never be.

In the morning she took him into the elm grove.
The trees were now in their light green and hung
down like a veil. New grass was springing up in
patches, and among it purple and white crocuses;
they always made her think of notes of music,
crochets perhaps. Ivy ramped over the overgrown
flowerbeds, where the stag-beetles lived and sometimes looked out among the dark leaves with their
satanic faces. She was afraid of them.

'It's beautiful here,' he said.

'Oh, do you think so? I'm so glad, because it's
my favourite place.'

She introduced him to the trees, talking to him
easily and naturally, occasionally almost forgetting
his presence. 'I sit here when I'm sad, here when
I'm going to dream something, here when people
have been beastly.'

She stopped, suddenly aware that these things
were among the intimate secrets of her being.

'Do you think I'm silly?'

He looked at her in his grave and courteous
manner. 'But no, why should I?'

She showed him the six graves where Lulu's
dogs and cats of other years lay buried, and where
she had buried the two Java sparrows who had died
during the very cold weather; it had been so sad

putting their little bodies into the earth. They had
died during the night in the bird-house; in the
morning she and Lulu had gone in and found
them dead.

'Have you always lived in Paris?'

'Yes, as long as I can remember. I have been
away to the country you know, in France, and to
the sea with my mother. Once we went to Spain
to see my grandfather in Madrid. But we always
lived in Paris.'

'Your mother's name was Anita, wasn't it?'

'No, Anita Teresa,' he said simply.

She should not have asked him that. He was
staring through the trees, probably thinking about
her, and she was dead. Perhaps he had loved her
very much. She understood what that felt like
because she loved Byng and Lulu like that. If
either of them should die she would feel like that
about it, but it was unthinkable that they should
die. At breakfast he had promised the family that
he would play to them, and she was wondering if
she would have the courage to ask him to play to
her, alone, before the others heard. She would see
how she felt about it when they had been round
the garden.

She took him to all the familiar places in the
garden and in the vegetable garden, and into the
field which also belonged to Linden, but where an
old cart-horse was allowed to graze. In the field
was a huge oak; it marked the boundary of a once
famous common, and a highwayman was said to
have tied his horse up to it while awaiting the
coach from London. Aunt Margaret said she was
sure his ghost came back at night and waited under

the tree with pistols in his hands. Coming away
from the field down the vegetable garden path, she
asked him while her heart hammered inside:

'Do you think, if you feel like it, you could play
something to me, alone?'

He looked at her and laughed. 'Of course.
When shall it be? Now?'

He seemed to think it strange of her to have
been so nervous about it.

She sat astride a chair in the top-storey room
and he took his fiddle out of its case, wrapped in a
bottle-green silk cloth.

The old, chestnut-coloured, mellow-looking
wood was highly polished. He took his bow and
looked at it, then he did something to the strings
of the fiddle; it seemed to her to be all part of a
magic formula. He drew the bow across the strings
and made three long notes while she watched his
fingers.

'Is there something you would like me to play?'

She thought of her favourite music which she
could get Aunt Gainy to play for her only very
occasionally.

'You like Bach, then?' He lifted his dark arched
eyebrows. He pronounced the word with a
guttural sound.

'I will play you some unaccompanied Bach. It
is possible I may not be able to play to-day, I
cannot always. One will see.'

His eyes were alert and darkly bright. Then he
played a lovely lively opening movement. The
charmed harmonies of the music which she loved
better than any other, because it gave her a feeling
of clearness and of deep emotional satisfaction, fell

across the room, rendered as Aunt Gainy had never
rendered them, with a lightness and roundness of
tone, a carefulness of phrasing, an appreciation of
their movement which Aunt Gainy had never
known. She knew this by the shapes they made in
her head, by the rightness of the patterns, by their
vividness and the way each of the designs was so
clearly cut, one out of another. They were cut out
like pieces of sculpture but that did not prevent
them from moving. They inter-changed and inter-
mingled with each other, but they were governed
by a main theme which rounded them all together,
which kept on creeping in and taking them up and
then letting them go again. She sunk her chin into
her hands. The music was drawing to an end. The
dancing, moving, intermingling forms were being
gathered in by a punctual, falling note. He took
the fiddle down and the silk handkerchief from
under his chin.

'I hope I have not made you tired,' he was
saying.

She shook her head. What could one say, what
was there to say? But there he was standing with
his back to the mantelpiece, the sun bursting
through the window, making a little path of light
over the bedsteads to his shoulder in its black cloth
covering. Do you like it? Does it please you?
What on the whole do you think of it? his eyes
were asking.

'It was lovely, I loved it, I wished you had gone
on forever.'

He smiled, pleased. He laid the fiddle on the
bed, the bow beside it, and came round to her.

'And what is it that you do?' he asked, sitting on

the bed and smiling at her. She understood that
the question was a compliment, but it was the
terrible question she had just been asking herself.

'I can't do anything.'

The full force of not being able to do anything
was the most deathly thing in the world. Things
locked up and unable to move were inside her.
She had felt them over and over again; in dreams,
in the garden with the trees, in bed when she had
sat up to kiss her knees good-night because there
was nobody else there to kiss. She had felt it in
music which had made her forget that she hated
her face because it was not beautiful, and now
someone had arrived in her life who already possessed the power of showing what he could do.
She got up and went to the door. She heard him
call her by her name, she was aware of him standing in the doorway of the room when she went
down the stairs, horrified at what he had done; but
she could not go back. She knew that she would
have to be alone to recover from the realization
that she could not do anything, and perhaps would
never be able to do anything. One would probably
get used to it as one got used to nearly all evil
things.

HE had gone out early after lunch to the tailor's
with Uncle Heston, and she took her now rather
neglected religious habit out of the box in the
wardrobe. It had been made for a children's fancy
dress party to which she had gone as a nun, and had
been very useful ever afterwards for her religious
games. She dressed herself in front of the glass,

being careful to put her veil on at the right angle,
before performing her duties for the day in Lulu's
room. Lulu's room was large and filled with things
of interest, sacred and profane. There were three
little altars, and it was her duty to change the
flowers and see to the candles.

Lulu had only become a Catholic after her
second marriage, and some of the family had gone
over to the Church with her. She was very devout
and always went to the two Masses on Sunday and
to the long evening service with the sermon and
Benediction at the end, which was the best part of
it. They used to go together, and she closed her
eyes as Lulu did during the sermon, then one could
think one's thoughts till it was time for Benediction. Lulu slept in a large double bed with four
pillows, and at the end of it a cushion. There were
shelves, cupboards, bookcases, little brackets with
curious old ornaments, and many different kinds of
pictures on the walls. Photographs of the graves of
those of her children who were dead, sacred
pictures, pictures of India where she had lived with
her parents when she was a child, and Chinese
prints. One of the altars, and the most important
one with the priedieu where she said her morning
and night prayers, was by the bed, the other two
were in recesses on either side of the wardrobe.

She changed the water and arranged the new
flowers very carefully, standing back to get the
right effect; then she lit all the candles. She was
going to have a service on her own at her favourite
altar, not the one before which Lulu said her
prayers, but the altar dedicated solely to Our Lady.
This statue had not the fat face nor the matronly

lines of the big one on the chief altar, but its face was tender and more compassionate; it looked down upon the world with its hands outstretched, a blue cloak hanging from its shoulders. She knelt and prayed, putting her hands inside her long sleeves as the nuns did at the convent. The candles burnt up, and there was a faint smell of lavender; one was always coming across it in unexpected corners in the room, for it was Lulu's favourite scent. She felt serene and holy and the rattle of her rosary fixed into her white girdle was pleasing. She was going to be a nun when she grew up; she hoped to be the sacristan who looked after the altar and extinguished the candles after Benediction. It had once been her practice to give the dolls Communion on Sundays with Omenatab officiating as priest, though sometimes she had been the priest herself. But once her mother had come up unexpectedly and had been shocked; had said that it was irreverent of her to play at such a thing. After that she had not done it, but she still sometimes heard their confessions, especially Omenatab's. As he would never own up to anything she was always obliged to accuse him herself of his sins; once she made him put his hand over the Catechism and say: 'I accuse myself of having broken all the ten Commandments.' She had not the least idea what sort of a penance to give him for it, but remembering the Sunday sermons, she had preached him one in Father Pindarin's slow voice.

She was beginning to meditate on Purgatory, and imagined herself dead and outside the gates of Purgatory and not at all liking the look of the

flames inside. 'Must I go in?' she asked the
guardian angel. 'I'm afraid you must. The flames
are not so bad as they look from here, you are
seeing with your earthly eyes, soon you will get
used to it.' There was a noise in the hall, then
voices. Someone came up the stairs with light
footfalls. It was Tim. He crossed the landing and
called out to her.

'Bon Dieu! Good afternoon, Sister, and what is
your order?'

'The Sisters of the House of God,' she said,
standing in the doorway, embarrassed, realizing
that he had never before seen her in this dress.

He began playing an imaginary fiddle, while he
walked about the landing imitating a street
musician, in front of her.

'I hope then you will say a prayer for me sometimes. I am a poor man who has to earn his living
by playing the fiddle in the streets, Sister.'

She laughed at his caricature; he had drawn in
his cheeks so that they looked hollow, emaciated,
his shoulders hunched as if from the cold. Suddenly he dropped the buffoonery and turned
round to go up the narrow top-storey staircase.

'I'm going to practise,' he said quietly.

Had she imagined it, or was there somewhere an
obscure rebuke? She extinguished the candles,
genuflecting before the altars, and undressed in
her room. She changed into her jersey and skirt
and went up to him. He was turning a page as she
came in. She sat down and waited till he had
finished the movement. Then she questioned
him.

'Don't you like my dressing up as a nun?'

He came over to her, still holding his fiddle and pointing with his bow. 'Show me your hands.'

She held them out, surprised. 'What's the matter with them?'

'There is nothing the matter with them. But they are not meant to be the hands of a nun, that's all.'

'But I was only playing.'

'Yes? That is what I am doing now. I'm practising in order that I may play one day.' He nodded to her in a significant, much older way and went back to his music-stand. He began playing a saraband, soft and slow with a swinging movement accompanied by little trills in the treble. And here she was sitting down and bowing to his authority. She allowed it to him because he had brought with him the long looked-for stimulation of the mind.

THE days of Dalius and Omenatab were over, and she had taken Pauline and Valentine downstairs to her room where they lived in the wardrobe. But the deputy-prince, once the greatest of her imaginary friends, so great that the only quarrel they had had was when Dalius had one day become too real and had frightened her, and the Lord Chancellor with his eastern vices, had retired into private life. She did not tell Tim, but she pretended that he was a renowned musician whom she had invited to come and make a long stay in Pomoroyal for her own pleasure. She sometimes wondered if the retired Chancellor smiled to himself in the darkness of the wardrobe in the top storey room; and once, in spite of the fact that

Dalius could not exist without her consent, she
came to her in the night and said: 'You have
deserted me for this fiddler.' In fact, Dalius cried
and she had to comfort her. 'I have been your
friend for years.' 'You are always my friend, my
dear.' 'I shall have my revenge. I know more than
this fiddler,' said Dalius, and went.

Spring was coming on. It was after Easter and
the chestnuts were out and her mother was preparing to join Byng at Malta, and went up to town
shopping every day. She herself was shortly going
to school, for the first time as a boarder. Mary
sipped her tea, and the steam from the kettle went
up in white puffs over the range.

'Ah, but you'll love the Sisters, you needn't be
thinkin' about that, Biddy. Faith, won't you be
comin' back to us in your holidays now that your
mother's goin' abroad again? Ah, we haven't lost
ye yet, we haven't.'

Frances came into the kitchen with a tray. She
stopped and laid the tray for a moment on the table.

'Come here, Frances, I want you.'

'La, Miss Louie, I must get finished.' But she
came. She put her arm round the slender waist,
the starched waist-band was uncomfortable.

'My Biddy has an enlarged heart to-day,' said
Mary. 'She's feelin' the need of expandin' it.
Isn't that so, avourneen?'

She nodded. Frances laughed and said she
must be going because she hadn't finished clearing
the table.

'So you've found a friend in your cousin? What
did I tell ye now? Make up your mind to be hatin'
a person before you've seen them, and the very

next minute 'tis you that will have to be changin' it.'

But she was melancholy to-day, nothing could move her. Mary drew her head on to her old fat shoulder.

'There my Bidden asthore, it's a long toime growin' up but it'll come at last, be believin' it now, for it's meself that's tellin' ye.'

There was a peppery smell about Mary, not unpleasant, but not restful. But she was not worrying about growing up; she had long got past that. She left a kiss on the burnt apple cheek and went out of the house by the side door. . . . The birds were singing, the grass was very beautiful. Her heart felt even a little soothed to see it. The elm trees hung down in the grove, thousands of little bright green eyes, and the air smelt of the river. She put her arms round a tall elm and leant against it. There were shoots growing out of the tree on either side and they touched her, so that it felt as if the tree put out its own arms to receive her into its embrace. She laid her forehead against it and smelt the sweet, woody smell. It seemed to her as she stood there, that the strong, steady stream of life from the tree encircled her, and a sensation of peace came dropping down very slowly through the leaves. Hush, hush, hush, sounded through the grove, like an inland summer sea made by the rustling of the leaves.

Tim was coming across the lawn wearing his new suit of English cut; she saw him through the trees. Over by the house Aunt Gainy and Uncle Heston were bringing out chairs to sit in the sun, and Lulu came down the steps from the drawing-room carrying a paper.

'Perfectly wonderful day,' said Aunt Gainy, in a high staccato voice which rang out all over the garden.

When Aunt Gainy said that she had a curious quickening feeling. The scene, the time, the place, even the words, went back years in her mind, they had associations of great happiness which she could not remember. Tim was coming to the opening of the grove; he knew where to find her. She noticed that he looked thoughtful, not very cheerful, he had been in the smoking-room with Uncle Heston.

'I thought perhaps we might go for a walk?'

'Yes, where shall we go? Shall we go to the cemetery? You haven't been there yet.'

He nodded. 'Do you mind if I go in and practise till you are ready?'

She saw darkness in his eyes, and the line in the middle of the lips grown very fine.

'Then you'll come and fetch me?' He went away.

She picked flowers round the garden for the graves of her adopted dead. The shadows of the trees on the lawn looked like warning fingers wagging up and down. Life, she knew, was full of dark pits and secrets people hid behind their eyes; hideous, cruel, bitter, painful secrets, they were waiting to spring upon one all down the line. One was always in the grip of that hateful power, authority. She desired above all things to be her own mistress.

Lulu was sitting in a garden chair, and she smiled into Lulu's grey eyes in which the past seemed to be forever rolling away. Lulu passed her hand over her head. She put her lips to the cheek faintly smelling of powder, still more faintly of something else and lavender. Lulu also kissed her.

'My Louie,' she said, and laughed a little as she opened the case in which her pince-nez lay embedded in velvet. She went back across the grass towards the house, it was soft and springy to the feet as if it were made of green elastic. Sometimes she felt as if they had some secret understanding between them; in spite of the fact that Lulu was her grandmother they seemed in some way to be equals, she had always loved her. The spring light was in the house, it came in through the coloured panes of the great window over the stairs, and one could see the trees swaying in green and blue worlds. Nurse was singing, 'Yip-i-addy-i-ay-i-ay', to Max who was making a wailing noise in the spare room, and strains of Beethoven came down from the top-storey, oddly mingling with nurse's nasal voice and Max's crying. She put on her hat and coat and borrowed a basket from Lulu's workroom for the flowers.

The trees waved in the garden in the wind. The two poplars by the gate stood like tall women shaking their plumed heads. The grass and the daisies swayed, while the heavy sweetness of the river and the pointed sharpness of spring fought together in the air. Now the brown palings of Linden were behind them, the chestnuts were on either side holding their white and pale pink flowers erect and towards the sky. It was a long way to the cemetery, they only spoke once, when Tim offered to carry the basket and she gave it to him. He walked beside her with one hand in his pocket. She herself was also occupied. For half-way up the avenue, the feeling of expectation had come to her. She had not had it for a long time; but she knew that it was only caused by the spring day, the yellow light among the heavy chestnut leaves, the wind, the shaking shadows.

Now they were at the cemetery. The adopted dead were people whose graves were either neglected or who had something interesting about them on their stones. Laetitia and Marion were both interesting and neglected. She explained this to Tim as they walked through the sea of graves to the older part where the sisters were. As she did so she wondered if it had not been lacking in tact to suggest the cemetery for their walk, whether it would not perhaps call up the sad memory of his mother. But he seemed to understand her feeling about the dead. One of the most satisfactory things about him was the way he took everything for granted. He did not say 'Funny little girl,' like other people. Or, 'How morbid,' like her mother. The only other person who had ever understood, and who had sometimes come with her to this place, was Aunt Margaret. That was because Aunt Margaret liked ghosts and was interested in what happened to people after they died. One of the most attractive things about Laetitia and Marion was that they had a piece of poetry on their grave, although it was otherwise so neglected.

TO THE MEMORY
OF LAETITIA ELIZABETH BARRON,
OF THE PARISH OF WICKHAMPSTEAD,
DECEASED THE 29TH MARCH, 1880,
AFTER MUCH SUFFERING,
AGED FORTY-ONE YEARS.

AND OF HER SISTER,
MARION AGATHA BARRON,
DECEASED THE 1ST MAY, 1881,
AGED THIRTY-NINE YEARS.
ON WHOSE SOULS, SWEET JESU, HAVE MERCY.

God Who so loveth flowers
Did call them hence,
First one, then two,
To seek their recompense.
The lovely flowers who faded in their prime
He gathered to His garden of all time.

Out of this poem after many nights of thinking
in bed as to why Marion had died so soon after
Laetitia, she had composed the story of their lives.
They had lived in an old cottage on the common
outside Wickhampstead. She had passed it very
often. A small squat chimney was stuck in the
middle of the roof and the cottage stood in a large
tract of ground now given over entirely to the
growing of potatoes. But the potatoes had nothing
to do with the sisters. In their time there had been
a garden there, for they were great gardeners. Any
day one passed one might have seen Laetitia,
before she got ill, hoeing in a long blue dress and
a large hat; and a little further away Marion, in a
sunbonnet, would be pruning rose trees. All their
relations were dead—which, she thought, must
have been very nice for them—and they lived alone.
One day Laetitia fell ill; she was very ill indeed,
and outside the porch the doctor told Marion that
her sister would die. But not yet; it might take years.

And it did take years. Laetitia would get a little better and then she would lie out in the garden and watch Marion weeding and hoeing, but she knew she was going to die, as one does know these things. Gradually she became worse and suffered a great deal, and Marion nursed her. One day, she said to Marion, 'Promise me something. When I am dead, don't leave this place. Stay here and make our flowers grow.' Marion promised. 'You must not be lonely,' Laetitia said. 'Because when I am dead I will always be with you.' Marion said nothing. She had a secret that she would not tell her sister; while she was nursing her she had caught the disease that was killing Laetitia. The day came and Laetitia died. Marion went to the funeral and covered the grave with flowers from the garden, and everyone was astonished because she did not show her grief. She was so calm and quiet, as if she had known everything from the beginning. She went back to her own life, and put the garden in order and planted out things for the summer and the autumn as if Laetitia had been there. But all the time she was very ill, and when it was finished she went to bed. The doctor said that she would die quicker than her sister because she had not taken care of herself; and so the next year she died, and they opened the grave and laid her with Laetitia.

It was a very sad story and every time she told it to herself the tears came into her eyes.

'What are you thinking about?' Tim was asking her, over the grave; he had been taking out weeds for her with his pocket-knife.

'Nothing, nothing, please don't ask me.'

The daffodils in the jam-pot stood up triumphantly among the tall grass.

'In a week from to-day I shall be going to school,' he said, looking at her. He shut his knife with a certain deliberate movement.

She stared. 'But why so soon?'

'My school begins before yours.'

If a thunderstorm had suddenly broken over their heads it could not have had a more darkening effect on the world. She sat and stared at the daffodils. Oh, Laetitia and Marion, did you also have to go to school or were you taught by a governess at home? Did you live all your lives in your garden thinking your own thoughts, or did you have to go away to be educated?

'I shall not be able to play the fiddle any more.'

'Why?'

'Because at English schools they do not like one if one is musical. Uncle Heston hopes I will grow out of it.'

She was not surprised. It was what one might have expected from a person who preferred music to come out of a gramophone.

'But you won't.'

'No, of course not, but I shall not be able to practise.'

She got up, she could not bear it. The iron fist had come down on them from nowhere, the rasping voice of authority. Do this. Go there. Do what you're told. Don't ask questions. It's all for your good. The eternal formula of unpleasant proceedings. One was never free. One was trapped inside this cage. They went back as they had come, in silence. But in the chestnut avenue she

put her hand into his, feeling it to be the only form
of sympathy she could offer him; he took it, holding it with his long fingers.   Outside the gate of
Linden, with the elm grove staring at them over
the brown palings, he threw back his head and
whistled in what sounded to her like a contemp-
tuous perfection the opening bars of a Bach pre-
lude she had often heard him play on the fiddle.

Hold fast. Hold fast. One must not cry. She sat
in the taxi holding on to her bursting soul in the
tightness of agony.   Lulu, her mother, and Aunt
Gainy were all coming to consign her to the school
gates. It was remarkable how people always came
to look on, on those occasions in one's life when
they should not be there.   When people died or
were married everyone came in crowds, when the
most decent thing they could have done was to
have stayed away. She did not mind Lulu. Lulu
was different.

Her mother and Aunt Gainy were talking
loudly because there was such a noise going over
the bridge. She stared out of the window and
watched the traffic.   Hold fast, hold fast, everything and everybody said.

'Cheer up, Louie,' said her mother.

'You'll be coming back to us in the holidays,'
Aunt Gainy said.

Lulu looked out of the window through her
austere, veiled eyes.

'I don't believe she really minds a bit,' her
mother went on.

Hold fast. Hold fast.

'She's a funny, independent little girl.'

'Oh, I expect she does, really,' said Aunt Gainy.
Lulu leant forward and touched her knee.

'Look, Louie, there's such an amusing man
standing over there with a monkey.'

She looked, and saw through tear-stricken eyes
a small monkey in a red jacket standing on top of
a barrel-organ and holding out a tiny top-hat for
pennies.

The chairs in the convent parlour had very stiff
backs; they were hideous chairs, upholstered in
yellow and red. There was a strip of red carpet on
the polished floor, and beyond the French windows
of the parlour ran a stretch of white cloisters;
a garden gleamed behind them full of trees. They
all looked self-conscious, but Lulu sat stiffly on her
chair, her hands clasped over the handle of her
neatly rolled umbrella; she was staring over the
grand piano at a picture of the Vatican hanging in
a frame of dark green velvet. The Reverend
Mother came in, a stout cheerful woman, and
shook hands. She was not at all sentimental and
something in her brisk, vibrant manner made one
pull oneself together and hold fast.

She took them round the garden. It was a
beautiful garden with a small orchard on one side of
it, and many winding paths with trees and hedges.

'A magnificent garden to have so near London,'
said Lulu.

The Reverend Mother smiled and said that they
thought so too. Now the moment was coming,
they were back in the parlour. She saw her mother's
tearful face, felt her moist kiss, smelt powder,
scent, silks. The Reverend Mother looked on as

if she were assisting at an operation of a not unusual nature and knew exactly what was to be done. Lulu lifted her navy blue spotted veil and kissed her. Her eyes were very calm, her gloved hand shook a little. Through the black coat, where it was crossed in a point, she could see the silver chain that always hung over Lulu's high-necked blouse, held together at intervals by three little amethyst brooches. Her mother was drying her eyes; Aunt Gainy was unbuttoning and re-buttoning her glove. The tall portress opened the door smiling, and they went out. Lulu was the last to leave and she was the only one who did not turn back and wave.

The portress closed the door and now she was alone at Mexican Gate.

'Come along,' said the brisk, surgical voice of the Reverend Mother. 'I am going to take you to your form mistress, Sister Mary Anselm.'

She followed her down winding corridors smelling of floor polish.

THE white cubicle curtains hung down in the darkness. She lay awake, strained and excited among strange surroundings. Strange sheets and blankets, and her head was on too low a pillow. All around unknown people were sleeping who knew each other but whom she did not know. She shut her eyes and saw Tim turning round at the gate waving good-bye, the cab waiting for him with Uncle Heston already there, his white gloved hands clasped over an ebony walking-stick. He sat inside the cab like fate waiting, a solemn,

unblinking owl. She imagined her own little room
quiet and lonely for her. The white bedspread on
the bed not turned back, and Lulu in her room
sleeping on her high pillows; the night-light burning on one of the altars under a blue shade. She
turned round and sighed. There was a wooden
partition on one side of the bed, and when she
turned she knocked it with her elbow. She would
go to sleep. She would dream of beautiful things
that would make her forget; of flamboyant butter-
flies and purple mountains. But now she was
running, running after the Reverend Mother
down corridors and passages. The Reverend
Mother's veil got caught in a nail on the wall.
She turned round to disentangle it and it was not
her at all, it was Lulu who had become a nun and
who laughed very much to see how surprised she
was. But now Lulu had vanished, and she opened
a door and went into a classroom. There was a
huge book on the desk, her desk. On the page
which was illuminated in gold, red, and blue, was
written: *The secret of happiness*. She read on and
discovered that it was something she had always
known, without knowing that she knew it. She
had a feeling of very great happiness, and turned
the heavy pages to see who had written the book.
On the title page under the title, which she could
not read because it was written in another language,
she read her own name.

'SHUT the door, please, Zara, and put a piece of
paper in it by the lock. We must have it seen to,'
Sister Mary Anselm said.

She watched Zara shutting the door. Her jet-black staccato-looking hair danced over her shoulders as she bent her head. Everybody watched Zara shutting the door. Then she came back grinning derisively at the form, with her back turned to the rostrum so that Sister Mary Anselm could not see her, and slid into her desk, putting her elbows on it and bending over her books. She had decided that she liked Zara and that perhaps one day when she was no longer a new girl they would become friends.

She looked up at the windows. Through them she could see the green quadrangle, across which was the nuns' part of the convent and the school refectory. The low, regular chanting of the nuns at office came over the cloisters from the chapel, Sister Mary Anselm was reading. Behind her spectacles her tired eyes were fixed on the print. There were a great many pictures on the walls, historical and religious, some of other countries; many were photographs of old French cathedrals. Sister Mary Anselm looked up suddenly, and said:

'Sit up, girls, sit up.'

Everyone straightened themselves except Zara, who did not seem to have heard her. Zara was the black sheep of the Lower School. She liked her pale, creamy skin, her dark bright violet eyes, the sharp, clearly-cut features, and the slender lively body which went with her bold character. The clock struck six and the Angelus rang in the chapel. They turned from their geography books and knelt on their chairs towards the statue of Our Lady.

'*The angel of the Lord declared unto Mary.*'—'*And she conceived of the Holy Ghost,*' answered the form in severe, matter-of-fact accents, which they kept up throughout the prayers.

After the Angelus they sat down. Almost immediately there was a knock, and Sister Bridget looked in.

'May I have Sybil for her piano lesson, Sister?'

Sister Mary Anselm looked surprised to see her, but she said: 'Certainly, Sister.'

A very fair girl with long plaits put away her books. Sister Bridget was causing a disturbance. She stood in the doorway, smiling. She was Irish and very pretty, and the white coif round her face only showed how pretty she was. She had a natural and infectious charm; one had the feeling that she thought she ought to dispense this charm always wherever she went. When she smiled and half shut her eyes, her long black lashes came over her lovely cheeks, and everyone was bewildered, surprised, enchanted; and her hands were graceful little things which she used a great deal when speaking. She smiled again and took Sybil away. After they had gone people dropped things and fidgeted. Only Zara had not stirred, she sat with stubborn elbows on her desk.

'I think you might take your arithmetic books now,' said Sister Mary Anselm.

Everyone except Zara changed their books.

THEY had come back from a long hot walk and there was a nail coming up through the sole of her shoe which had been painful all during the walk.

The nail and Beatrice Sheringham's conversation about the number of maids they had at Sheringham Park had made her tired. Beatrice's father had just been created a peer and she was the Honourable Beatrice Sheringham.

The cloak-room was a long stone half-basement passage called for some reason now forgotten, the 'Coalhole'. At the end, near the door leading out on to the garden, people were laughing. Zara was washing her hands when suddenly she threw some water, scooped in the palm of her hand, across the shoulders of the most sedate member of the third form.

'You know you could get into a row for that, Zara.'

Zara laughed and made grotesque figures with her legs while she dried her hands, and several people gathered to look on.

'Sister Anselm's quite right about you,' said the sedate member. 'She said the other day that where you really ought to be was not in a convent at all.'

'Well, where? Choke it up, Mary Ann, my soul isn't a fragile article like yours.'

Mary Bertrams paused. 'She said you ought to be in a reformatory.'

There was a shocked silence from the four girls looking on, then laughter.

'It only shows the poor darling doesn't know what people get sent to reformatories for,' said Zara, now doing gymnastics in front of Mary.

'You ought not to speak of a nun like that, it isn't respectful.'

A black figure was coming down the steps of the Coalhole.

'Far too much noise in here,' said Sister Mary Anselm. 'And I'm surprised to find that it's you who are making it, Mary.'

Zara stooped to get her shoes, with a subdued noise in her throat.

SHE was weeding in the new girls' garden, while the Honourable Beatrice was standing behind and telling another girl how she hated gardening because the damp earth got into one's nails, when there were shrieks of laughter. Zara appeared among the trees from the direction of the Coalhole in fancy dress. A black felt winter school hat was pinned to resemble a three-cornered hat, someone's coat hung loosely from her shoulders to give the impression of a cloak, and she was whirling a hockey stick with a long red streamer round it. She went round the playground making wild pagan gestures and extraordinary whistling noises like the wind.

'Is anyone brave enough to come with me?'

'Where to?' several people asked cautiously.

Zara dropped on one knee. 'I'm the devil and I'm going back to Hell, but I want a few companions first.'

A circle gathered round her, laughing. 'Take care, Sister Anselm's coming.'

Zara paid no attention. 'Will anyone come to the bottomless pit with me?'

When Zara said this it reminded her so much of her own games that, without thinking, she ran forward and broke through the circle. The group stared at her, but Zara jumped up, took her hand and dragged her through the trees.

'You're a lot of cowards, you wouldn't come if God Himself asked you!' shouted Zara back at them, seizing her one disciple. She let herself be dragged towards the Coalhole.

'Hide quickly.'

In a cupboard in the laboratory they hid. There was a terrible smell in the cupboard. Someone came into the Coalhole and called them: 'Zara and Louie Burnett. Sister Anselm wants you, you must come to her at once.'

'Dilly dilly, come and be killed for pretending to be the devil,' said Zara. 'You're new, aren't you? This will mean a row.'

After what seemed a long time, because the smell was so bad in the cupboard, they came out, and sat on the long table that went down the middle of the room fitted with all sorts of curious things, and talked about the school. Zara was rather conscious of making an impression but perfectly sincere. When the bell rang for prayers they went softly to the door.

'Now for it,' said Zara, her eyes full of darkly bright lights.

A very faint smell of limes came through the windows as they wrote their Sunday letters; Sister Anselm had just gone out of the room to speak to someone. She was writing to Tim.

'Doesn't Louie Burnett remind you of somebody's maiden aunt?' said a voice from the back of the room.

'I wish some of you reminded one of anything so pleasant.'

'You're merely being rude, Zara.'

'So are you, fidgety Phil.'

'I should have thought Louie could speak for herself without you butting in,' said Mary Bertrams at the next desk.

'You never think quite enough, Mary Ann, for goodness sake turn your silly little nose out of my direction, I don't like it.'

Mary Bertrams said something about board-school manners and shrugged her shoulders.

'Well, if Mary's got a silly little nose, Louie Burnett's got fishy eyes,' came from the back of the class.

'Better than having two little black holes in one's face like a pig,' said Zara, turning round and fixing the girl who had spoken with her own dark handsome eyes. She felt a painful blush creeping over her face.

'Now, for the Lord's sake shut up, and let me finish my letter,' said Zara.

There was a pause and pens worked over paper.

She had learnt that it was dangerous to emerge from traditional obscurity into a friendship with a brilliant and rather daring personality. It exposed one to the crude witticisms of persons, who though lacking in every other kind of perception, seemed to possess the facility for putting a finger on one's weak spots; and when Zara set herself up to be the champion of her stupid sensitiveness they were more entertained than ever.

'But really, Louie Burnett, do tell us why you

part your hair in the middle like that? It gives you such an old maidish look,' said Sybil.

Her heart thumped with fear. 'Does it? I like it parted in the middle.' Her voice sounded to her tight and prim, and very much like an old maid. Everyone looked up from their letters and laughed.

'Perhaps she wants to be an old maid,' suggested somebody, with that kindness more killing than any cruelty, and which she always associated with Aunt Elise.

'Pat Sybil's little freckled face for her,' said Zara. 'She loves having her face patted. That's what Sister Bridget does when you're a good girl and know your piano piece, isn't it, dear?'

Sybil jerked her pigtails. 'Let your little friend speak for herself.'

'I shan't,' said Zara.

She got up and stood over Sybil; she was just bending down to pat Sybil's cheeks in fine imitation of Sister Bridget when Sister Anselm came in.

'What are you doing out of your place, Zara?'

'I was just showing Sybil how much nicer she'd look if she did her hair differently, Sister.'

'Kindly go to your place.'

Zara went.

Time swung slowly round at Mexican Gate. It was only her third week, and Sister Bridget was conducting Wednesday's choral class in the recreation room. They sat on the hard-backed benches and shared copies of the score for an operetta they were going to do at the end of the term. Sister Bridget rolled up her sleeves and showed her small white wrists encased in linen. She tapped on the table in the middle of the room.

'Now girls, I'm going to try out your voices in order to cast you for parts. As I point my stick at each one in turn she will stand up and sing a few bars. Florrie will accompany her on the piano. Marie Bertrams, begin *Annie Laurie*, please. Thank you; sit down. Mary Priddle, continue. Thank you; sit down. Now Phyllis, open your mouth, my child, wider, wider. That will do. Come, Sybil dear, thank you. Now, Beatrice, don't you know *Annie Laurie*? What do you know, my dear? Don't you know one tune? Nothing at all? Surely you know *God save the King*?'

Beatrice blushed. The form giggled.

'Silence, please, girls,' said Sister Bridget, lifting her baton. 'Then sing "ah", my dear, a nice round "ah", as if you were very surprised about something. That's right. Zara, I know your talent, but for the sake of argument let us hear it.'

Zara stood up and sang without any affectation. She had a pleasant deep quality in her voice. Now it was coming to her turn. She was already beginning to tremble.

'Now, Louie.'

She got up trembling and sang through the first few bars, holding on to the bench with one hand.

'Go on, sing out, don't be so nervous,' said Sister Bridget.

The colour went flaming up to her face, and her knees shook under her.

'Thank you. Very nice timbre. That will do.'

She left them for a moment and went over to speak to Florrie at the piano.

'Whatever's a timbre?' asked several voices behind Zara.

'A quality of tone,' said Zara, without turning round, but Sister Bridget had seen her.

'Who gave you permission to speak, Zara?

'Nobody, Sister, they wanted to know what timbre was.'

'Then they should have asked me. Timbre is a characteristic quality of sound produced by a voice or an instrument,' she told them across the room, tapping her baton on to the palm of her hand.

She lightly stood poised against the piano, her veil thrown back, the smallness of her hips showing in spite of the heavy folds of the habit. She was like a piece of delicately tinted china. And she could keep order, and did, too; even Zara yielded her a sulky obedience. For she had noticed that Zara definitely did not like her, and that Sister Bridget was by way of liking Zara because she thought her an odd, brilliant child. By carefully watching Sister Bridget on many occasions she had observed that, although she dispensed her smiles right and left as if she considered that the world was a sad place and must be cheered up, and was conscious of her own ability to add to its cheer, yet she reserved her real devotion and almost fanatical admiration for talent in any shape or form. Now she was going on up another bench, pointing her baton at each one in turn, and Zara sighed.

THEY were walking round the garden smelling the sweet smell of grass mixed with flowering limes. She had been chosen for a part in the operetta.

'It's only because she's got that goody-goody look,' someone was saying among a group under the trees.

'Hush,' said Mary Priddle, and the group began talking about something else.

'That's you,' said Zara.

'Zara, have I got a goody-goody look?'

Now for once and all she would get it out of her. Her elbow was squeezed, Zara's only gesture of affection.

'You've got a sort of poet look. That's what they mean. You needn't take any notice of them, they're jealous.'

The lengthened shadows of the trees lay across the grass, and over the hedge one could hear the voices of the Upper School practising their bowling on the asphalt. Sister Bridget's approval had somehow taken the edge off her maiden-aunt appearance, and she had noticed a certain changed attitude towards her in the form. It was as if for the first time they acknowledged her as a person, who, if they did not much care about her, had a personality of her own, because that personality had been allowed to her by an authority which they respected. At prayers she and Zara knelt together. They faced the mantelpiece in the recreation room on which stood a statue of Our Lady of Succour. The May dusk came into the room through the long windows, Zara's chin was resting on her hand, her lower lip protruded slightly; her eyes were gravely, firmly, and thoughtfully looking straight ahead of her. Somehow it seemed more the pose of study than of prayer.

SHE woke in the very early pale summer morning. All around lay a white and gold quietness; something that one does not expect of life except in its richest moments. She waited for a tram to rattle down the long road outside Mexican Gate, but there was silence; nor did the early bell ring across the cloisters for the nuns. She did not want to destroy the wonderful feeling as if one were lying in a magic circle. She turned round and the wall-paper seemed unfamiliar. The quilt was soft and heavy. Then she remembered what had happened. Lulu had taken Combesmere for the summer, and she was at Leathley for the holidays.

Beyond the white railings of the balcony the garden sloped down a hill, and she could see the trees in the garden of Barbican opposite. And still further away and below it through the trees she could catch sight of a long silver streak flowing between wide green banks—the river. Tim was still asleep when she went into his room, the blind half-way down the window, flapping against the woodwork. A strand of soft black hair had fallen across his forehead. His hand bounded up under the sheet as she touched him and he sat up as if someone had struck him. She drew back into the doorway. He laughed when he saw her.

'I'm so sorry, I didn't know where I was.'

'It's Leathley, Tim.'

'Yes, I know. For the moment I thought I was at Hanton.'

His room faced the other side of the garden which ran up the hill in terraces. On the last terrace one could see the wire netting of the tennis court, beyond it Leathley Hill went on still a few hundred feet further. He got out of bed and flung his arms over his head.

'What is the time?'

'I don't know.'

She stood looking at him, he seemed different. Could it be that a few months of school life had made him change? Or was it she who had changed? She stood there deeply embarrassed, she had come in so eager and excited to share the joy of being at Leathley with him. She was looking forward to acting as showman to the place that was to her like a dream place. All she said was:

'You'll be able to practise.'

'Yes, I know, thank God.'

He put his feet against the window, built low into the wall, and looked out on to the garden. She wanted to ask him if he liked Hanton and what it had been like, and if he had been able to practise, and to tell him about Zara. Yesterday there had been no time for conversation; they had come down straight from London in the train with Aunt Gainy, and strange people in the carriage. She could not say a word.

'What is the matter, Louie?'

She shook her head. Then she turned and went out of his room.

SHE was very tired coming up from the river. The soft rhythmic sound all day in their ears and the gentle motion of the launch cutting through the water had made her sleepy. They had been out all day with Lulu and Uncle Philip, who had come down for a week with Uncle Heston, and had been shaken out of his usual moroseness for the day. Now he was coming up behind more slowly with Lulu. Tim took her arm and helped her up the hill.

They were passing Leathley Church and nine clear grave strokes were being struck. An old rose colour began spreading itself over Leathley Hill. Tim was carrying Lulu's blue square cushion which she always had behind her back in her chair in the launch.

'I will sing to you to make you go to sleep,' he said, smiling at her.

And he sang in a low voice a French lullaby, but as he had translated it, it did not rhyme. It was about the fishing ships coming into the bay and the mother rocking her cradle. One could imagine the peaceful evening, the graceful red sails of the smacks coming in over the pale, pearly-looking water. Now the mother was lighting the candles in the low house, they flared up and shed their green glow in the dusk. The coloured squares on her apron gradually faded with the light as she stood in the doorway looking out over the quays. He paused while they were passing old Mrs. Bortley's Georgian house; a square red brick building. It was the manor house, and Mrs. Bortley owned nearly all the land round Leathley. She was a masterful old lady who drove a high pony trap, and wore very hard-brimmed hats.

'Go on,' she told him.

Now the clouds were gathering in the bay as it were from nowhere, they made the pale, pearly water turn black. The mother's hand trembled on the cradle, the red sails shook in the wind, the candles wavered and suddenly went out, blown by a gust that swept through the house, and the mother started up and ran to the door crying with fear. Would the smacks get in before the storm? But the song did not answer the question, and now they had reached the top of the hill and opposite was the old *Cup and Beadle* Inn. It had once been a posting inn; a hundred years ago people had stopped to change their horses here on the way to London. There seemed to be a great deal of excitement in the bar. They could hear the voices of farmers and villagers mingling together, glasses being rattled and chairs moved, heavy boots stamping on the tiled floor. Above it all, some-one suddenly roared out: 'I don't care if I do, Garge.'

And a wave of laughter seemed to rock over them all.

They had to wait for Lulu and Uncle Philip who were a long way behind.

'There's going to be a war,' said Tim.

'How do you know?'

'I heard Uncle Heston reading about it out of the paper.'

The old rose colour had now spread all over the sky, but the sun had disappeared. It had slipped behind a bank of clouds from which it sent down its rays like a picture of the Holy Ghost descending on the Apostles.

As they entered the gate, which creaked because

it wanted oiling, and went up the steep path, Uncle Heston came out on the stone verandah waving to them. Aunt Gainy was sitting in a chair, her racket laid across her knees.

'What news, old chap?' shouted Uncle Philip.

'War will be declared by midnight,' Uncle Heston called back, triumphantly.

They all went up on to the verandah and he told them what he knew from the bulletin in the Post Office, in his slow voice. Uncle Philip was very excited.

'What did I tell you, my dear chap?'

Lulu got up from the chair in which she had sat to listen to him.

'That is bad news, very bad news,' she said. 'And bad news can wait.'

'But what else could we have done, Mother?' Uncle Heston asked in a puzzled and rather horrified tone.

She shook her head and began to go upstairs. As if she did it on purpose, she went up more slowly than usual.

Tim was finishing something that ended with a long note in the treble, a no-ending at all, behind her in the drawing-room. Then he began to play again. She half listened and half did not listen, his music forming a background to her thoughts, and her thoughts were about Barbican, the house opposite. For years and years it had been shut up. It had been shut up when she was five years old and Lulu had taken Combesmere for the summer just as she had done this year. And Barbican was her dream-house. She had hidden in that garden and played in those verandahs; and here and there where a shutter had been left open or had come unhooked, she had looked in at the dark rooms. She used to wander round the garden and talk to the trees and dream her stories, Dalius had also been with her there. An evil-looking witch of a woman had come once a week and had gone over the house. She had hidden in the bushes and watched her, but she had never been caught. Now, after years of neglect and desolation, the owners of the house were coming back to it and she had not been able to take Tim over to see it. Doors and windows were flung open. People came and went. Pantechnicons arrived from London, and the builder was making repairs to the porch. Poor Barbican looked down with forcibly opened eyes at the unwelcome activity; the war had brought its owners home from abroad.

Tim had stopped playing and Lulu and Aunt Gainy came into the room. Lulu's silver chain clinked against her belt as she settled herself in her chair.

'Lulu, who are the people who are going to live at Barbican? What are they like, and how many of them are there?'

Lulu laughed and opened her paper.

'I don't really know them, my darling. They're the Berringers from Weir Park in Langthorne. I think Miss Berringer owns the house. Weir Park now belongs to her brother.'

She put her pince-nez on the bridge of her nose and now she was going to read. Aunt Gainy was sitting at the piano frowning at one of Tim's accompaniments while he stood behind her point-ing out something. Then he leaned over and played several bars over for her himself with one hand. Aunt Gainy nodded and he took up his fiddle.

She moved her stool further into the room to listen to him. Aunt Gainy was still making little lines in her forehead. The pink frill down the middle of her blouse tossed to and fro as she moved her hands; it was too long and got in her way. Whenever she made a mistake she apologised with a nervous laugh, and Tim said: 'It doesn't matter, Auntie.'

His bow went on serenely over the strings. The room was full of that beautiful tone like a charm that fell upon the senses. Sailing over the flatness of life, it broke through the hard, bitter places. A passion caught for a moment by art and held for a certain space of time. She had a feeling as she sat with her chin in her hands that nothing mattered. That nothing could hurt one. The past and the future faded out, and there was nothing but the present in which they were both contained and kept forever.

AND now it was the last night of the holidays and Lulu was coming to say good-night. She had left the door open so that she might hear her coming along the passage. After a long time an even step sounded on the stairs, pausing on the top stair as if Lulu stopped to take her breath, then continuing slowly but with no hesitation. The smell of lavender began to come nearer, and with it a tinkling sound: the knocking of the silver acorn hanging on Lulu's

chain against the buckle of her belt. As a very little
girl she used to unscrew the acorn and put dried
leaves inside it. There was a rustling of a stiff silk
petticoat, a soft hushing as the folds of the skirt
came together, and Lulu was in the room. She
stood at the foot of the bed.

'My darling, I'm so sorry it's the last night, but
we'll be able to look forward to having you again.
Even if your mother does come home because of
the war, she will, I hope, come and stay at Linden.'

Lulu smoothed the pillow with her ringed hand,
the wide palm, the fingers that turned slightly back.

'Good-night, my Louie.'

She kissed Lulu's soft scented cheek. For a
second the hands pressed her shoulders, then the
rustling and hushing sounds started again and the
door closed, shutting away the last comforting
smell of lavender and the tinkling of the acorn.

She sat up in bed. She could see the stars outside, because she always slept with the blinds half-
way up to break the terrifying dark. The tears ran
down her face. It was not the thought of going
back to school, the thought of leaving one's leisure
which one wanted so much. It was the thought of
her mother coming home again because of the war.
They would all go and live somewhere in a furnished house. There would be no Lulu. There
would be sudden fits of temper, unjust punish-
ments and the usual misunderstandings; and there
would be no Byng to mitigate them, for Byng's
ship was going to the war. She could not bear the
idea of living alone with her mother. The servants
would go and come. There would be everlasting
altercations between nurse and her mother, and

cramped and awful moments when she would be appealed to for a love which she could not give.

Byng had called her his last love. Tall, fair-haired Byng, with a queer, crooked mouth, leaning against a tree filling his pipe after a picnic which they had had together, no one else there. They often went out by themselves for the day. Byng called it 'taking a day out of life'. 'You're my last love, Babbams, and don't believe anybody who tells you that the last love isn't the best. It's the love of one's vision,' and he had laughed. She had not quite understood the last part, but he had told her not to bother about it. So she was Byng's last love, and on those days when he got into still, cold rages and began to pack his trunks when he had decided to go away forever, she would go downstairs, sit on them, and ask him to stay because she was his last love. At the end of his leave she alone saw him off at the station. He would kiss her and call her his darling and his sweetheart, his only lady in the world, and promise to send her presents wherever his ship went. And when she got home there would be a terrible row going on in the house and nurse would be leaving.

She lay and thought about it, about the years of her childhood which were behind her, until she could not bear to be alone and think any longer. She got up and went into Tim. It was thick darkness in his room.

'What is it, what is the matter?'

She stumbled through the darkness and found him.

'I don't want to live in furnished houses. I don't want to live with mother. Oh, Tim.'

He held her shoulders. 'But you're thinking of things that may not happen.'

'Oh, but they have happened. They have happened.'

She sat on the bed and leant against him in her grief.

He said nothing.

Then he said: 'I will come and put you into your bed.'

She got into her bed and he put the bedclothes over her. He bent over the pillow.

'Shall I kiss you?'

No, she could not face the idea of him kissing her. It was a strange, frightening idea.

'Then shall I kiss your hand?'

She put her hand out of the bed and he kissed the fingers.

'Don't be unhappy. I was unhappy when my mother died, but one gets over it. One *must* get over it.'

He seemed to be talking to himself in the middle of the room. Then he went. She lay still, while her mind twisted itself into tortuous shapes. She heard them come up to bed, and heard the little brass-faced clock in the hall strike twelve. The soft bed might have been a rack upon which she was stretched. In the distance there was a humming noise below Linden on the road. Two white streaks of light shot across the room and a gate swung back with a long, yawning sound. The humming continued, only further off. A car had gone into Barbican opposite. She dozed. She was walking along a narrow white ribbon suspended over a gorge. All around were great mountains and the mist hanging on them. It dangled in the air like white beards. She dared not look at them. Somehow she knew she must try and get across the ribbon without falling into the gorge. Rocks were sticking up in the air, their pointed edges waiting to receive her, and she could hear quite distinctly the roaring of a river that was passing at a great speed below. The white ribbon was beginning to break. It was old and the strain of having her walk across it was too much for it. One of her feet slipped through it and now she began to fall hundreds of feet through the air. A very beautiful voice spoke above the noise of the river, she heard it even while she was falling.

'Don't forget to shut the gate,' it said.

But now she was very near the river; the bubbling water rose to meet her and hammered in her ears.

II

SHE took the book from Zara's hand and sat down in the chair facing the needlework class. Everyone's heads were bent over their work. Each person sat at her own small table. The afternoon sun trickled in through the windows throwing up high lights on Zara's shining ebony hair as she stood at Sister Boniface's desk.

'And now what will you do since you have given your occupation to your friend, eh?' said Sister Boniface, peering at Zara over her spectacles.

'Whatever you like, Sister.'

'But it is always the same with you. You do not like what I give you to do. Needlework is not your métier, eh? It is extraordinary, but your brains do not seem to go to your fingers.'

'Certainly they do,' said Zara, stretching out her well-shaped fingers. 'But not where they are concerned with a needle and thread. There is something I wish you would allow them to concern themselves with, Sister.'

'And what is that?'

'The choosing of your literature for the needlework class. I haven't the privilege of knowing who chooses your books, but they are frightful, perfectly frightful, Sister.'

Sister Boniface threw up her head and made a noise like a snort. 'But how am I to know, my good Zara, how am I to know these English books?

You do not mean that they are immoral?'

'Not in the least. I should say morality was the strongest point in their favour. I was speaking of their literary, their intrinsic value.'

'Intrinsic, eh? You are being witty, I suppose. You would have their intrinsic value to be literary rather than moral?'

'Certainly. A work of art may have a moral bias, but it can be a work of art without one.'

'Iconoclast!'

'Not at all. Artists are often persons whose morality you would censure, Sister, for being different from your own.'

'Indeed! But I am an artist myself. What do you call this?' She held up her work.

Zara bowed. 'Without a doubt you are. I am standing at this moment admiring the amount of morality you are putting into every stitch.'

'Tiens! Impertinent! But you were always bold. Well, you can choose me two books for Friday and I will look over them. But mind, *rien de choquant*.' She winked at Zara.

'I protest. You do my intelligence an injustice.'

'Go along, you, with your intelligence. I say that it is a pity it does not extend to your fingers.'

'And I maintain that it does.'

'Very well then, take these and wind me some balls.' She drew out a drawer behind her full of skeins of wool.

'I shall need a companion for this work, unless I use one of your chairs.'

'No, no, take one of your companions, take Marie-Thérèse.'

Zara went to the back of the class and began winding wool with a ginger-haired Belgian girl. Now that the conversation immediately beside her had stopped she went on reading the book that Zara had been condemning, more or less sensible of the text. Bonny loved to argue with Zara; although she pretended to think her a dark *méchante* girl, as she had once called her when they were in the fourth form together. Zara had risen behind her desk with a very straight face. 'It was God who gave me the colour of my hair, Sister,' she had said. But Bonny had been ready for her. 'Indeed, I hope it was so.' That was five years ago when they had first come up from the Lower School. Now when one looked at Zara one realized something about her. She was like a well-cut diamond. Two years back she had got a little stout, but now she was growing again, shooting up, tall and slender, a certain hardness about her chin and sometimes round her mouth. She had a hard, resilient quality; the world would never get very much out of Zara, she would look at it with those analytical eyes and decide exactly how much everybody and everything was worth. She did not care, she could do most things well. She was a scholar and learning came easily to her, she was not afraid of anyone. Bonny had been right, she was bold. But what boldness, how much she envied it herself. Now that Brenda had come up into the Upper School, Zara's diamond-like quality was more striking than ever beside Brenda's mobile face; it was intensified because Brenda was so much more mobile than other people.

IT was Saturday afternoon after tea, and nearly everyone had gone into the garden. She was turning out her locker because she had lost a book. Sybil was arranging her music, having got permission to practise on the grand in the recreation room; it was the best piano in the school. Zara came through the room humming.

'Hello, Sybil, are you going to indulge your propensity for work, on a Saturday afternoon?'

She went across to the piano and looked at the music.

'It's a Ballancz sonata in E minor,' said Sybil.

Zara sat down and played through, with much less practice but with many more times art, the short sonata which Sybil had been studying during the whole of one term. Sybil, standing by the piano, sighed.

'Why ever don't you take up music, Zara? I suppose you have heaps of talent in your family?'

Zara leant back against the music chair. 'Because I'm going to do something else.' She played over three bars in the treble. 'That second movement's too flimsy.'

'Are you criticising Ballancz?'

'Certainly. Why not? Criticism is the current coin of a work. Ballancz wrote this second movement when he was either feeling sick or had had a row with his wife, it's quite unequal to the rest of the thing, pulls it down to an almost mediocre level.'

Sybil looked at the ceiling. Zara wheeled round on her. 'You don't think that Ballancz wasn't affected by the ordinary things of life just as we are? You don't imagine that artists live in a sort of celestial dream, that they don't have rows with their wives, and that a badly burnt piece of steak isn't enough to choke a sonata to death?'

'I don't know,' said Sybil, with a certain stubbornness in her voice.

Zara got up. 'Then you can't be an artist.'

She took Sybil by the shoulders and pushed her gently down into the chair.

'But don't let me deter you by my patter. You sit down and go at it hard.' She put her hands behind her back and walked up and down behind Sybil's chair in imitation of a professor giving a lesson. 'If I might suggest, Miss Manley, I should say you have reached a stage when it would be advisable to think a little less of how you're doing it, and a little more of what you're doing. Feeling, you know; emotion. After all, feeling can't be entirely ignored. It's out of feelings that things get made. I think one ought to feel things —as well as do them well.'

Sybil laughed. 'Really, Zara, why don't you give music lessons? I believe Sister Bridget said something like that the other day.'

'Did she? Well, what better authority than Lady B.? Never mind me, my dear, I talk a lot of rot. You go on working. If you work hard for the next ten years, or perhaps more, you may at the end of that time begin to be a good pianist.'

Sybil sighed. 'Oh, I'm fully prepared for it to take longer than that.'

Zara turned on her. 'Well, you shouldn't be then, for that makes you lazy mentally. You should be prepared for it to happen at any moment, knowing that it won't.'

'Oh, go on, Zara, and let me practise,' said Sybil putting down the loud pedal.

'I'll be gone, prestissimo!'

They went out together through the Coalhole. 'Imagine her being fully prepared for it to take longer than that! You'd think she'd got two or three hundred years to live. Come on, my heart, let's go into the sunlight.'

The autumn sun was streaming over the asphalt. They stood on the edge of the playground and looked at everybody. In the distance members of the fifth and sixth forms were occupying the two tennis courts and a group of people were watching them. Several people were attending to their gardens, some were sitting under the trees sewing; but there was no one anywhere with a book in her hand.

'Come and sit under the trees,' said Zara, 'and watch the tennis players. It must be peculiar to have such a passion for a game that one's always practising one's service or one's backhanders even when one's doing something else. The other night I saw O'Reilly's shadow on the curtain in the bath-room, I thought she must be having a fit. But no, she was only practising a stroke with an invisible racket in her hand; and then they fall in love with tennis champions and try to acquire a style like the beloved. I wonder what they'll all be doing in ten or twelve years time; husbands, children, or per-haps some of them will be earning their living. Ah,' Zara closed her eyes and leant back; 'and what shall we be doing? Because it's not so very far away; this war won't last for ever, and then——' She broke off and sat up. 'It's a good thing Sybil hasn't got two or three hundred years to live, because she'd never make a pianist, she's not even musical. It must be some queer strain of personal ambition or some deep desire for a superiority which they haven't got, which makes certain kinds of people go in for things they haven't the slightest talent for. And you once let her call you an old maid; it's she who's the old maid, creatively and spiritually speaking, Sybil's a born spinster. She may marry and have dozens of children, but that won't prevent her remaining a spinster for ever. You once let that silly little thing, whose pigtails I used to pull, be rude to you about the way you parted your hair. Well, we've paid her out for that. That loud pedal was definite, wasn't it? How irritating she must find me, she wouldn't take any notice of me if I wasn't musical; but I am, and she can't get over the fact that I am and that I haven't got any ambition about it. She can't get over the fact that I play the piano to please myself. And that's the way with all the little Sybils of the world; they don't realize that it's love, not ambition, that makes an artist.'

Zara sat back again; her well brilliantined hair was drawn straight over her head, her features might have been cut out with a chisel.

The ping-pong of balls on the asphalt courts was a dreamy sound across the purple light of the afternoon. The trees had been losing their leaves, and they lay distributed over the paths. The long look of autumn lay on the convent buildings, a deeper lemon in the sunlight, a longer shadow slanted in the shade. Far, far distant, forgotten memories seemed to be in the air. There had once been a time of wonderful happiness, long ago, not in her life, but in whose? She knew now that this had been feeling of expectation she had had as a child. It was not expectation; it was in the past, but the autumn air was pregnant with that past. She was thinking about the two or three hundred years that would be not Sybil's or Zara's or hers, because she herself would so much have liked those two or three hundred years. She wanted to be able to dream in quietness, just to look at things for years and years; the most important thing to be the particular slant of a shadow on a hill. She wanted to understand the architecture of the trees, to be able to spend time indefinitely looking at them. Above all things she wanted time; time to grow slowly. But she was not going to be allowed it; she had known that for some time. In the world a great wheel was grinding men to pieces. She hated the war, rebelled and fought against the hysteria that was everywhere; but they went on being killed. Masses and prayers were said for them in the chapel. Awkward moments occurred sometimes in the dormitory at night when condolences had to be offered to people who had suddenly been bereaved; and yet, although outside the world was being shaken in the grip of war, here time kept its slow and steady pulse. Autumn did not come any quicker because thousands of men were being killed. It made no difference to the shadows or to the trees losing their leaves. There was a certain waning look about the sky very much like the look she had noticed in Lulu's eyes as a child. It was as if Nature held on in spite of man to something that was always there. But perhaps, after all, she was only an indolent dreamer who wished to be allowed to dream.

But what great happiness those poems hidden in the bottom drawer of the chest of drawers in the cubicle gave her, when every night she took them out and read them over and over again by the gas until the last bell was ringing, and she had not undressed and Aniseed came up the dormitory to ask what she could be thinking about when everyone else was in bed. And then, because one could not go on reading them, one said them to oneself while one was undressing. Finally one went on repeating them in bed to oneself. Then one day they would suddenly seem too puerile and childish for words and one would put them away in disgust at the bottom of the drawer. But later on the comforting thought would come. One day one would write better ones. She felt quite sure about it. Ah, perhaps it was like that feeling of expectation. When the day came one would find it had been in the past. No, no, no. Surely the day would come when one would write better ones. But perhaps she was only an indolent dreamer. What a shot in the dark it had been the day Jehovah had shouted at her in the Latin lesson. It had come to her turn to translate, and she had simply not been there; for two seconds she had not felt that she was in the room. 'What are *you* thinking about?' Jehovah had shouted. 'Writing a sonnet on a Robin Redbreast,' and everybody had laughed except Zara, who had smiled. But nobody knew anything about those poems. Jehovah's energetic, needle-pointed mind had found her out without Jehovah's knowing it.

Then there had been that evening when she had been reading under the gas, and Zara had come up softly behind her. The next day she had suddenly longed to show them to Zara, but it had been an awful moment after she had made the decision and Zara was looking forward to it. It had been like unfolding the most intimate secret of one's life. She had not felt able to be there while Zara read them. She had put them into her hands and had run the whole length of the cloisters until she telescoped into Sister Bridget carrying a cup of milk to one of the sick nuns. Zara's reception of them had been so gratifying that she had accused her of being too kind and Zara had been hurt. How ridiculous it was. But after that she had repeated them to herself for days, had been able to think of nothing else, until they had once more become puerile and childish and had been put away.

'What's happened to our golden halo?' said Zara.

'She's out for the afternoon.'

Zara smiled. 'Although the golden halo has succeeded me in your affections the dark-haired devil would like to say she thinks its she who knows you best.'

'No one has succeeded you in my affections.'

'Ah, the golden halo plays the harp, but the dark-haired devil only bangs her cymbals.' Zara lifted her arms high above her head and beat a pair of imaginary cymbals in the air. She got up and pulled Zara off the bench.

'You know that's not true; so come and play Brahms to me instead.'

THERE was a literary altercation going on in the Coalhole between Asta, a sentimental and over-mannered girl in their own form, and Spains from the sixth. Spains had literary blood in her family. One of her great-uncles had been a famous novelist. She herself could not stomach any literature that had not been mellowed by several centuries, and confessed to finding her great-uncle a little too modern. They were both washing their hands.

'Ah, but Rossetti,' said Asta heavily, over the wash-basin, 'Rossetti wrote some beautiful things.'

'Rossetti?' said Spains, drying her hands, and peering over her glasses at Asta. 'I thought he was a painter.'

There was a hushed moment. No one at the basins quite knew whether Spains, though it was inconceivable, did not really know that Rossetti had been poet as well as painter; or whether it was some advanced form of literary swank which might be above their heads, for she was known to move at home in intellectual circles. Spains went up the steps towards the Coalhole door with a book under her arm; it could be nothing but one of the early novelists, perhaps Fielding, or it might have been Sterne. She turned in the doorway.

'I don't consider that anyone has written any poetry worth reading since Milton.'

Asta, who had a great respect for Spains' literary ancestry, was crushed.

Going up the stairs she met Brenda coming down in very secular-coloured clothes. Gold and green and blue seemed to float around her in an almost ethereal manner; she had just been out for the afternoon. She held Brenda's hands in the

middle of the stairs and looked up into the lovely
mobile face and the light, clear, green eyes.

'Oh, I've had such an afternoon, old fellow.'
Brenda had a lilt in her voice that sometimes made
the tears come into one's eyes.

'You look like a peacock in green and blue and
gold.'

'Shall I spread my tail and strut upon your
terrace?'

'I haven't got a terrace. But if I had, you certainly should. I shan't let you go, my peacock.'
But Brenda's hands were wriggling out of her own.

'Oh yes, you will, old fellow, because you see I
must go and tell the Archangel I'm back. I'm
jolly glad I'm back, O mercy me!'

The mobile mouth made a grimace; the clear
eyes had an expression of half comic, half real
dismay. A soft strand of hair fell across her face,
and Brenda had wrenched herself away, and passed
her running down the stairs.

She went on up more slowly. Zara had called
Brenda a golden halo. Did the saints wear those
kind of soft radiating clothes? Clothes that hung
in folds around slender, still growing limbs,
beautiful clothes with gold lace, clothes that were
the colour of elemental nature moving in the wind,
sunlight pouring down upon it, making patterns
of light with leaves and foam? Yes, in the Beatific
Vision, perhaps. When they entered the religious
life they dressed themselves in dark clothes; they
gave up external beauty to follow a cross and
beautify instead the soul. Strange, inverted vision.

Zara had left the door at the end of the practice
room open. She was playing a Brahms valse. She

played the tender lyric with its old-world feeling with a delicacy and roundness of tone that would have made Sybil sigh if she had not been deeply occupied in putting a little emotion into the Ballancz sonata in the recreation room. Yet it was played with such an emotional control, such a detachment, that as she stood there listening at the end of the corridor, she wondered if it was not an intellectual criticism of the very emotion which it aroused and expressed.

HEAVY yellow fog hung on to the windows; it was a dark November day. One felt as if the blood must be congealing in one's veins. They sat at their desks over a history paper which Aniseed had given them early in the afternoon. The gas burnt overhead; sometimes it made a melancholy noise in the pipe. She was always frightened when she could not see the world; it made one feel as if one was in a cold but stifling Hell.

Aniseed sat hunched up behind her desk on the rostrum, her thin, pointed face coming out of her coif, her long nose looking downwards, her small bright eyes were fixed on her book; she was reading her office. Aniseed always reminded her of a kind, but strict little bird. Somebody was practising hymns in the practice rooms. The sound, allied to the heavy yellow day, was like an inarticulate cry of despair, a series of stifled sounds of misery. And down below, the Lower School were having choral class. Every now and then they stopped and began something over again. But at least their noise was cheerful, there was a

certain amount of good will in it; as if they hoped
eventually to make something coherent and com-
plete out of the number of times they were stopped
by that sharp tapping of Sister Bridget's little stick
on the table. And she knew that their cheerfulness
had something to do with Sister Bridget herself,
with the little Irishwoman's smile, and the lifting
of those white wrists in the air. She thought it
curious that nearly all the girls now looking at
Sister Bridget in the recreation room would come
up through the school just as she and Zara had
done. What would be the end of them? Where
would they go? What would they do? What
would happen to them when they had grown up
and gone into the world? Would they settle down
to an easy or uneasy mediocrity, or would they
branch out and discover something for themselves?
Aniseed's bird-like eyes were on her and she turned
back to the history paper, but she was not interested
in it. She was far more interested in wondering
what would happen to the little girls in the Lower
School who were sitting there just as she and
Zara had once done, while Sister Bridget pointed
her baton at them.

A black figure suddenly appeared outside the
glass in the top part of the door and someone
knocked. Aniseed fluttered across to the door like
the mother bird safeguarding her young; she did
not wish them to be disturbed at their papers. Now
there were two black figures standing there talking
to each other on the other side of the glass. She
could not bear the desolation of the day any
longer, and called across to Zara. Zara had
been covering sheet after sheet with a swift

pen, and turned and smiled over her shoulder.
'Chèrie?'

But Aniseed had come back into the room and
was coming over to her.

She spoke rather nervously. 'Louie, my dear,
will you go to the parlour?'

She got up and put her papers together. She
could not think who had come to see her; but any
diversion that would break the feeling of being
stifled inside a yellow Hell was welcome. Zara
smiled at her as she went to the door.

'It's your cousin,' Sister Rosalie said.

Was it imagination or was there a strange expression on Sister Rosalie's face? She was too
relieved that the afternoon had been broken to
wonder about it.

Tim had been shown into the best parlour. The
parlour with the polished floor, the strip of red
carpet, and the chairs with their hideous patterns,
where once, years ago, she had sat waiting for the
Reverend Mother, and Lulu had looked so sternly
at the picture of the Vatican over the piano. He
rose in the gas-lit room; a tall, immaculately-
groomed young man, with his hair parted on the
side. Once in the holidays, when she was fourteen,
she had been in love with him. There had been
five or six days when she could not bear him in the
room, and could not bear the room with him out of
it. She had avoided him, and at the same time was
miserable when he had not been there. After a few
days of it he had asked her what was the matter.
She had told him quite honestly that she thought
she was in love with him. It was in the large, cold
billiard-room at Linden. He had laughed at her.

'I don't think things are quite as simple for you as all that. Do you mean to tell me that you would stand here in cold blood and tell me so if you really were?' 'Yes, I think I might.' 'Then I know that you wouldn't. Come, you and I are too fluid to be too serious over these things.' And suddenly the whole thing had evaporated, and they had become friends again. She went over the room to him and put her hands into his. His hands were trembling. She looked at him, observing the cut of his waistcoat and the stripes on his tie. They were far too sensitive to each other for her not to know that he had brought her bad news. He held her away from him so that their arms were both stretched out separating them like a gulf.

'What is it, Tim?'

'I'm afraid I have bad news for you.'

She wanted to say: 'Don't tell me, please, keep it from me, I never want to know.' But she said nothing.

'Byng's ship has gone down.'

What did that mean? It did not mean that it had gone down. It meant that it had been blown up. And now what was he saying?

'I'm so sorry to have to come and tell you this on this rotten day.' Apologising politely for the weather. It was so like him. The gesture of courtesy that one might have expected from him; no one else would ever have thought of it. In direct opposition to the rude brutality of the world. The gesture of manners, the days when people wore flowing cloaks and swept the ground with their hats.

She took her hands away from him and went to

the piano seat. She knelt with one knee on the
hard upholstery and stared over the piano at the
picture of the Vatican. In that moment she was
swung out into space and the world seemed to cease
to exist. She was leaning against iron-grey railings
on the deck of a man-of-war in mid ocean. There
was a high wind blowing and a grey swell on the
sea and the ship pitched. There was nothing at
all in sight but the sea, and a grey sea it was. Byng
had told her to stay there and he would come to
her in a minute, and so she would stay, although it
was extremely cold. The wind seemed to scrape
one's cheeks. She moved her knee against something and found it to be the hard, raised pattern of
the piano seat, and that she was looking at the
picture of the Vatican which hung inside its velvet
frame over the piano. Tim came across the room
to her and put his hands on her shoulders. The fog
seemed to be lifting outside, because it was lighter.
She leant her head against him and let her hand lie
in those exceedingly beautiful fingers—fingers
that hardly looked practical enough to belong to
a musician, to the hand of a performer. The end
of the world was in the parlour with the stiff-
backed chairs. It had been brought to her by the
most civilised of people.

My father is dead. My father has been blown
up. That was nothing; fathers were blown up
every day. It was the gesture of war breaking
across one's quiet dream, throwing its shadow over
one's life. One was not going to escape, one would
get over it, but something would have been done
to one's inheritance. One would inherit a maimed
world. The dark day, the fog, the feeling that the

blood was congealing in one's veins were all part of
Byng's death. They had been waiting here for
her for years. Years ago, when she had been a
nervous little girl waiting for Reverend Mother,
the parlour had known. She was crying, her tears
were pouring down on to Tim's hand, his other
hand was over her head.

It was her last term, and as she went along the
passage to the dressing-rooms, her mackintosh
trailing over her arm because she had so many
things to carry and could not pick it up, she heard
Zara singing in a clear, resonant contralto:

'*C'est le dernier jour d'amour, c'est le dernier
jour.*'

The voice faded away as Zara went into the
dormitory. In the dressing-rooms everyone was
unpacking after the holidays. From a group of
younger girls at the end of the room Brenda
suddenly rose from her knees in a navy blue dress
with a light green belt, which was only kept into
position on her slender hips by two little strips of
braid. It was, of course, only the school uniform
except for the green belt; but on Brenda it looked
something quite different and special. The sober
navy showed up the clear skin, the light soft hair,
the high cheek-bones with their vivid colouring;
and underneath that rather puzzled forehead
where there were three distinct lines that childhood and adolescence had already given to her,
her eyes were deep set.

'Oh, it's Louie. Oh, my dear old fellow!'
She ran forward throwing her arms out, then

remembering where they were, brought her hands together instead in a subdued clap.

'But, poor old thing, you do look so sad. Whatever's happened, old fellow? Has the bottom fallen out of your world?'

It was said with just that inflection in the voice, that mingling of comic dismay and real tenderness that made the tears come into one's eyes. She hung her things up in her cupboard while Brenda talked to her. Among the younger group someone began to sing:

> '*O the French are in the bay,*
> *Said the Shan Wan Waught!*'

The others took it up, joining in seconds and thirds; it was one of the things they had learnt last term with Sister Bridget, and they sang it well. There seemed to be a great deal of excitement for the first evening of term. A very small person suddenly appeared in the doorway and clapped two small brown hands together. It sounded like a shot through the dressing-room. The singing stopped.

'Lord, Jehovah,' said Brenda, under her breath.

A perfectly oval face with a skin like parchment and very bright eyes looked out from the circle of a white coif.

'I cannot think what the meaning of all this festivity and vocal display is. Had I been a stranger listening to you on the landing I should most certainly have thought I was in an academy of dramatic art. I know you all have very beautiful voices, but I should prefer to hear them exercised at the proper times. I should hardly have thought the holidays had been long enough for you to have forgotten that silence is requested on this landing.'

She whipped out the sarcasms, turned round and went out. A general sobriety rested on everyone and the unpacking went on in silence.

'Sciatica,' whispered Brenda in her ear.

THE half past eight bell began to ring over the cloisters. The silver, gong-like notes floated across the lawn on to the playground, and Jehovah's small figure appeared suddenly through the trees beside the tall poplar-like form of the Archangel. It was time for prayers and she went in with Zara; the spring evening was very still. They went to their lockers to get their veils for chapel. Jehovah, standing by the desk at the end of the room, could hardly keep still, she shifted from one foot to another.

'Don't forget your gloves for Mass in the morning,' she shouted. 'Some of you don't seem to realize that gloves are intended to be worn.'

Either sciatica or a bad spell of indigestion was affecting Jehovah's nervous system.

The bell was tinkled and they went out along the cloisters and turned up the stairway to the chapel. She dipped her fingers in the holy water stoup and then realized that she would have to go into chapel with Di Van Anderman, Zara was close behind her with a South American girl. She went in, leading the way with the hard, expressionless beauty. It was nearly dusk. A faint smell of incense and flowers still lingered in the air; the sanctuary lamp hung down with its silver trappings, one red and glowing eye among the shadows.

The dying daylight came in through the coloured windows; Saint Agnes looked down from one immediately on her left, and next to her, Saint Cecilia. The noises of dresses touching each other, of footsteps on the stone floor, of jangling rosary beads and creaking benches stopped. Jehovah went into her stall and made the sign of the cross. There was a pause. The school seemed to be drawing a deep breath as if they were all getting ready to dive off a spring-board, then in a low, throaty, but gradually rising key they began to break the silence in the chapel.

'O *Almighty God, author of our being, omnipotent and eternal good.*' She had heard it hundreds of times. She sighed and let her body relax beside Zara on her right. She was glad of the shadowy, silent place; the voices that one knew so well were like a protective wall around one.

'*Receive us, O Lord, this night into thy keeping . . .*'

The long preliminary prayer went on. Sometimes she caught the words and sometimes they escaped and her own thoughts came in between them; but now it was coming to an end.

'*Receive our souls as we devoutly hope of Thy mercy into Thy everlasting kingdom.—Our Father who art in Heaven,*' continued the voice of the school, now more coldly certain.

It was growing darker. Night prayers were long. Zara by her side was only an outline whose shoulder reared itself a little above her own; they were all only outlines, white shadows huddled together, the starched smell of newly laundered veils around them. There came the pause for the examination of conscience. Nearly everyone

covered their faces with their hands, but Zara's
chin was firmly raised. Her attitude at prayer was
the same as it had been years ago when as little
girls they had knelt together on the hard forms in
the recreation room. It was the attitude of critical
contemplation. Now they were saying the act of
contrition, asking forgiveness for the frailities of
the body. Her mind was not there, she was
distracted, thinking of other things.

The cool, snowy curtains hung down in the dormitory; the lime trees outside the windows made a
sighing sound. She went into her cubicle and laid
her things on the bed. She unfastened her curtains
that in the day were always neatly hooked to the
partition, and now she was alone in a small world
of her own. The bell for the nuns began to ring
in the chapel, and a tram rattled down the road
outside Mexican Gate sounding its ping-ching,
ping-ching. Someone was pouring out water from
an ewer into a basin; the ewer was heavy and
the water trickled in slowly. Jehovah had been
standing on a chair which someone held for her,
trying to light the gas. Suddenly it flared up
with a thin, piping shriek, then settled down into
a dull yellow glow. It lit the dormitory, and sitting on the bed she saw her own face opposite in
the mirror over the chest of drawers, a thoughtful, brooding face.

She had become used to the contours and
peculiarities of that face. One no longer mourned
the fact that one was not beautiful. The rats-tails
were sleek and smooth over the head. Time had
been kind to them. She had been kinder to them
than time; she had cut them off. When she was

fourteen she had burst into the furnished sitting-
room and had laid those rats-tails before her mother
wrapped in tissue paper. 'Oh your *beautiful* hair!'
She had stared at the blonde woman in amazement.
'It *never* was beautiful.' 'What will Byng say?'
But on Byng's last leave he had said nothing at all.
He had put his hand up the back of her head and
stroked the sleek hair. His last love might do
what she liked.

There was a powerful smell of tooth-powder in
the dormitory. A Parisian girl was talking in the
next cubicle half in French, half in English,
recommending her face powder.

'Oh, but I do get such terrible pimples,
Henriette,' said somebody in a Dublin accent.

'Mais pourquoi? It ees because you use that
varneeshing crême, I tell you c'est affreux; je vous
dis Jeraldeen . . .'

The voices died into a whisper because Jehovah
was passing up the dormitory.

She sank her chin into her hands. It was over
two years since Byng's ship had been blown up.
The war was over. They were back at Linden;
but what a changed Linden. The war had affected
Lulu's income and Byng's death had affected
theirs. The last few days of the holidays, the interview with Uncle Heston, trustee of the family
affairs, in the dining-room. 'You know, I'm afraid
you will have to earn your own living. We are
all very hard up. The war has knocked us pretty
badly. Your mother hasn't much, I know, not
enough for you both, and I can't allow your
grandmother to help you. I know she wants to
send you to a university. Of course, while she

lives she will probably oppose your doing anything, but she can't last for ever. I should advise
you to look out for something.' 'Yes, Uncle.' Why
did you say 'Yes, Uncle,' like that? Are you going
to let them trample on you? He paused and wiped
his mouth; clean-shaven elderly owl, in well
tailored clothes, keeping his fat down with special
diet.

'Perhaps you'll pick up some nice young man,
my dear,' he smiled.—Woman's proper sphere.—
'Tim, of course, can do what he likes'—pulls the
silk handkerchief out of his sleeve—'although I,
personally, think'—they always personally think,
these people, a kind of safeguarding of themselves,
no responsibility attached in the event of anything
turning out differently—'it's madness going in for
music.' Tim had gone to Paris, on his own three
hundred a year to study the fiddle under Bidaud.
He was of age now, and the little he had was not
under Uncle Heston's jurisdiction, it had come to
him from his Spanish grandfather, the deceased
jeweller of Madrid. 'Yes, Uncle?' What again,
'Yes, Uncle?' What a beautifully marked silver
pot it was, that one with the maidenhair fern that
always stood in the middle of the dining-room
table. Hand-wrought by some artist; a loving
hand had made every little dent in it, had made
those impertinently curly fishes' tails that curved
round it, very careful and slow. 'Of course, I
know you want to go in for literature.' A pause
here. He tapped his fingers on the table. 'But
such an overcrowded profession nowadays. Journalism, newspapers, and all that sort of thing;
besides, you're a woman, my dear.' Pause and

smile. 'Yes, Uncle.' Then suddenly, like a
rapier: 'That doesn't necessarily mean I'm an
imbecile, Uncle Heston.' Good heavens, who was
it who had said that? A very slight flush had come
into the elderly face. 'Oh no, I am well aware of
that. I am well aware that your grandmother
encourages your aspirations. But she forgets that
times are changing. We live in an industrial
civilization. Our sort of people are going to the
wall, we must take what's left to us and make the
best of it.' Final, that; but then one can talk about
making the best of something when there's something there to make the best of. 'I am sorry to be
so depressing.' Well, at any rate he'd realized that
he'd been depressing. 'But I thought you'd know
better where you are.' A touch of realism one
would not have thought possible in him. The lack
of money was a hopelessly unromantic question.
One either had, or one hadn't, sixpence in one's
pocket. One sometimes thought that the only
good thing about it was that it made realists of
people who would otherwise have remained entirely romantic and out of touch with life to the
end of their days.

Someone knocked on the partition. It was Zara
outside the curtains. She came in, in an amethyst-
coloured dressing-gown, with her hair knotted at
the back of her neck.

'Could you lend me your keys, dearest?'

She handed her ring over.

'Going to bed to-night, Queen of Hearts?'

That was the ridiculous name Zara had invented
for her when Brenda had come up into the Upper
School.

'There is a tear under your right eye. Shall I take it away?'

Zara had a clean handkerchief out of her pocket and was taking away the tear. She did it as carefully and as gently as if she were brushing dust off a piece of brittle glass. The analytical eyes were looking into hers, searching hers, trying to read into her brain.

'Nothing the matter?'

'Nothing. I was only thinking.'

'You have sad thoughts, then?'

'They're gone now.'

Suddenly she longed to say to Zara: 'Sit on the bed, let me kneel down and tell you what it is; let me make my confession to you. Let me tell you that I'm afraid, I'm a coward. I don't want to go out into the world and earn my living. I don't want to have to say good-bye to a quiet scholar's life, to smooth, civilized hours round a Wedgwood teapot. I want to be able to watch the evening in the sky, to dream on some far hill, to make things slowly out of patterns that I have been finding for years. I don't want to feel cramped, jostled, frightened, herded among thousands of people; to work among the noise of machines, the incessant clamour of traffic vibrating on the nerves. I don't want to be terrorised into a set formula of life. I am afraid. Be my mother. Let me tell you that I'm afraid. It's so good to be able to say that sometimes to someone who will not immediately want to take advantage of one's weakness.' Instead she said absolutely nothing.

'Good-night,' said Zara.

She felt Zara's kiss on her forehead. She heard

the quick footfalls over the floor. She undressed. Jehovah stood on a chair and turned the gas out.

'*Into thy hands, O Lord, I commend my spirit, Lord Jesus receive my soul.*'

Jehovah was saying the last prayer as she went up the dormitory, a hint of weariness in her voice, more like the end than the beginning of term.

She washed in cold water in the darkness. She heard Jehovah go out of the room and the Parisian next door immediately begin to talk to her neighbour.

'Jeraldeen, to-morrow I will show you the photograph of my American boy.'

The lime trees outside were sighing; a sad but peaceful sound. Couldn't one go back instead of going on? She got into bed. All around was nothing but white bed and the smell of clean counterpane from the foot of it, neatly folded. One of the things one got one's next door neighbour to do was to help one fold one's counterpane. It used to be an excuse to talk in the dormitory. In the old days she and Zara had always helped each other fold their counterpanes. 'Who's talking there?' Aniseed would call out when they were in the fifth form dormitory. 'I was only asking Zara to help me fold my counterpane, Sister.' How ridiculous it had been. But they used to have great fun over it. A long, long time ago, when she was fifteen.

THEY all stood round in silence while Jehovah told them the news in the small room where Sister St. John did the school accounts. She kept her eyes on the mantelpiece where there was a statue of St. Anthony in bronze. They had been called away in the middle of evening preparation by Jehovah. Jehovah was nervously fingering a pencil on Sister St. John's table. A huge red book with *Ledger* written across it lay on the table. She understood now the meaning of that attack of temper in the dressing-room.

'I have been allowed by Reverend Mother to tell those of you who have come up through the school, and who may be interested in Sister Bridget's future welfare, that she has gone to the Continent to teach music in her secular capacity. You, of course, all understand that the matter is absolutely confidential; it is not to be spread among the lower forms. Those who had private lessons from her will be told at our discretion.'

She was examining the cut of Zara's frock while she listened; somehow it took the edge off the agony of those cold words. Now that they were in the sixth they could dress more or less as they liked. Zara's dresses had long straight lines, there was sometimes a suggestion of a ruff over the wrists; she had evolved a fashion of her own. The long lines showed up the nicely shaped breasts. Now it was over and they filed out one by one into the passage; they walked carefully, as if they had just seen a dead friend before she was put into the coffin. After ten years of the religious life Sister Bridget, whom Zara had always called Lady B., had gone back into the world. She followed Zara. They left the others to go back to the classroom and went downstairs. Zara shut the Coalhole door

and put her back against it; she struck herself
between her breasts.

'Mea culpa, mea culpa, mea maxima culpa.'

She stared at her. 'What *do* you mean?'

'I mean that I have been guilty of an error, of a
lack of sympathy.'

'But I thought you never liked Lady B.?'

She was remembering things years back, when
Zara had refused to respond to those smiles and
had shown open disapproval of the little Irishwoman's charm.

'Yes, I know, that's just it. I didn't quite
approve of the way she used to throw her charm
about. It sometimes annoys me about you Celts
—your desire to please. But oh, I've been wrong,
I've been guilty of a lack of intellectual sympathy.'

Zara sat down on the stone step and rocked herself to and fro with her hands round her knees as if
she was in pain.

'But it's not your fault that she has gone, Zara.'

'No, it's not my fault, but it is my fault that I
have behaved like a Caliban. Two terms ago I was
playing in the practice rooms, amusing myself,
you know, as I often do. Suddenly up comes Lady
B. from her music-room. She said to me: "I wish
you would come to me for piano lessons, Zara.
There may not be much that I can teach you but it
would be such a pleasure." I got up of course
and said that I would have come to her long ago,
but that music wasn't serious with me, I was a
trifler, and that I thought it would be too dis-
heartening teaching people who didn't practise,
and so on. I knew what it was. She wanted to
give lessons to somebody who knew something

about music. She wanted to talk music occasionally, to play over things and discuss modern composers, and there I was in my intellectual priggishness, saying, this will never do. Oh, Louie, oh, Lady B., wherever you are, forgive me.'

'But still I don't see. That was only one instance after all.'

'Yes, it's only one instance. But it's quite enough to have behaved in one instance like that. I've shown a lack of insight that I would severely censure in other people. I don't believe it's the big, I believe it's the small things that make people take a definite course of action, even after years. It's the gradual accumulation of little drops that go to make a stream against which they eventually break themselves. I've been one of those little drops in Lady B's. life. I shall not forgive myself.'

Zara was crying, Zara who never cried, who used to boast when they were in the Lower School that she could not cry. She sat down on the step beside her, but her own thoughts were going round, groping out wildly in darkness for some solution.

'But God; she had God?' It came of its own accord out of her mouth.

'I'm going to say something terrible to you,' said Zara, through her tears. 'God was not enough. Let me lean against your fluid and flexible soul and ask you to forgive me for what I did to your countrywoman.'

When Zara was really agitated her manner became slightly exaggerated. She put her arm round her shoulders and they sat there. Zara was not at all ashamed of crying. She did it in a

sternly practical manner to relieve her emotions.
She did not want to cry herself, although she was
sorry. Although it was a shock that Sister Bridget
had gone without any warning, without saying
good-bye. That creative personality which, whenever one met it in the corridors or cloisters, had
stopped to make some kind of amusing observation, had never let anyone know by look or gesture
of its intended departure. The little wrists had
been lifted to conduct the choral class with the
same liveliness, the smile had never varied, the
voice had sung in the choir in chapel as if it were
to belong to God for the rest of its days. The
charming little creature from the stormy, fanatical
island across the sea—her island too—had gone
away, driven by what lonely reasons to find her
happiness, or at least her life in her secular
capacity. Cold, brutal words on that brisk tongue;
and underneath, Jehovah was sorry. Even
Jehovah was sorry, because no one could help
liking Sister Bridget, not even Zara, who had
disapproved of her.

'They'll never get another music mistress like
her,' said Zara, blowing her nose. 'She *was* a
musician.'

BRENDA came to her in the evening recreation and
said she had something very particular to say, she
wished to speak to her in private. But when they
had climbed up and settled themselves in the little
turret place over Sister Boniface's needlework
room, she began talking about her childhood. An
old farmhouse where she used to stay as a child

when her mother was ill. The old woman who used to put her to bed, how she always smelt of apples.

'That sharp, spicy smell, you know, old fellow. Whenever I pass a fruit shop or get a whiff of that smell somewhere, I can't help thinking of my funny old woman and her blue apron. And her rough hands, and the room with the beams in the ceiling. And how I used to wake in the morning and hear the cows making such a noise outside, and the cuckoo calling.'

She laughed a little uncertainly as if she was afraid she had said something poetical.

'Quite romantic, wasn't it, old fellow? But I do love farmhouses so.'

She began to wonder if anything else was coming; but she waited because of the more than usually flushed look on those cheeks. From below they heard the shouts of the Lower School at recreation, and from the Upper School tennis courts the sound of balls going backwards and forwards, a uniform, springy, elastic note; pong-pong, ping-pong; pong. The ball went into the net. Someone else started serving. There was a long smashing sound, then another volley and the even noise began again. Everybody except herself and Zara played tennis whenever they could get a court, there were long waiting lists at every recreation. In less than two weeks she and Zara would have said good-bye to Mexican Gate. They would have become old girls; they would have gone into the world, and the time of hovering on the edge of rather pleasant uncertainties as to the future would be over. She watched Brenda, sitting near her, a beautiful mobile image. Those green eyes had lately been restless and troubled. Now it was coming. She looked at the evening light among the lime trees.

'Old fellow, I want to tell you something, I'm not going to leave it till the last. I'm going to enter the order.'

'Yes, Brenda.' On another stratum of consciousness she had known it for a long time; perhaps Zara had known it too when she had called her a golden halo.

'I think I've always wanted to be a nun. Of course, I'm not old enough yet, but when I'm twenty-one no one can stop me. You don't disapprove, do you?'

'No, of course not. I think you're quite right if you feel you want to.' But it hurt to think of beautiful things going into dark clothes. But one must not be an absurd, sentimental fool. It was her life and she would be happy in it. It was a practical, thoroughly workable life. The grave clothes of mortality, the insignia of the grave were words, only words. There were three deep lines on Brenda's forehead.—I've been hurt, I want to shrink away. Something seems to have been left out of me.—But that was not what Brenda was saying, she was saying: 'I think I've always wanted to be a nun.'

'But you love life so. You enjoy things so much, colour, music, beautiful clothes.'

'Yes, yes, I know, old fellow, I do. But I think it's only Our Lord who knows what love really is. I've always loved Him very much. He only asks that one should love Him and that's what I want to do always.'

Jehovah was clapping her hands for prayers, and she took Brenda's hand and they got down from the turret. The ping-ponging on the courts had stopped. Zara was coming up the path towards the Coalhole as they came down, and there was something in her face when she saw them that made her wonder if she did not know what Brenda had been telling her. They went into the Coalhole and Brenda darted away, Zara always frightened her. Zara began taking off her garden shoes. While she did it she sang to herself something that was utterly out of keeping with the slightly sardonic expression on her face, an expression not devoid of a certain suggestion of quite good-natured humour. She sang a tender little German song which had a tender little refrain at the end of every verse.

THEY knelt and the priest and a small boy in a cassock came in with the censer. The organ spilt a soft phrase on the air. There was a movement in the choir and leaves were turned over. As it was the last day they could go into chapel with whom they wished, and Brenda knelt on her right, while Zara was on the other side. A blue, feathery volume of sound rose into the vaulted roof. The clear, fluted voices of the school mingled with the voices of the nuns in the choir, and very remarkable in its absence was a voice one knew so well. After the first hymn they began the litany. The priest knelt in his white and gold cope on the altar steps before the white eye in the monstrance. The incense ascended round the altar.

'*Kyrie eleison,*' sang the choir.

'*Christe eleison,*' answered the school.

'*Christe audi nos.*'

'*Christe exaudi nos,*' sang the school, answering the choir.

Then the choir led the gentle, persuasive melody of the litany.

She shared Brenda's hymn book and thought in quiet amusement how the white veils of the dark-haired devil and the golden halo were touching her on either side, were united by her own neutrality in the middle. '*Ora pro nobis,*' Brenda was singing from under her white veil. Clear voice, clear eyes, clear soul gleaming through a gold, blue and green dress. No, no, shining through an ashen cloth in a rich whiteness like alabaster. What was it that shone like that? Was it perhaps Brenda's body that shone like that? And on the other side of her, that well-governed, well-produced contralto that could sing little German songs so perfectly; while one always felt that suspended behind that voice or those clever hands on the piano was a learned mockery. Perhaps one was being too sophisticated when one thought that. Perhaps the complicated, sardonic personality really did appreciate those melodious little peasant-coloured melodies; but far more likely that it knew that those simple little songs were not simple at all, that it was only the gift belonging to a complicated personality that could express them, that no art was simple.

Now they were bending their heads in the second line of the Tantum Ergo. The white veils bent all along the line like an uneven sea; for a moment all their voices were in unison. They

raised their heads again, and saw in the gold
monstrance with its jewels the white disk who was
God. An almost terrifying thought to think that
God looked at one out of a white disk. Zara's black
hair shone under her white veil. How much did
she believe and know, this dark-haired devil, who
for reasons of her own was going back to Austria,
to the land of her forefathers which she had not
seen since her early childhood, when her parents
for diplomatic reasons had left it. She was going
back to live in Vienna with three maiden aunts,
gently declining old ladies of another century.
Benediction was over. The chapel was full of
incense and the smell of lilies. The priest and the
young acolyte went out through the iron gateway
separating the chapel from the cloisters; the heavy
chain of the censer could be heard jangling as they
made their way to the sacristy. And now the school
stood up to sing the hymn they always sang at the
end of term. Again she shared Brenda's hymn
book, and again the clear voice sang beside her.
The Sacristan came in to extinguish the candles,
her heavy chapel veil drawn over her face. She
remembered how as a child it had always been
her ambition to be the nun who had charge of the
sacristy, and to be able to put out the candles on
the altar. What had stopped her life from taking
the same direction as Brenda's? Didn't she also
want to run away from the clang and clash of the
world? Yes, and no. She wanted something in her
manner of life and of living that neither the world
nor religion could give her. That she knew. What
it was she wanted she did not know, or at least
not consciously.

'Be with us still in the dark shade,
As in the light of day.'

Brenda was singing. And in her young voice there already seemed to be something of the consolation of religion, something of that unique and tender quality of divine forgiveness. The hymn was finished, and they knelt a moment before going out of the chapel.

III

THE brass tray spread itself over the upper end of the table with the Wedgwood teapot in the centre, and behind it Lulu sat back in her chair swinging her black satin bag gently to and fro. She had grown smaller. She seemed to have shrunk into herself. It was very strange. The black hair was still piled on top of the head, the eyebrows still delicately pencilled, and there was a very slight tinge of carmine on the cheeks. She had always fought against getting old. The silver chain with the three brooches still fell over her small compact bosom, and the little acorn dangled on the end of it where she tucked her watch into her waistband. But she was much, much smaller. She was shrinking away.

Feeling her gaze, Lulu smiled at her over the tray. She was glad to have her back. But the smile was rather sad, sadder than it had been in the old days when she had been a little girl. Opposite, her mother sat in a black and white blouse. She was getting very stout, but mourning suited her clear skin and her light hair, now with one or two white streaks in it. And next to her Aunt Gainy, in a pale grey dress, was cutting cake, looking many years younger than her age, a suggestion of pettishness and nervous irritability round her mouth, and that was all. There was a certain ingenuousness about her. She had never quite grown up.

'I hope you won't find it too dull here,' Lulu said.

'Oh, you needn't worry about Louie being dull, she likes reading too much.'

'I know that, Evelyn dear; but one wants social intercourse as well as books.'

'Well, she's got us, Mother. You're not very complimentary.' There was faint antagonism in her mother's laugh. Lulu moved in her chair.

'I meant perhaps younger society.'

'Oh, you needn't worry, Louie's very self-centred.'

'I shouldn't have said she was at all,' said Lulu. And now she was angry. She leant forward and the silver acorn struck the edge of the table. Uncle Philip's cup was still waiting for him on the tray. He had not yet come down from his afternoon sleep. She had long ago discovered the rather sad little secret of his life. For years and years he had been steadily drinking and sleeping his life away. Even the war had not shaken him out of it. He had been tactfully invalided out of the service many years ago, and she had often in the holidays met him in the evening on the road coming home to Linden, and had helped him home. Yet in his sober moments he was a likeable, cynical, amusing person. He used to say that old Mrs. Boddleman, who lived only a few doors away and was known to be a gossip in Wickhampstead, spent her time in climbing on to the flat roof of her villa and watching the bedroom windows through a pair of field-glasses. Uncle Tony was on tour in the provinces; he had not been found fit enough for the army during the war, for which Lulu had been devoutly thankful. Now Lulu and her mother had gone out, and she was left alone with Gainy. The dining-room windows were open at the bottom and a smell of flowers came in. A bee hummed and accidently came into the room, hitting itself against the window. The silver fern-pot stood in the middle of the table on the yellow Indian tea-cloth.

'Everything's just the same, Louie,' Aunt Gainy said with a sigh in her always rather agitated voice.

'Except for Frances, of course; sad, wasn't it? So sudden, poor girl. Quite upset Mother. Of course she wasn't a girl, you know; she was well over forty. And she'd been with us so long. The doctors said she ought to have had the operation years ago.'

So everything was not the same. Frances was dead. Kindly, willowy, decorous Frances, in her immaculate white afternoon aprons which she had always taken such pride in ironing herself because nobody could do it so well, was dead; had died in hospital after a short illness; the girl who was well over forty. When Aunt Gainy had gone away, she got up and went in to Mary. Mary was coming from the direction of the scullery with two curling-pins sticking out either side of her head.

'Och! my Biddy, 'tis yeself, and meself in curlers!'

She pulled the old chair from the table and got out the red cushion. There were pouches under the green eyes; but the burnt-apple face was if anything a little redder. Perhaps it was that drop she was fond of taking, that as the years increased became increased with them. Mary sat opposite in her rocker, leaning forward, one hand on her old fat knees, while the other slowly unfastened a curl.

'Ah, it's a real tragedy; an' there's no one to fill her place. This girl we've got here, och! She gets on my nerves sometimes, I feel the devil himself rising in me, an' it's the to-do I have not to keep givin' her a piece of me mind; an' it's smash, smash, smash, ye'd think we'd not be havin' a cup or a glass left in the place. An' if there's a man around, off she goes like a rocket an' you won't be seein' her for dust. A high-falutin' filly with not an idea in her head. But what would you be doin' now with a name like Alberta? There's a name for ye, avourneen.'

There was silence in the kitchen. Outside the shrill calling of birds to each other went from tree to tree. The sunlight charged through the kitchen window in layers of light. The gentle, half-amused, mildly shocked 'Oh la! Miss Louie,' seemed to leap into speech in the silence.

' 'Twas meself that followed her to the grave, an' 'twas meself that they ought to have been shovellin' in, not her. 'Tis the shockin' age I am. Now, I wouldn't like to be tellin' you how old I am, Biddy, but I shall be here till I drop; I couldn't be lavin' now that money's scarce. It'll not be said that a Mullins would do a disloyal thing like that. I did think once, ye know, I'd be goin' back to Kilkenny.'

She laid both curlers, now extracted, on the table. On either side of her head where the curlers had been, the hair stood up in a little bunch as if it were standing on its hind legs and bowing.

'But life has changed, avourneen; the old life will not be comin' again, I'm thinkin'.' She stirred her black tea.

'An' what is it now you'll be after doin'?'

'I want to write, Mary.'

But as she said it she wondered if it was what she really did want to do.

'An' what is it you'll be after writin' about, if I may be enquirin'?'

That was it. She didn't know. She had not the least idea. Her mind was completely blank; a frightening feeling. Poetry was different. But prose. What could one write about in prose? People, things, feelings, impressions. How could one write about these things? The idea of sitting down and saying to oneself: 'Now I'm going to write about such and such a thing,' was as bad as saying: 'Now this time, I'm going to have a really good sneeze.' One tried hard, very hard, and the sneeze knew one was trying, and it simply didn't come off. It escaped. That was just what happened. Laughing at one all the while for being so serious about it. Now if you hadn't tried quite so hard you might have had a really good sneeze. The fact was one had frightened it away. The green eyes were looking at her over the cup.

'I'm thinkin' it will be comin' in its own toime,' said Mary. 'I'm thinkin' it's like cookin'. For it's not out of books an' it's no one that can be teachin' you how to be a good cook, avourneen, an' if anyone ever tells ye that 'tis, you mind and be tellin' them that you know a certain Mary Mullins that knows better. 'Tis the cruel and wicked nonsense that they're all for teachin' these poor girls

nowadays at the cookery schools. Take three eggs,
four ounces of butter, four ounces of lard, an' add
a little vanilla flavourin' while you're about it, an'
they think that makes a cake. Faith, 'tis pitiful.
'Tis not all the recipes in the world that will be
makin' one good cook, Biddy.'

She stretched out her right hand and looked at
the thin coating of dough which was sticking to
the index finger.

'Shall I be tellin' ye what makes a good cook,
Biddy? Well then, I'll just whisper it in your in
case that Alberta's standin' with her ear to the
keyhole, an' I'll not be havin' her hear it. 'Tis no
less thing than the spirit of the Holy Ghost. Och!
the angels'll be havin' me up for profanity. But
'tis that I'm tellin' ye truly.'

She began to pour herself out a second cup of
dark brown tea into the breakfast cup. Then she
stood up and drank it with one hand laid across
her bosom whose undulations were visible under
the black cotton blouse. The blouse was held
together at the neck by a brooch with a gold bar
on which her name was written. Her first love
had given it to her, but she had forgotten how
many years ago.

She went into the drawing-room and found
Lulu sitting alone in her chair reading. The chairs
were in their summer cretonnes. Ulysses was
trying to catch a bird in the garden. She could see
the grey whisk of his tail appearing occasionally
round the fir tree. She stood with her back to the
mantelpiece and looked at herself in the gilt-
framed mirror opposite and disliked herself. Disliked the navy-blue clothes, the blouse with its

circular collar, the little buttons that ran the whole way down to the waist. Disliked her nose, her mouth, her eyes, her maiden-aunt appearance. A maiden aunt with a well-groomed head. After many years one had conquered those rats-tails. It was really quite a triumph to have done that. She would not have to be so morbid about her appearance. It was morbid, this desire for beauty; make the best of what one had. Be thankful one hadn't a cross eye. Tim would have had to spend his time making the sign of the cross before it because he was superstitious about such things. Lulu was looking up at her. Where she had taken her pince-nez off her nose there were two little red marks.

'Would you like to come down to Leathley with me for a few weeks early in the autumn? I shan't have been away this summer. Heston can't grudge me that.'

She sat down on the floor beside Lulu as she used to do when she was a little girl.

'Yes, Lulu, I should like to—so much.'

SHE was going upstairs when Uncle Heston stopped her.

'By the way, that little matter I spoke to you about a few months ago—have you been thinking about it?'

'Yes, Uncle.' Hand on the bannisters. Had she been thinking about it? 'I'm going to start at Bengartens' Commercial Training School in the autumn.'

'A very good idea. Excellent.' He passed his hands one over another, a habit he had had for years which had always irritated her. It was such a good idea that he could not have thought of a better one himself.

'Why are you beginning to look like a little boy?'

'I'm not, Uncle.'

'Yes, you are. You've cut off your hair, and you go about in a boy's blazer.'

'It's a school blazer.'

'Well, it looks very masculine. You won't get married if you aren't careful.'

Voluptuous old man. Perhaps it was some voluptuous streak in men like Uncle Heston that made them dislike women cutting off their hair. It hurt their vanity to think that at the critical moment a woman couldn't pull down her hair and say: 'I am yours.' She had robbed herself of a characteristic feature of feminine abandonment.

'I don't want to get married.'

He was walking across the hall smiling to himself.

'And if I did there's only one man I'd want to marry, and he wouldn't care if I was bald.'

Irish temper. Touch of her mother. But the smoking-room door was shut, he had not heard. She went up into the spare room. Max was playing behind an arm-chair, talking to himself in some game. His sandy hair and green eyes were like Byng's. And on the mantelpiece Byng looked out of a silver frame. A photograph taken on his last leave in an easy, smiling pose. Was there something gently ironical in that smile? Was there something rather sad in those eyes? Perhaps if he had lived he would have disappointed her. Perhaps

it was a good thing he had died. What a terrible
thing to think about one's father. 'Oh, Byng,
forgive me, I didn't mean that.' But the smile was
still gently ironical. He was just going to take out
his pipe and begin filling it. 'It's all right,
Babbams, I'm dead, I forgive you for that thought,
I shall live as a romantic figure in your memory;
and you will live as my last love.' Her mother
looked up from her book. She was going to ask
her if she would be able to pay for her tuition in
the autumn at Bengartens' Training School.

In the autumn she was going to start life as a
stern realist, rushing about with a portfolio under
her arm and a pencil behind her ear, taking down
letters in shorthand in a business office.—I am a
business woman now.—Powdering one's nose and
going out for coffee and biscuits in the middle of
the day. Leaving twopence for the waitress on the
marble-topped table. Perhaps one would have an
egg. Coffee and biscuits did not seem very much.
That was why most of those little girls looked so
thin. Perhaps they spent it on silk stockings, or
perhaps they hadn't got it to spend. But before
then she was going to allow herself just one summer
back in the world of romance. There was going to
be a sense of finality about that summer; and since
it had to be, it should be a beautiful sense of
finality. It was the end of something. A certain
kind of gracious life was coming to a close, the life
of leisure, of ease, of perceiving delicate nuances in
feeling, in manners, of listening to music, even
though it was not played by an artist like Tim.
She was going back into the land of childhood.
She was going to recapture all the old impressions,

like the feeling of richness and expectation on certain days. Perhaps poems would come to her which would not be like the sneezes that would not come off, but which would arise out of a pure, emotional response. She was going to turn the key on the future and lock herself up. She would watch the evening sky from the elm grove as if she would never see it again; and perhaps she never would see it again in quite the same way. She would examine every leaf as if it were a work of art, carelessly thrown off by the tree. But she would not be deceived about that work of art; the tree had not sprung up in the night, it had been standing in the grove quite possibly for a hundred years.

'Yes, I think I could manage that,' her mother was saying.

Max was making impish grimaces behind the chair. Suddenly she wanted to lean forward and say to the blonde woman: 'Let's be friends, I'm so sorry we haven't been friends all these years.'

But she could not say it. Now her mother was asking about Tim.

'Have you heard from him lately?'

'Yes. He's working very hard. He's made a friend called Bernard Bocarro. They've been going about together a good deal.'

She knew about Bernard from Tim's letters. He was older than Tim. He was a linguist and had acted as interpreter during the war. He had been all over the place. Nowadays, he gave occasional lectures on old musical instruments; his father had been a collector and connoisseur.

'That must be very nice for him. I think it's a

pity he's gone in for music, but that's his own look-out, he certainly plays very well.'

Now that she had got over Byng's death her mother was in many ways happier, except for the problem of money. The marriage had not been a success. They had never been very happy. Now that she was grown up she realized this. Through the spare room windows she could see the elm grove and the tops of the trees waving very slightly. There was a shrill persistent piping from one of the trees.

THE equinoctial gales swept round Linden. The wind took the leaves up and twirled them into spiral columns just for fun; then there would be a lull, when the trees rocked uncertainly and the leaves would flutter trembling in a corner. A pause, a moment of fearful expectation, and then it would come again round the house, howling. A bough made a sawing noise, and the garden groaned. She heard it from the billiard-room. It was a good place to read in. There were shelves all the way round, and nobody ever came in to play billiards nowadays. She sat in a huge, dusty chair by the fireplace. There was a very old gramophone with a cold in its voice which knew only a few old musical comedy songs and sang them like a hoarse old man. She put the records on occasionally and sat and listened to the terrible noise it made, but after a time it would become too desolating; there would be something almost unpleasant and evil in its mockery of sound.

She had been reading for some hours when the

wind began to break in on her mind. There was
something savage in the way it tore round the
garden and shook the windows; then it would sigh
and moan and make horrible stunt noises in the
air. She got up and put a record on the old
debilitated instrument standing on a table near the
windows. Her mother and Max were away, Aunt
Gainy was away, only Lulu and herself and Aunt
Margaret and Uncle Tony were in the house.
Aunt Margaret and Uncle Tony were rather like
ghosts, as they appeared very rarely at meals, one
only met them occasionally in the hall or going
upstairs, or perhaps for a few minutes at night.
She turned the handle of the gramophone. Tim's
last letter crinkled in her pocket, written on thin
notepaper in his fine, though erratic hand. The
disc began to move. Out of the old rusty horn a
hideous nasal sound started quite close to her ear.
She sat on the table listening to it; the voice that
was trying to sing a once popular song did not even
sound human. She would see exactly how long she
could stand it. Outside the wind was rushing
round the house shaking and banging the windows, then it started sighing and heaving and
making a movement like a high sea. Suddenly,
out of the horn came a shrieking 'Yah'—a louder
and more human note than the noise it had been
making. There was a rumbling in the box, and it
stopped. It was a very dark day. It had been
raining, and it was really difficult to see to read,
and the 'Yah' had upset her. The billiard-room
looked very cold and large and the wind outside
seemed to be trying to encroach upon one's mind
so that one could think of nothing else. It sounded

as if it were heavy with centuries. As if it were full
of voices that were trying to break into articulate
speech. She got down from the table, picked up
her book and ran. At the door she turned and
looked back into the room. It was cold and still.
The big billiard table in the middle, the lamps
hanging over it with green shades, the books all
round on the shelves; here and there where one
had been taken out there was a gap, and several of
them were falling against each other. The place
had suddenly got on her nerves. She wanted to go
to somebody, to be near somebody.

Lulu was sitting in the drawing-room with her
reading-lamp turned on, her book in her lap;
she was dozing as she often did in the afternoon.
She went in quietly and sat on the sofa. Lulu
woke up and saw her.

'Isn't it a dreadful day, my dear?'

'Yes, it's awful.'

But what was the matter with her? Why had
she been frightened? It was that dreadful yahing
sound that had come out of the old horn, and the
crying in the wind that had followed it. She sat
back with a cushion behind her and began to
read.

THEY walked over the white stone bridge in the
autumn sunlight. The air was like a diamond
through which one could see for miles. Lulu
walked very slowly. The sunlight lay on the lock
and the lock-keeper's house; a pair of blue
drawers was hanging on a line outside the house
with a striped shirt beside it. Under the bridge

the river looked very clear in its pale, pearly half-tones, but on either side the trees were scarlet and yellow and some of their leaves were floating in the water. They skipped over the weir, dancing in the white, lacy froth. On each side of the valley the hills rose, Leathley Hill higher than the rest, now purple and bronze, and away on the left stretched the downs. For once everything stood out, every detail was clear to the eye. The roads, the houses scattered over the hills and in the valley, the farm-house, the dark brown, newly ploughed fields, even the horses and the cows, and particular clumps of trees, and over everything was a purple and blue look.

They went into the post office and Lulu bought some stamps. Miss Princeling looked over the counter at them. She had been the postmistress for twenty years. What she did not know about the residents of Leathley perhaps even God did not know. Her long nose with the gold-rimmed spectacles on its bridge was as inquisitive-looking and as sharp as a bird's beak. One felt that she was one of those people who were in the habit of saying that if they liked they could write a book about their experiences. But it was not so much the experiences that Miss Princeling had had as the experiences she knew other people had had. The information that she had collected over a period of years from every means at her disposal. She asked Miss Princeling who was living at Barbican.

'Oh, Miss Berringer's still there. A solitary lady. Lives all alone except for visits from friends or her brother. She never comes into the village.

Mrs. Hildermore does all the shopping. The lady-housekeeper, you know.'

She laid that emphasis on the *lady* part of the housekeeper that gave one to understand that she herself did not consider the housekeeper a lady.

'Between ourselves, not my idea of a congenial companion.'

So Mrs. Hildermore and Miss Princeling were not friendly.

She left Lulu, who wanted to read, in their rooms, and went for a walk by herself. She went up Leathley Hill and turned on to the road towards Combesmere. She was going to have a look at Barbican over the fence. She was going to look in on the house and garden which had always attracted her as a child when the house had been empty. Opposite a thatched farmhouse roof on the way up, an old willow was growing on the bank, some eight feet above the road. It leant over, trying to grow out of the field to which it belonged. It had a Rabelaisian face and was always laughing. It leant so far forward that one could not help thinking that perhaps one day it would crash into the road and kill someone travelling in a car towards London, or some one only walking up the road. Perhaps that was why it was always laughing; it knew that it was somebody's fate.

She had come to the cross-roads and the fence of Barbican was in view, the trees in the garden, the ilex that stood by the house like a sentinel. She was going to look in near the back gate, the high garden gate in the fence; some newly-planked steps were leading up to it. She climbed the bank

and looked over. A twig broke under her and the
dark brown wooden stain of the fence came off on
her hands. A smell of wood-smoke floated in the
air. Leaves crinkled and curled by the wind were
sailing down from black branches. The quiet
autumn was falling about the garden, and the
house still wore its look of deep melancholy. It
was the same as it had been in her childhood
except that the garden was now looked after. As
she stood there a step sounded on the gravel by the
greenhouse. The figure of a woman came round
the greenhouse and stopped to look at her. She
was wearing an old gardening jacket, and her light
brown, faintly chestnut hair was bound round her
head in two small tight plaits. Very youthful blue
eyes looked out of the face. She got down off the
fence and crouched on the bank, though it was not
an unforgivable thing to want to look into another
person's garden. The gate in the fence opened; the
lady in the gardening jacket came out on to the top
step and asked her if she wanted to see the garden,
would she like to come in. She got up, explaining
who she was, and why she had wanted to look at
the garden.

'Won't you come in?' said Miss Berringer,
holding back her dog, an unwieldy sheepdog
whose hair fell over the eyes.

She went in rather dreamily, and Miss Berringer
locked the gate. She had thought it was one of the
children from the village who had come to damage
her chrysanthemums, and was on the look-out for
them; that was why she had come so suddenly
round the corner by the greenhouse. The sheep-
dog smelt her clothes. But it was most unusual for

people to ask one into their gardens because they
had seen one looking over the fence. Now Miss
Berringer was showing her round the garden,
telling her about the chrysanthemums quite un-
concernedly, as if they had met in an ordinary
manner. The oval face, the slight drawing in of
the lip, the pale complexion, the rather sensitive
features were not familiar to her, but the voice was
quite familiar. It was the voice that had broken in
upon her nightmare years ago just before she had
touched the river in her fall from the white ribbon,
and had said: 'Don't forget to shut the gate.' She
had woken up and had realized that the noise of
the car coming out of the gate had been the river
in her dream. It was the voice that had woken her
when she was falling in that horrible deathly way
through space. She was quite sure of this, she had
far too good an ear for sounds not to have remembered that voice. Miss Berringer said that gardening was now one of the few hobbies left to her;
once she had owned racers and had her own racing
stables; she said with a certain roguishness that
she had been a great gambler in her time. Then
there was a drop of half a tone in her voice.

'One can lose a lot of money on the turf,' she
said slowly, 'too much.'

She lifted her head and her eyes were looking
over the house, and in spite of their youth there
was something like hopelessness in them. Then
she smiled again, and in the smile there was that
roguish quality which had been in the voice.

'It was considered rather daring in those days
for a woman to own horses. I'm afraid I've done
a lot of daring things in my time. Of course

now women can do nearly anything they like.'

But could they, she wondered? What consti-
tuted doing what one liked? Power, money,
perhaps in certain cases, only the art of getting
away with it, which was certainly a great art.
Perhaps what women had always had to rely on,
the art of charm; but what great charm they often
had to exert to get away with so little. Miss
Berringer was talking again. She was fond of
wood-carving; she had a little shed where she used
to do her carving. And now she understood why
she had been so promptly asked to come in; Miss
Berringer was lonely. This perfectly charming
woman with her roguish smile and her natural
manners wanted somebody to talk to. She remembered Miss Princeling on the lady-housekeeper.
Miss Berringer asked her to stay and have a cup
of tea, and now that they were going towards the
house she saw that a woman in a yellow dress was
watching them from the verandah. There was a
loose black belt in the middle of the dress with
which very angular fingers were fidgeting. She was
a tall, dark, lean woman with a big nose. She was
like one of Cinderella's ugly sisters; it was not so
much that she was ugly as that she was unpleasant.
Miss Berringer introduced her to Mrs. Hildermore.

'Ethel, Miss Burnett has come to pay me a call.
She used to spend the summer at Combesmere
when she was a child, and wanted to have a look at
Barbican again.'

So the situation was delicate. She had come to
pay a call, even though she had come in by the back
gate. Miss Berringer asked Mrs. Hildermore if

they could have tea; the angular hands pulled
again at the black belt.

'Miss Burnett has to get back to the village
before five,' said Miss Berringer. A slight note of
authority had come into her voice.

'Very well, certainly.' But if one had not known
that the words meant very well, certainly, if one
had been a stranger from another country and had
not known the language, one would have thought
she was refusing. They went in from the verandah
through French windows into the drawing-room,
where a fire was burning in the bricked-in
fireplace.

'I hope it won't be too hot for you, I feel the cold'.

She said it would not be in the least too hot, she
felt the cold herself. On either side of the fireplace
hung a set of old prints. The room was full of old
things; things picked up here and there as the
years had gone by. And hung in a corner over a
cabinet as if it had been put out of the way, was a
portrait of Miss Berringer when she was young.
Except that the contours of the face seemed
rounder, there was not very much difference from
the Miss Berringer who sat in front of her. The
eyes were as youthful now as they had been then,
and there was something in them that was both
present in the portrait and in the living person, a
certain readiness to be surprised and charmed.
Although the mouth was sad, although that little
corner of the lip had been drawn in, as if the
surprises that life had had to offer had not been so
charming as those youthful eyes had hoped, yet
there was a certain childlike expression in them,
a genuine capacity for happiness.

'I lost my mother three years ago,' Miss Berringer was saying. 'Since then I've lived alone. Ethel stayed on as my housekeeper. She nursed my mother in her last illness. I miss my mother very much. As one gets older one doesn't make friends so easily.'

The sheepdog stretched itself full length on the hearth, holding Miss Berringer's foot between its two paws on the floor. In the pleasant old room there was a feeling as if time had been arrested. It held the atmosphere of the past. Of a past that had had its moments of happiness and excitement and daring, and of sorrow; the carrying of her mother's coffin over the threshold; of disappointments over friends; perhaps of decrease in her fortunes, and now what was happening to Miss Berringer's life? It was sinking down into loneliness and the cultivation of beautiful chrysanthemums. Mrs. Hildermore came into the room behind a nervous maid carrying a tray, and the atmosphere became immediately charged with an antagonism which seemed to be oozing out of every pore in Mrs. Hildermore's body. Miss Berringer, absentmindedly took a cigarette out of a box and lit a match. Mrs. Hildermore was pouring out the tea.

'Barty, dear, *must* you smoke just before your tea?'

'No, I suppose I oughtn't to,' said Miss Berringer, putting it back and carefully blowing out the match which she had just struck. 'Don't you think I'm obedient, Miss Burnett?'

'Well, it's your throat, not mine,' said Mrs. Hildermore. 'One or two lumps, Miss Burnett?'

But she could not help feeling that what the

woman really wanted to say was: 'May I take you
out into the back yard and shoot you?' Miss
Berringer was smiling across at her as if she was
trying to take her attention off Mrs. Hildermore.

'I like your dog.'

'Yes, he's a fond old fool, Carlos, a silly old fool
Carlos, aren't you?'

'He's really too big for a house dog,' said Mrs.
Hildermore.

It was an extraordinary tea-party. The feeling
of uneasiness and awkwardness grew more striking
every minute. After her second cup of tea she got
up to go because it was nearing their own tea-time
and Lulu would be waiting for her. Mrs. Hildermore rose to shake hands as if she was unwilling to
perform the act of courtesy, and only did it out of
consideration for Miss Berringer; one must not
think for a moment it was because one was a guest.
The air was colder outside now, and now the
clearness was draped with a blue vaporous haze
which came winding up the valley like a scarf
trailing among the trees. Miss Berringer saw her
to the gate with the sheep-dog following them.
Behind them the firelight glimmered against the
windows in the dark interior. She wondered if
Ethel was watching them behind a curtain.

'I hope you'll come and see Barbican again, I
think the poor old house needs friends,' said Miss
Berringer, unfastening the gate.

Then they shook hands gravely, taking a long
time about it as if it were an important ceremony
which had a particular significance; as if they were
both taking in each other's personality over the
handshake.

BARTY had called; it was a thing which, according
to Ethel, she never did. For years she had neglected her social duties in Leathley; she never
returned anyone's calls. Ethel had been in the
habit of leaving years' old calling cards in a dusty
brass tray on a table in the hall to remind her, and
Barty always used to manage to spill a few of them
on to the floor when she passed. 'Don't want to
know the county. I'm exclusive.'

But that had been years ago; the cards in the
hall were now several years old. But she had called
on Lulu at their rooms and now they were all
sitting in the old drawing-room again. Lulu had
taken a great fancy to Barty, who liked old people,
and knew how to charm them by pretending to
them that they were not old. Lulu liked this
because for years she had hated the idea of getting
old. She did not feel old except that she could not
walk so quickly and did not always hear everything that was said. But she still read a great deal
and kept up her languages. Life was still full of
interest for her though it was saddened now by
things she had never thought would threaten it.
Barty's brother was staying with her for a few
days. He lay in a long chair with his feet bolstered
up on a footstool. He was drawing caricatures.
He was an almost permanent invalid and had a
man to look after him. For years Dimpy had been
his valet, and now he had become his nurse; a
quiet-mannered little man with a certain look of
a delicate constitution, he came in and out of the
room as quietly as a woman. Ethel was like an evil
spirit temporarily quelled behind the teapot.

She sat back in her chair by the window and

watched them all.   The roguish smile was in
Barty's eyes as she leant forward talking to Lulu
by the fire.   Lionel had a look of her too.   His
curly grey hair waved over his head; there was
something about both of them that reminded one
of incorrigibly wilful children.   He drew a
caricature of Ethel with a hook nose that annoyed
her very much.

'But that's very unkind of you, Sir Lionel, I
haven't got a hook nose.'

'Oh well, you never know, you may have one
one day.   It's not meant to be true to life, you
know.'

He drew one of himself with Dimpy standing
by refusing to give him another whisky and soda
because he had already had quite as many as were
good for him.   He drew Barty when she was a
young woman, bribing the driver of a hansom to
let her drive the cab down the Strand when she
was in evening dress and going out to dinner.
Then he seemed to get tired and lay back looking
at the fire.   Barty came round to where she was
sitting and put her hand on the back of the chair.

'Don't go back to town.   Come and stay with
me if your grandmother can spare you.   Can't you
both come and stay with me?'

'No, I'm afraid not.   I should love to, but I
can't.   I have to go back and work.'

'I'm so sorry,' and Barty sighed.

The days of driving a hansom cab down the
Strand were over.   She knew that.   She realized
that.

'I'm so sorry, but perhaps you'll come and see
me sometimes.   One can't be *always* working.'

And the smile was again roguish. She came of generations of leisured people who could not be always serious.

'I feel like a ghost looking at you all.'

'Oh, my dear child, you're much too young to feel that,' said Barty, laughing.

But there was nothing patronizing in her 'my dear child', only something caressing and affectionate.

'But I know what you mean.' And she looked back into the room; her eyes were thoughtful.

'I feel like the ghost of to-morrow.'

'Poor little ghost!' Barty was laughing again. She laughed, but she understood.

'Never mind, there *was* a yesterday.'

The old rebellious spirit, the young woman who had driven the hansom down the Strand in evening dress was looking out of her eyes. Damn it, there was a yesterday!

BENGARTENS was a square stocky building. From the outside it sometimes reminded her of a smaller type of prison. There were two entrances. One for the men and the other for the women. She went in by the women's entrance down the steps into the basement where the cloak-rooms were, and got a ticket for her clothes. Four old women had charge of the cloakrooms, they had mysterious brown paper bags on their chairs in which they kept their lunch; but whenever there was a large number of people in the cloak-rooms the paper bags used to be hurriedly put under the chairs as if they were forbidden things.

'Now, dearie, don't leave your case on the radiator, you never know who's about down 'ere.'

The old woman who looked after her section of the cloak-room was always talking about people 'taking things'; she had it constantly on her mind.

She went out and immediately fell in with a stream of people also going up the stairs. People of all descriptions came to Bengartens for a commercial training; well dressed people, shabbily dressed people, people of indefinite age whose fortunes seemed to be on their last legs, and who had suddenly started taking up a business career. Little girls and boys who hardly looked as if they had left school, who were going into offices as stenographers or clerks, and still had the world before them unhampered by traditions. On the first floor the congestion began. It was the second work-hour of the day, ten o'clock, and the changing of the classes was beginning upstairs. In the middle of the building was a lift, but it was far too small for more than a few people to get into it and was generally only used by instructors. But round and round the lift a narrow stone staircase went up to the top floor, and the traffic of people trying to come down, and other people trying to get up at the same time, was always intense. At every hour a bell like a tocsin sounded from the middle of the building and all the doors would spring open on every landing as if they had only been waiting for that bell, and a stream of people, hot air, voices, would pour out on to the cold stairways. The first few days she had been terrified before this rushing herd on the stairs, but she was beginning to get used to it. An instructor would come out on every landing and hold back a section of the crowd with his arms, while those nearest the stairs would go down first.

She waited on the first floor staircase for the people to come down. Everybody had to flatten themselves against the wall while the others passed. Now they were beginning to climb. They were on the second floor. Then there was another block. Cheap scent, powder and a peculiar hot smell that always came out of the classrooms, flooded the landings. She had to go to the top of the school because she was only starting her course. That was the way things went at Bengartens. As one became more and more efficient one went lower down the building; it was as if Bengartens were saying: 'The sooner you do this the sooner I'll let you out.' So that when anyone had become a really fast shorthand typist with a first-class speed certificate, that meant that they had arrived at the first floor, and there was the bright world waiting for them outside. The doors were all tabulated with their subjects; now they had passed the speed test rooms and were going higher. Commercial French, Commercial Spanish, Commercial German; Advanced Commercial French, Spanish, and German. Book-keeping and Accountancy, and Business Methods. And now they were pushing up and had come on to the fourth floor; Shorthand and Typewriting rooms numbered and tabulated were all round. One more push and they were on the fifth floor. A sigh from everyone. The tocsin had stopped clanging. It made speech impossible even if one had known anybody to speak to. There was a hushed moment as if the landings were glad of having disgorged their load into the classrooms, and now she was walking behind a small boy in a shiny navy blue suit. They all showed their cards and numbers on entering. Everything was done by cards, tickets, and numbers. If one wanted a pencil from the shop downstairs one got a ticket from another counter before one could buy the pencil.

She sat down at a typewriter and put her case on the floor; she always tried to get the same machine, because one got used to a machine. She had become almost fond of the one she always used, and a few mornings back when the little boy with the shiny suit had had it she had felt extremely annoyed with him. A small girl with a very much powdered nose was sitting next to her. She must have been quite young, she had a blue hair-ribbon on her head. Dimly back in the past she also remembered wearing a ribbon herself, exactly at that angle. The typewriters were in rows very close to each other. They had covers over the letters so that one could not see what letters one was striking. That was called touch-typing. Whenever one thought one was not being watched one lifted the black tin cover and had a look to see why one had been putting down a bracket and a note of interrogation instead of the letters O and P.

Miss Swangstee banged her ruler on a wooden stand in the centre row of machines; she conducted the class like an orchestra, except that she used her voice as well as her hands. The thing was to keep the rhythm. If one fell out of the rhythm the whole class was pulled up and Miss Swangstee shouted down the room: 'Who's putting the rhythm out

like that?' One trembled and put up one's hand.
Everybody else looked triumphant to think that it
had not been them. On the other hand if it was
somebody else who had put the rhythm out one
felt most superior.

'Now,' said Miss Swangstee, banging the stick,
'A light, brisk touch. Don't look under your
covers, please. See how many people can get this
exercise right.' Miss Swangstee was so accus-
tomed to having to speak above the noise of thirty-
five to forty machines going at once that she
always shouted. On her first day, when she had
put the rhythm out, and Miss Swangstee had
shouted, she had really thought that she had done
something unprecedented and frightful, and that
she must be one of the stupidest people who had
ever come to Bengartens; but after it had happened
to three other people she realized that it was only
Miss Swangstee's manner. Now they were at it.
An extraordinary hammering, roaring noise began.
The vibration tingled in one's ears. But as one
was helping to make it oneself one didn't mind so
much, and Miss Swangstee was making as much
noise as she possibly could with her ruler, but the
ruler had been quite outdone by the typewriters.
One could only see it but could not hear it.

'Now take your exercises.' The rhythm was over
for to-day, everybody's bells tinkled and new
sheets of paper were put on to the rollers; they
were all going to make noises on their own.

Miss Swangstee went behind to talk to Mr.
Band. What Mr. Band did no one quite knew,
but he seemed to be copying lists of numbers on to
sheets of paper. He was an elderly man with a

walrus moustache, and he was rather fond of Miss
Swangstee. Miss Swangstee used to indulge him
in between the time they had their rhythm and the
time she came round to give them individual attention. She was a swarthy young woman with deep
eyes. She looked as if she had gipsy blood in her.
She had a very well produced chest and wore
blouses with a good deal of lace on them, and a
chain round her neck with medals on the end of it.
She was evidently a Catholic. She also wore an
engagement ring, but she was not engaged to Mr.
Band because he was already married and had
children. She knew this from a girl who had just
left room number one for room number two, and
had heard Mr. Band one day tell Miss Swangstee
that one of the children was ill.

She was so interested in trying to do her exercise
that she forgot the time. Miss Swangstee came
round and corrected all the exercises in the same
voice that she had given the rhythm. Then the
tocsin began to ring the hour and there was a
sound of doors opening and the stampede beginning on the stairs. They got up, put the typewriters in order for the next people, shut their cases
with a snap and filed out one behind the other.

'Good morning, Miss Swangstee.'

Miss Swangstee gave everyone a nod, and stood
waiting with her ruler in her hand for the next
class. Now for the shorthand class on the next
floor.

'Stand back, please, will you kindly stand back
there.'

The people from the fourth floor were trying to
get upstairs, and of course they were trying to get

down before the others had a chance to get up.

The shorthand theory room was like heaven after the noise of the typewriting room and the rush on the stairs. She sat down at an old, much-scratched desk; people came and went here, there were no regular hours of rush. She opened her books. *Jem Waite has caught a lot of fish in the stream.* *Did you see how many fish Jem Waite caught?* The whole exercise seemed to be about Jem Waite catching fish. The thin instructor who smelt of violet scent came round and signed her card. He had spiky fingers. His hands were always blue, and his hair was getting very thin. He spoke carefully as if he found words difficult. One felt that he had acquired his education with difficulty. He looked as if for years he had been attending night schools and had gone to bed late and got up early to take some long train journey to work. About nearly everyone at Bengartens there was a thin, nervous feeling, as if they were always rocking uncertainly over the edge of something. He was sitting down beside her, but he did not sit down with any ease, one felt he thought that he ought not to be sitting down. He corrected one of her exercises and then showed her one or two more difficult things in the next. Then he passed on to somebody else, and his halting voice was on the other side of the room talking to a spinsterly lady whose low-necked blouse showed her thin chest, and who constantly punctuated his frequent pauses before a word with shrill cries of, 'Oh, I see!'

The charming creature was sitting in front again this morning with a friend whose hair was still in

plaits.   She had noticed the charming creature
before.   She was wearing a green dress this morning.   A tall, boyish girl with a certain lackadaisical
look about her, she reminded one of a good
fashion drawing.   It was not that she was wearing
anything very wonderful; it was just that she
seemed to have the art that Brenda had had, of
making a very simple dress look quite extraordinary.   It was in her carriage, her head, a certain
presence, a consciousness of being somebody, which
stamped her once and for all as belonging to a
certain kind of people.   She had been trying to
turn round for the last five minutes without
appearing to do so, now she did it quite openly,
and put her hand on the edge of the much-
scratched desk; there was a large ink stain on her
middle finger.

'Hello! I was just saying to my friend that the
less one has in one's head for this sort of thing the
better for one, don't you think?'

The voice had an accent that fell on the ear very
differently from most of the voices that one heard
on the stairs or in the classrooms.

'How far have you got?' the charming creature
went on.   'Of course, one ought to learn it at school
with one's alphabet.   Look at that child over there,
that's the age to come.'

The charming creature was quite young herself,
but she was certainly not a child.   Now she leaned
still further over.

'Oh, I'm a bit ahead of you.   You haven't been
here long, have you?   Noticed you on the stairs;
fearful crush, isn't it?   I always try and come up by
the lift.   My name's Jonquil, and this is my friend

Williams. Her name's Mary, but Williams is quite enough here. I feel we really ought to call each other by our numbers. You can call me by mine if you can remember it.'

What a fitting name for her. She was exactly like a tall spring flower, and her hair was really brown, not a non-committal colour like most people's, like her own. She had not given her Christian name; it was probably Peggy, Dolly, Betty, or Kitty.

'Isn't that man with the violet scent pathetic? Do you think he puts it behind his ears too? Don't you think he looks as if he'd never had quite enough to eat?'

Certainly Jonquil looked as if she had always been splendidly nourished. One could see her as a spoilt and lovely little baby sitting up in her pram in a huge blue bonnet, while people stopped to admire and ask her nurse whose child she was.

'What typing room are you in? Oh, I've gone to number three. How do you like Swangstee? Isn't she amusing? Does she still flirt with the walrus? Poor things, I expect it's awfully boring doing that sort of thing all day.'

The violet-scented instructor was looking down a row of desks.

'I don't know what your name is, Miss—er— over there, but please attend to your work.'

Williams, on Jonquil's right, was really working very seriously. Jonquil turned round, but in another moment was back again.

'Where do you lunch? At the Patisserie? Oh, good; shall we all go out together to-day?'

Shall we help Jem Waite pull his boat into the

bay? If the tide is too low the boat will stick on a sand bank. What a weighty boat Jem Waite has got. Jonquil was turning round again.

'Isn't Jem Waite awful? He goes on for pages like that, but one gets rid of him on page nineteen; then Archibald Smith starts. Archibald spends his time shipping or trying to ship bales of cotton to Mr. T. L. Jones. Mr. T. L. Jones is an equally annoying man, he does nothing but repeat himself.'

It was a November day. Outside one could hear the traffic. Sometimes there would be a block and one could hear the taxi drivers shouting to the drivers of some dray. Horns would be blown; engines would hum. Sometimes a rich, raucous voice would request somebody else to take their bloody little bus out of the way. Now the tocsin was beginning, but she had still another hour to do in the theory room. Jonquil and Williams were going.

'See you later,' said Jonquil, putting up now two ink-stained fingers.

She strode to the door, her dress looking quite remarkable on her beautiful figure.

She sat in the Patisserie and ordered a fried egg. She had turned up two chairs on the other side of the table. The Patisserie was a long narrow room with tables on either side, and the waiting was very spasmodic. It was patronized to a certain extent by Bengartens because it was near the school, and also by business girls from neighbouring offices, but most of the students went to the other cheaper restaurants in the row. She had one day seen Miss Swangstee sitting with a friend at the table she now occupied, looking most melancholy over a book in her lap which she did not seem to be reading, as she never turned a page. While by her side, the friend, a shabby little woman with meek and wretched eyes, had sat patiently waiting until Miss Swangstee should come round from her mood. It was so unlike the vigorous, loud-voiced Miss Swangstee in room number one that for a few minutes she had not recognized her. Outside the glass she could see a green coat and a small green hat; a tall, queenly figure was walking in with Williams behind in navy blue. Williams had only just left school. Everybody in the shop, even the waitresses, stopped to watch her walk in and look round with the air of one who knows someone is waiting for her. Then she saw the chairs and the table in the corner.

'Ah, there you are, Burnett.'

They sat down, Williams an adoring friend, but rather nervous about her own prospects. She hoped to go in for journalism, she had newspaper connections, she really wanted to write, but, well, everything was journalism nowadays, wasn't it? She asked Jonquil why she had come to Bengartens.

'Oh well, you know, useful. Mother thought it might be useful. One never knows. Things not what they used to be, and so on. I think I shall really go on the stage. And so you haven't written a novel yet?'

She was disappointed. Her mother was a novelist.

'I should so like to have been useful to you. Know heaps of writers. Don't do anything in that line myself. Yes, please, what *are* we having, Mary? Poached eggs on toast and two coffees, and *do* you think you could serve us a little more quickly to-day? Yesterday I had to wait three-quarters of an hour for one cup of coffee. No, I know it wasn't *you*, it was that other waitress, with the—er—well, that other waitress.'

The girl with the brown stain on her apron was saying that they were very rushed at this hour, while she took away the remains of somebody else's meal.

'Yes, yes, I'm sure you are; too bad. You look as if you were short-handed.'

The girl was completely won over; she said they should be served at once.

'And what do you think of Bengartens?' said Jonquil.

She looked round the shop as if she were wondering whether she was being indiscreet, and then answered her own question.

'Quite an interesting place, isn't it? But I don't think I could stand it for very long. The way everybody rushes about. An hour at a time is quite enough for me. Don't know how you can do two hours' theory on a stretch, but then I've no concentration.'

The waitress was putting cups of coffee down, and the fried egg she had ordered was on the tray which the girl was balancing on her arm.

It was a December morning, the air was crisp like the cracking of a whip, and stung one's cheeks. She remembered how it had always seemed to her

as a child, like a knife being held over one's
head with the words, 'Behold, you shall be cold.'
The buses were slipping about the streets because
of the frost. She walked up to Bengartens slowly.
Lulu was not very well. The cold weather affected
her chest, and for the last three days she had been
in bed. A stout man in a coarse apron was standing in the door of a fruit shop rubbing his hands.
There were rows and rows of oranges behind the
glittering glass window, and tangerines in silver
paper. Tim was coming back for Christmas, he
had left the date open because of Bernard, who was
also coming over. Zara had gone to Vienna. Had
gone off without saying good-bye, she had written
instead. 'Don't come and see me off, I couldn't
bear it. We won't say good-bye, but au revoir.
God bless you,' Zara said in the letter. An ironical
last line from Zara who, one suspected, did not
believe in God. What she meant was: May all
good go with you.

She had arrived opposite Bengartens but she
could not cross the street. A long stream of traffic
was passing down. She looked up at the square
grey stone building. She had become so used to it
that she hardly ever looked at it now. She just went
in solemnly into the women's entrance down into
the basement and had her clothes locked up by the
old woman. But now the glittering look of frost
was on it, and suddenly it seemed a very cold, a
very grey, a very hard-set, steely place, overlooking
a crowded street. It stood there solidly with an
eyelidless stare on its face. There were no curtains,
only blinds which were always pulled so far up
that they might not have been there during the

day-time at all. There was a squat grey stone
cupola at the top. It was rather like a head
without a face appearing between two square
shoulders.

Now there was a block in the traffic and she
could pass over to the other side. She was now in
the second typewriting room. But she had been so
slow in getting those first exercises right that she
had remained with Miss Swangstee until she had
almost become an institution. And Miss Swangstee had become quite fond of her. She had hung
on to her among a crowd of new people who came
every week, she even got to know her name. She
used to take a special pleasure in calling her Miss
Burnett. She became what few people ever became
to Miss Swangstee, to whom faces and people were
very much alike except for their sex, a personality.
They had been towards the end so intimate that
she knew all about the young man to whom Miss
Swangstee was engaged. He had a job in China.
And on those days when she was very depressed,
and her voice seemed louder than usual above the
rhythm, it was because she had not had the usual
fortnightly letter from him. Once she had even
said that she sometimes thought the marriage
would not come off, and she had been so sorry for
Miss Swangstee. She had thought of pressing her
hand as she had filed out with the others; but at the
last minute she had not been able to do it. Something in the way everybody marched out putting
up their cards to show their numbers had put her
off, and Miss Swangstee had stood looking very
severe, nodding to each one in turn and standing
with her ruler ready for the next class. But now

she had left room one, and was in room two, where there was a male instructor.

It was because of her incapacity to do things quickly when she was being hustled that she stayed so long in the first two rooms. It had always been the same. At the day school as a child, later on at Mexican Gate. Whenever anything had had to be done very quickly, in the shortest possible time, she had never been able to do it. Even if she had known it quite well, the suggestion of having no time left had made the whole thing go out of her head. Panic, death, had seemed imminent, and the whole thing immediately became a monstrous impossibility. So she would be a slow-coach, plodding slowly through Bengartens, whose one idea was to teach one to do things as speedily as possible. And now she was in the speed room with Jonquil for shorthand. Williams had once been with them too, but Williams, who always looked nervous, and seemed to have time worrying at her back, and who had worked more and talked less in the theory room, had been ready to depart to a higher speed room long ago. She had been most upset when one morning at the end of the hour, a list of those who were ready to move into another room had been read out, and her name had been among them. 'What shall I do? I shall have to leave you.' She had been nearly crying. She was a very nervous girl. Jonquil, who was quite immoral about her own progress in speed, but who felt able to face life in the speed rooms on her own, had said: 'Look here, it's *you* who are going to be the journalist, not me, so don't be absurd. We're bound to meet on those cursed stairs, and anyway, we always go home together.' So now they were alone without Williams, plodding along in the first speed room. The most cheerful hour of the day was when she met Jonquil at the door and they both went into the room together. Now she was climbing the stairs, slowly, among swaying rows of people, and the eleven o'clock bell was ringing. People talked although the bell clanged, and the singular thing was that one got used to hearing the bell and yet talking against it.

A cold sunlight was streaming through a window on the stairs. It fell over the forms pressed close together on the wall, allowing the other people to come down, and it made a curious impression. It made the shoulders of all the people who were in the dark part of the stairs look as if they were all moulded into one uneven, rolling mass which was trying to push up the stairs. It was like an impressionistic study of shoulders pushing against a colossal wheel. At last they were up. Jonquil was waiting at the door for her.

'Wasn't it a bore, had to walk up this morning, the lift's not working.'

Then she smiled, and they went in and sat down to wait for the instructor, who seemed to be doing addition in a note-book. It had been very cold on the stairs, but in the classroom the radiators were on and the room was if anything a little too warm. Jonquil looked radiant with red cheeks, though she was yawning because she had been to a dance and had not got home till three o'clock. One always felt the steady flow of health in her body.

They had the usual reading and dictation, followed by the usual corrections, and they both had nearly the usual number of mistakes. Jonquil yawned through the hour. When the twelve o'clock bell rang they were both glad. They were due at other classes. The door was already opened and people were crowding out; the cold air from the landings met them in gusts, the crush was beginning. A great many people left at twelve o'clock. They waited on the top stair. Voices rose all around them against the clanging of the huge bell.

'Well, we lose each other soon, don't we?' said Jonquil. 'Meet at lunch.'

For they were beginning to go down. Suddenly in front of them the crowd swayed. There was a shriek from the floor above. Something black flew down inside the closely-barred cage of the lift, something that flung out around it as if it were a bird trying to fly. The bell was still clanging.

'Good God! What was that?'

The crowd on the stairs surged round the iron bars.

'What was it?' cried a hundred voices.

A girl was shrieking on the top floor in hysterics. Intense excitement seemed to have collected in the atmosphere in a few seconds. People pushed behind and in front of them.

'What was it? What was it?'

'A girl got into the lift on the fifth floor and it's not working, it's out of order, it wasn't there.'

'But the door—it's an automatic door,' said someone.

'Well, there's nothing very automatic about that,' said Jonquil in a clear voice above the crowd.

She felt her heart bounding up inside her, they were being pushed towards the cage by people behind who wanted to look through the bars.

'I'm not going to look,' said Jonquil, taking her hand. 'Make room, will you, get out of the way.'

A sharp, male voice spoke from the landing below:

'Will you all kindly go to your landings in as orderly a manner as possible?'

Somehow or other they were going down the stairs amid a sea of eager, horrified, astonished, interested, and excited faces. Everybody was asking what it was. Jonquil dragged her after her. Everybody asked them what it was as they came down, and as they pushed by without answering, the next people after them were asked. All idea of going on to the next class was abandoned. All they both wanted was to get out. They went in silence into the cloak-rooms.

'Whatever's happened, dearie?' the old woman asked.

'Don't know,' said Jonquil.

They took their hats and coats and put them on in the passage. Then Jonquil took her arm, but a crowd of people had suddenly blocked the basement, they could not get to the door.

'Please make a gangway.'

Two men were carrying something down the steps into the women's cloak-rooms. It was the limp figure of a little girl with a bow on her head; her hair was all over her face as if it had been blown round and round.

But now they were out in the street. They were standing outside Bengartens. People were talking in groups. She looked up at the grey stone building staring across the congested street.

You did it. You did it. You killed that little girl. You great big stone beast!

She took Jonquil's hand and now it was she who was dragging Jonquil. They began to run. They ran down the wide pavement, nearly knocking down people who were coming up, or merely passers-by looking into shop windows; groups of students coming up from colleges round about stared at them.

'For goodness sake, Burnett, don't run like this. People will think we're wanted by the police.'

Now Jonquil was holding on to her, restraining her from rushing across the street in front of a motor lorry. Anywhere. Anyhow. Away from the neighbourhood. Far, far away among quiet old houses, centuries old, standing in squares full of trees.

'Look here, we must go and have some lunch,' the slow, cultured voice was saying.

'Well, let's go to an old place. Somewhere very old. Somewhere monastic. Somewhere where there aren't any shops.'

'Well, I'm afraid we can't have lunch in a church. Stop a moment, I've dropped my only good pair of gloves, and I've got to go and see some friends of mother's to-morrow.'

Jonquil was picking up her gloves. 'You know it was only an accident, Burnett. Horrid, of course. Poor little kid. But I expect it was instantaneous. Now let's be sensible, and take a bus. I know a really nice old place, you'll love it, trees and church too, quite handy. We'll go in

and have a little service on our own afterwards.
Mother and I go there when we're feeling hard up.
Not to the church, I mean the little place.'

Now they were sitting on the top of a bus, the
cold air skimming over their faces, and Jonquil
was taking out a bright green purse.

'I've been collecting green things for years.
Isn't it rather nice?'

She took the purse because Jonquil handed it
to her, but she was not looking at it.   Even its
colour conveyed nothing to her.

'I'll never, never go back.'

'Oh well'—Jonquil stretched out her legs—
'one will, of course. But I'm damned if I shall ever
use that lift again. Of course, it's not the lift's
fault, because it wasn't there.'

But she did not listen. She was looking over
two streets at the spire of an old church. It stood
up like a piece of frozen lace in the air, in a pale,
frozen-looking sunshine and a glitter of frost. And
now the quarter was being struck, and a set of
chimes rang in the tower. All around the church
the traffic was hurrying in a quick stream; but the
chimes took their own time in an easy swinging
motion. There was a cheerful, reassuring intonation in their mellow voices. As if the old church
were saying: 'This does not matter at all, this does
not matter at all. I am too old to worry about this.
I was here long before all this bustling began, I
shall keep my own pace of time back in the
shadow of the centuries.' And she remembered
the sharp-tongued tocsin clanging the hour at
Bengartens. The black thing falling inside the
bars of the cage. A little girl in a dark blue

crumpled dress with her hair wound round and round her face; only a quarter of an hour ago she had been alive.

'You know I don't think you eat quite enough,' Jonquil was saying with something like a public-schoolboy tenderness in her voice.

'I'm always telling Williams she ought to eat more. I'm sure nervous people ought to eat a lot. Now it's different for me, I'm as strong as a young horse.'

'Good-bye.'

Jonquil waved her hand and smiled while everybody around looked at her. Then she went down the platform. The green coat disappeared behind the bars of the barrier into a crowd of people all waiting for trains. The carriage was thick with tobacco smoke. She had got the last seat in it. There was not even room for a very small person to have squeezed in anywhere. The glitter of frost had become obscured inside the beginnings of that pale yellow Hell which she knew so well. Fog was coming over the city. The train was packed with people going back to their homes in the suburbs, men behind newspapers and pipes, women knitting or reading. There were two other women in the carriage besides herself. One of them, a young woman with very pink stockings and very high-heeled shoes, was reading an old novel of Ouida's. It had a paper cover on which some dramatic situation was depicted; a woman with long hair hanging almost down to her knees was walking about a landing in a night-dress or tea-gown as if she were Lady Macbeth. The other, an elderly woman in black, was knitting with bright red wool.

It had been very kind of Jonquil to see her off. They had spent the afternoon going round the old squares full of trees as she wanted to do in the morning. After the first few minutes of shock and natural reaction, Jonquil had got over what had happened at Bengartens in her wholesome school-boy way. 'Horrid, of course. But it was only an accident.' She sat firmly into the space which was allowed her. She was wedged in by the pressure of bodies on either side. The train stopped at every station of the line, but nobody in the carriage had yet got out. They sat stolidly puffing at pipes, rust-ling newspapers leaves, or changing the position of their feet, which they had to do very carefully so as not to hit their next-door neighbours. Some-times they did hit them and apologized, and the next-door neighbour said: 'It's quite all right,' in exactly the same kind of voice as the person who hit them had spoken. Then more newspaper leaves were turned, or somebody coughed.

The atmosphere in the carriage was exactly like the atmosphere in her head, except that in the carriage it was more resigned. It had reached a settled state of block. But in her head the state of block was rebellious. During the two months she had been at Bengartens she had been very slowly getting used to things that had at first struck her as being absolutely unbearable and like a nightmare. Noise. Hustle. The proximity on the stairs. She had even got used to talking against the clanging of the tocsin. And that was what Bengartens had intended. Bengartens was trying to mould an

unwieldy mass of humanity into an efficient me-
chanical system. First of all it would train out of
one little fads and fancies; then it would gently,
tactfully, attack the personality behind those little
fads and fancies. Because of her slowness Bengartens had had a little more trouble with her than
it had with many people. But it was far too strong
to be defeated even by a person as slow as herself;
and in some things it had begun gently, per-
suasively, to succeed. But would there have ever
come a day when she would have thought the
clanging of the tocsin a beautiful sound? Would
have preferred it to the sound of the chimes in the
tower of the old church? That was of course
carrying it too far. Long before that could have
happened she would have left. Now the woman
who had been knitting with the red wool got out
on to a cold, dark station and the door was shut
again. Jonquil was too healthy to be affected by
Bengartens. She had rejected it at once. She did
not take it seriously. She called everything that
her healthy instincts rejected, amusing or pathetic.
But as for ever becoming a part of them, or in the
least like them, she would not have entertained the
idea for a moment. Bengartens would never have
any success with Jonquil because she felt herself to
be a long way superior to it.

It was very cold, even in the carriage with the
pressure of bodies around one. Outside the fog
was settling in patches. The lights in the stations
seemed to be a long way off. Figures walked like
ghosts through the mist. Now one of the men was
getting out; he turned up his coat collar and went
out into the thick and cold yellow air. The train

went on. She would run away, she would be a
coward and run down to Leathley, and stay with
Barty. Barty had said she might come whenever
she liked. Far away in the quiet valley where one
could see winter coming over the downs, and the
river winding cold and grey for miles between
skeleton poplars. There one would be able to
think. Why not run away and recollect oneself?
But what about those fees that Bengartens had
already put into its pocket? What about Lulu
being ill? One could not run away. They were
drawing into Little Wickhampstead. Doors were
opening. She took her case and got out into the
cold night. Wickhampstead was of a retiring
nature. It tried to draw back among its cedars by
the river and evade the spread of the city; and up
to now it had been more successful than other
places because it was an odd, out-of-the-way place
full of large old houses, once the property of the
wits of another age. But it could not evade the
builders. It could not gather itself together and
jump into the Thames and swim down to Leathley. It had to remain where it was while the builders
erected modern villas in their hundreds over its
old gardens and commons.

She went down the chestnut avenue. Her mind
was now a tomb. It felt as cold as the air outside it.
It was in the grip of a paralysis which was creeping
over it. A worm was burrowing in it. The yellow
Hell and the white fog from the river were getting
into it. She opened the gate. She could hardly see
Linden, but she saw the light in the hall and the
lights above in Lulu's room. The front of the
house was otherwise in darkness. She went slowly

up the steps and took out her latchkey. But as she put it into the keyhole the door was opened for her. Somebody was standing in front looking at her. It was Tim. After wandering for some hours in a half-lit tomb it was surprising to open a door in the tomb and find that it was daylight outside and that the sun was shining.

'You look tired, where have you been? I expected to find you here.' But all she could say was: 'Oh, Tim, Tim, Tim.'

The sense of being shut in had broken down, and out of it her rebellious soul was pouring. They went into the blackness of the smoking-room and she sat in a cold leather chair.

'Why isn't there a light in this room? And are there no fires in the house? Is this a house of the dead?'

'No, no, but we can't afford to have fires in every room, and something has happened to the light in here.' She hoped he would go on raving, being angry with everything. To hear somebody with a voice like that—full of warmth, light, depth of tone; a living timbre that made the words, 'Is this a house of the dead?' sound magnificent. A voice to which words meant something. Nothing automatic about that voice. A real living person who lived with every part of his body. With his voice, his hands, his gestures, even with the words he used.

'Oh, Tim, Tim, Tim.'

She was rocking herself on the black leather seat of the chair, her hands between her knees. The hall light made a yellow pathway across the smoking-room carpet, and she could see him standing by the mantelpiece with one arm on it,

standing there in a dark suit, watching her while
she rocked in her agony. He did not know that
she had just been wandering in a tomb. People
in the sunlight didn't.

'I didn't know you were coming back to-day.'

'No. Bernard and I only decided at the last
minute. And may I ask what you have been doing
to get yourself in this state?'

He was angry. When he was angry he always
spoke English with a faintly Latin intonation.

'Nothing. Nothing. Only I saw somebody
killed to-day. It was rather upsetting, but it was
only an accident.'

There was a noise outside the window. Somebody stumbled past. Uncle Philip going out down
the dark road. She could not answer his question
properly because what was there to say, what had
she been doing?

'What do you want to go to this place for?'

'Because I shall have to earn my living, I must
learn to do something.'

'You have no other gifts, I suppose?'

No, she had no other gifts. She might have had
them in the past. Perhaps might have them in the
future; but at the moment she had nothing in the
world. Something snapped in her head and she
cried, rocking herself, it made it easier if one
rocked. He went past her into the dining-room.
He was moving about on the other side of the table.

'Is there anything to drink in this house?'

'Yes, somewhere in the sideboard.'

He was back, sitting on the arm of her chair
with a wineglass of Madeira, one of the few wines
they kept in the house nowadays. Recollections of

a horrible nightmare and leaning against the now-dead Frances, of praying that one might die before one was twelve because life was too frightful to be lived. Devils with slits in their faces walking over one's body. One of the most horrible nightmares she had ever had. He was taking the hair away from her forehead with a soft, almost feminine hand. She wanted to tell him everything. One could tell him everything. There were no set boundaries to his temperament. He had grown up long before she had. His childhood hardly existed. He had been born into the troubled life of two passionate and deeply sensitive natures. There had always been difficult situations, and a struggle against insufficient means. There had been the last three years of his mother's life which she had spent in excesses trying to forget his father's death, and then her illness. He had nursed her and looked after her; when he was fourteen and had come to Linden he had already begun to grow up. One could tell him everything. But she could not tell him that she was afraid of turning into a machine, that she was afraid of Bengartens' clanging tongue, that she had only realized it to-day. She would just sit quietly in the darkness of the cold smoking-room and listen to him talking about Paris and Bernard and Bidaud. And Bernard's sister, who was a painter, and pictures, and music, and a new concerto he had for the fiddle. She had begun to forget that there actually existed people who made words sound beautiful when they said them; quite ordinary words which they endowed with a part of their personality. Jonquil had been delightful; like a spring flower growing impertinently in

Bengartens; refreshing because she was repre-
sentative of people who could always hold their
own wherever they were. But not even she had
made words what he made them. She had worn
her clothes beautifully, had spoken with a certain
charming languor, but Tim got inside the words
and made them his own as he made things his own
on the fiddle. They went upstairs together to see
Lulu.

'I'm so glad you're back.'

One would have to be careful and not say it too
passionately, or he would suspect that something
was very wrong. Critical dark eyes were looking at
her as they went up the stairs, a hand holding her
own as if he were trying to tell by the pressure of
her hand in his what was in her mind.

Lulu looked smaller than ever in the big bed,
because the hair was not piled on top of her head.
Her mother had been reading the paper aloud;
Aunt Gainy was sitting near the dressing-table,
sewing. She kissed Lulu.

'Dreadful night, isn't it? You can come and sit
on the sofa, Tim,' her mother was saying behind.
'Had a successful day, Louie?'

'Yes, quite ordinary.'

'You look rather pale, my dear.'

'It's only the cold, Lulu.' She sat down by the
bed. The firelight danced about the room. There
was a faint colour in Lulu's cheeks. Perhaps it was
from the fire, or perhaps she really was better to-
night. Her mother was asking Tim about his
doings in Paris, and he was telling her those things
he thought both suitable and interesting. What he
said was rather like a book which had been

expurgated for use in schools, interesting and picaresque, but with the vital flavour of the author left out.

Aunt Gainy looked very young sitting under the lights over the dressing-table. If she had only ceased wrinkling her forehead years ago, one would have thought on meeting her that she was a very pretty woman. The old photographs on the wall near the bed showed what she had been like then, her shoulders emerging from a white lace dress. And high up on one shoulder was a bunch of flowers as they were worn in the days when she had been a young woman. She had been Lulu's favourite, and she had had piano lessons from some of the best people of her day. It was the child part of her that still played the piano; played it quite well if she had taken the trouble to practise, though she had only a slight musical gift. But she lacked continuity. Nearly everything that she did went up in little bits and unfinished ends. She never finished reading a book or even a paper; some explosion always occurred in the middle which prevented her. Something or somebody had been forgotten and had to be attended to. She was worried by a hundred little things. Now she was sighing.

'I shall have to go and light that stove.'

'Can't it wait till later, my dear?'

'No, the room won't be warm if I leave it.' She got up and folded her work.

'Can't I do it, Auntie?'

'No. Thank you very much, Louie. I forgot to put any oil in the thing.'

Now she was going out of the room. Tim got

up to open the door for her. Aunt Margaret was
outside. She had just been going to knock. She
came in and rubbed her hands.

'I see you're holding quite a reception.'

Lulu did not hear and she had to repeat it, which
made her nervous, and she laughed to hide it.

'Oh yes, it's all one can do when one's sick.'

'Very cold. Very cold. The best place to be in
is in bed.' Then she saw Tim, who was waiting
to shake hands with her.

'Oh, how d'you do, Tim, I didn't know you'd
arrived. Very glad to see you. Very glad. I
suppose you've been having a gay time, eh?'

She laughed and gave him a slow wink. A faint
flush had come into her face on seeing him. It was
his manner of shaking hands, as if he had been
waiting to see her, and only her, since his arrival.
She knew quite well that it was only his manner,
but she could never quite get over it, and it always
made her flush in exactly the same way whenever
she had not seen him for some time. He was now
asking her to sit down between himself and her
mother on the sofa. She hated sitting very close to
people. But as he had asked her she felt she could
not refuse. She had once said that he was her idea
of a charming young man. She had come back
into the room to say it one night when they were
going to bed and had been talking about him. She
had said it in a whisper so that no one but the two
of them should hear.

Her mother was asking if she had been out for
her walk to-night in spite of the fog.

'Oh yes, just a short walk, you know, for the
sake of health, eh, Tim? A short, brisk walk.'

'I shouldn't have thought this sort of weather was good for anyone's health. Give me a good fireside,' said her mother.

Aunt Margaret sat on the edge of the sofa with her arms folded in black, tight-fitting sleeves. She always wore black with a high neck. She kept in a more modified form to the fashion of her girlhood. As a girl she had been very handsome, before an illness had taken most of the colour out of her face and hair. She was a tall woman, long-boned, with nearly aquiline features. In the passage leading off the landing outside, some of her old drawings had hung for years. They had been done before she was twenty and before her illness. They had marks of unmistakable talent in them. She had never been taught to draw, she had done them alone and unaided, but for some reason, after her illness she never did any more. She had forgotten all about them. She never looked at them or noticed them on the wall. Now she got up from the sofa very carefully and came round to the bed to see Lulu.

'How are you feeling this evening? Do you think you're any better?'

'Yes, I do feel a little better to-night,' said Lulu. 'Have you got a cold? You sound as if you had a cold.'

Aunt Margaret drew back, laughing. 'Me? Oh no, I haven't got a cold.'

The door opened and Aunt Gainy came in to ask Lulu what she would like for her dinner. On the sofa she could hear Tim telling her mother that he was going to share Bernard's flat with him for some months in London. So that was what was going to happen. And where was Bernard's flat? Bernard's flat was in one of those old squares around which she and Jonquil had been walking, because he was telling her mother so. Her mother was saying that it must be charming, she loved those old houses.

'I hope you'll ask me to tea, Tim.'

He said he would be delighted if she would come to tea, and he hoped that Louie would be able to come round when she left her school in the afternoons. It would be nicer for her than having tea out. Her mother said she was sure that Louie would like to do that. That would be very nice for her. She felt for a moment as if she were again a little girl and someone had asked if she might be allowed to go to a party. But this was only Tim's way of getting round a situation. She could afford to sacrifice a little independence and dignity, and to be a little girl again.

Bengartens had an enemy who was going to live in an old square. Winter and early spring. Blue evenings full of music. Lights through the trees across the square. . . . Thank you very much for asking me to your party, especially for getting permission for me to come . . . a little girl sitting on the edge of a chair, her hair drawn on to the top of her head and tied with a bow. A memory of not being allowed to ride a tiny tricycle belonging to some children whom she used to go to tea with, because their mother, in asking if she might ride it, had not made quite clear what it was; and her mother, always too hasty in her conclusions, had thought it must be some kind of a push chair, and had said she thought she was really too old for that. She remembered walking by the side of that tricycle and longing to ride it. The children had been so nice about it, and both their mother and nurse had thought her mother rather foolish. Tim was looking at her from the sofa, soft lights in his dark, critical eyes. . . . Don't you think that will be most satisfactory? I don't think I have made any mistakes there. . . . No, he would not make any mistakes. He belonged to the dangerously gentle people of the world who knew exactly upon what ground they were treading. Alberta was ringing the gong. She did it as she did everything, quite differently from Frances. She gave it a series of jerky bangs, so that the sounds became confused and all ran into one another like smothered thunder.

'You'll have to go down now, won't you?' said Lulu.

Her mother had dropped the paper and the sheets had all fallen out of their places. Tim was bending down, picking them up and putting them in order. Her mother was laughing.

'Thank you so much, Tim. How careful you are.'

IV

It was the New Year. Lulu sat in her place at the head of the table, a shawl draped loosely round her shoulders. She did not like the look of the thing, but there it was, she had been ill and did not feel very well. She was bending now to listen to Edie who sat on her right hand, and whose idea of being sociable was to talk all the time. But for years Edie had been getting deaf and now she had an ear-trumpet or some apparatus very like it, and Lulu could not bear speaking into the thing. It seemed disgusting to her that anyone should parade their physical infirmities like that. She couldn't think how Edie could do it, especially as she wasn't yet an old woman. Aunt Margaret said she must be getting on though. She knew for a fact that Edie was six years older than herself; how she kept so young-looking she couldn't think. But then she was a small-boned, fat person, and when you had fat it didn't show so much, and she did something to her hair. Lulu thought that being talked to was better than trying to talk into the dreadful thing, so she was letting Edie talk; but the look in her eyes was distant and worried. She was probably thinking about Uncle Tony; he had come home just before Christmas, and had taken to his bed. He refused to give any explanation to anyone. He said he wished to be left entirely alone. Aunt Margaret said she had heard him groaning in

the night across the landing of the top storey.
Lulu had asked the family doctor to see him, but
when he came downstairs, and spoke to her alone
in the dining-room she had come back very
worried. Meikle said it was only nerves, and that
the best thing to do was to take no notice of it but
to send him up his meals. That would mean more
trouble for the servants. But Alberta did not
mind, as long as it was a man she had to look
after, Mary said.

So he was the only member of the family who
was in the house and was not at New Year's dinner. Aunt Elise was up for a few weeks, and had
arrived for the New Year. She had such a large
family that she and Uncle Kenneth could never
both go away at the same time; also he disliked
leaving home nowadays, he had grown morose
and did not want to see anybody. Daisy had also
come up. She was the eldest of Aunt Elise's
family, and however much one might have disliked her as a child, one could not ignore her looks.
She had a great look of Lulu when she had been
young. Men always liked her, and huge South
African cousin William was sitting by her, putting
forth all his rather primitive charm. He reminded
one of a large dog wooing a kitten, and who was
very conscious of his superior bulk and thought
the kitten must be too. But Daisy was a good deal
more sophisticated than William, who had been
brought up to believe that all women were the
same, and were attracted by immense physical
strength. She had already had several mild love
affairs in the county town where they lived, with
men who had more attractions to offer. She flirted

mildly with him over the pulling of crackers, but she was far more interested in Tim, who was drawing corks with Uncle Heston near the window. One could see this by the way she looked at him when he filled up her glass, then she would look across the table and smile. The smile meant: 'He's very charming, I suppose he's yours?' Aunt Elise looked at him too. And if one could have had a cross-sectioned view of a part of her brain, one felt sure one would have seen her asking herself why he should not marry Daisy, even though they were first cousins. Now that they had no son, the title would inevitably come to him when Ken died.

The great disappointment of Aunt Elise's life was that they had no son. She had been trying to have a son for many years. It was too late now. But on the way against many struggles, and means that were not adequate to keep a large family, she had had eight daughters. Now her gaze, like Daisy's, had graduated from Tim to herself across the table, and she smiled that smile one had known all one's life, insidiously kind. They both thought that she was the one whom he would probably marry. And why? Daisy was certainly her superior in looks. One might be finicky and talk about fine points like ankles and finger-nails, because Daisy had had a habit of biting her nails in her teens, for which she was now very sorry; but even then, it was Daisy and not herself who was handsome. It was because of Tim's manner that they thought this. He meant them to think it. He behaved to her in front of them as if there were undoubtedly some intimacy between them, and had been for

years. It was all done only by look and gesture.
An eyebrow lifted occasionally during a conversation, consulting her as if they were in the habit of
sharing every thought. A slight leaning forward,
if he thought she wanted anything. A looking
round the table for something she had asked for
which was probably by his elbow, and which he had
his hand on, ready to pass; but which gave the
impression that he would have gone to the end of
the world for it, had it not been there. Yet it was
all done in such a way that the rest of the family
who saw their behaviour to each other every day,
did not notice anything out of the ordinary. It
was taken for granted that they were fond of
each other. They had known each other far
more intimately than Daisy had ever known either
of them.

So nobody noticed anything extraordinary. But
Edie did. Edie thought herself very observant and
keen-sighted. She was always telling one interesting little things that she had noticed. She kept an
eye on them now, while she talked to Lulu and
held the ear apparatus for Lulu to talk into. She
was a cousin of Lulu's on her Scottish side. Her
face reminded one of an eager, spiteful little bird.
but it was a pretty little face. She must have been
a pretty little feminine woman. Her husband had
died many years ago, and she had had a good deal
of trouble with him, because, as she owned quite
shamelessly, with a suggestion of indulgence in her
voice—she was always indulgent towards men—
he was rather too fond of his 'coffee.' Now she lived
alone in rooms on very small means; but she was
always cheerful and talkative. Lulu said she wished

Edie didn't talk so much. She came on Sundays sometimes to lunch and tea. She was always saying that she had a great capacity for happiness, and that little things pleased her. But one suspected that being poor, and living in a position of expectation from various relatives, she considered that she was far more likely to have those expectations realized by appearing cheerful and interested in everything than by being melancholy and letting things go.

Now glasses were being raised, and they were all drinking Lulu's health in sherry. Uncle Philip was down in an old suit and carpet slippers. He hated new people in the house, even though they were relations, and confined his remarks to his end of the table to Uncle Heston and Aunt Margaret. But after three glasses of sherry, he unbent, and asked William about his fruit farm. Aunt Margaret had a coloured collar on her dress in honour of the occasion. She sipped her sherry slowly and held up the glass now and then to have a look at it. Uncle Heston was his usual well-tailored self. As he grew older he became more of a dandy. Max, who had been put at a small table by himself because there were so many people there, and because Lulu thought he would not make so much noise, came round and squeezed himself in between Aunt Gainy and her mother.

'Well, I hope it will be a very happy New Year for everybody,' said Lulu.

Aunt Elise leant forward from her place on the other side of Edie, and smiled.

'Thank you, Lulu, very much.'

Aunt Elise and all her family had always called

Lulu by the name which she alone had made up for Lulu when she had been a very little girl.

'And I hope, Tim, you're going to give us some music afterwards.'

'I really think I have had too much sherry to be able to play well enough to satisfy you or myself, *ma tante*.'

Though he knew very well that it was inevitable, and that he would have to play something later on in the drawing-room. Aunt Elise liked being called *ma tante*, and she liked it to be thought that she knew something about music.

'And you, Aunt Gainy, would you be able to play after this sherry?'

'Ah! put it there, Tim,' laughed William, who had not the least idea that Tim could have drunk him under the table with ease.

Aunt Gainy laughed also, and said she did not think she had had quite as much as all that, and that she thought she would be able to play for him.

'What about making a move?' her mother was saying to Lulu. She was getting tired of sitting at the table so much longer than usual.

'Yes, yes, I was just waiting to see if everyone was finished.'

Lulu got up slowly, holding her shawl across her chest, and hanging her bag on her arm. They were going to make a concession to convention this evening and leave the men behind. Uncle Philip rose unwillingly to his feet. Why all this beastly ceremony just because there were a few more people in the house? Tim was standing at the door, Daisy dropped her handkerchief and William bounced down to pick it up. Beside Tim he

looked like a large country cousin who had not yet
learnt to control his movements in proportion to
the space allowed him to move in.   As they went
through the hall she saw Alberta whisking round
the top of the stairs with a tray. Her permanently-
waved hair was nearly standing on end with the
excitement both of the occasion and of having so
many young gentlemen in the house. She blushed
whenever she came near Tim, but one felt that
William was her idea of a Hercules among men.
Mary said that the permanent wave had been
given her, free of charge, by one of her young men
who was a ladies' hairdresser.

Ulysses was sitting in his place by the fire when
they went into the drawing-room. He was now
getting very old, and disliked strangers as much as
Uncle Philip did. Daisy knelt down to stroke him
but he growled at her.

'I think you ought to go to bed, Max,' her
mother was saying.

'No, please, just a little longer, you said I could
stay up later to-night.'

'Well, only a quarter of an hour more then,'
said her mother.

Max had, long ago, learnt to get by cunning
what he could not coax out of her, and retired into
a corner behind the ottoman. He wanted to hear
Tim play. Not that music had for him the attrac-
tion that it had always had for her, but that he
thought Tim wonderful. And Tim was very kind
to him. Sometimes when she looked at him and his
green eyes reminded her of Byng, she felt pity roll
up for him inside her. He was naughty, and spoilt
by her mother, but there was something extremely

sad about him; she did not know quite what it was. Now they were all lighting up, Daisy was offering her a cigarette. She had a pale blue cigarette-holder through which she was smoking. How fond people were of pale blue, she disliked the colour herself except in certain combinations. Aunt Elise was talking about Uncle Ken to Lulu. Aunt Margaret had come in for a few minutes because of the occasion, otherwise she never sat with them in the drawing-room. She was choosing a chair for herself behind. Aunt Gainy got up to rearrange one of the curtains; it had become hitched up in something and Alberta had not troubled to see to it. When she pulled it back for a moment one could see the sky and the frosty night full of bright, hard-looking stars. Edith had settled herself on the sofa, and her mother was now talking into the ear-trumpet. Lulu looked relieved to have got rid of her at last. She found herself sitting next to Daisy.

'I hear you're taking a course at Bengartens Commercial School, Louie?'

'Yes, Daisy.'

She had begun to forget that Bengartens existed and that she would be soon pushing up the stairs again to the clanging of the iron tongue. Tim had been playing Bengartens out of her system.

'I hear it's a very good place for that. Quite one of the best. Of course I learnt what shorthand I know on my own.'

She remembered that Daisy was somebody's secretary.

'Oh, really, did you?'

Why talk about these things? She did not want

to know how Daisy had learnt to help Jem Waite
pull his boat into the bay, or to write letters
beginning: Dear Sir, I am in receipt of your letter
of the 19th inst., for which I am much obliged—
useful and necessary as they might be. She must
pull herself together and admire something
belonging to Daisy.

'What a delightful little holder.'

'Yes, it's rather sweet, isn't it? It was a birthday
present.'

She took the cigarette out of it to demonstrate
its charm when not in use, which was to hang
by a ring from the chain she wore round her
neck.

'I like your ring, I was admiring it at dinner.'

Goodness, she had forgotten the ring she always
wore on her little finger. They must try something else.

'But I've had it for years, Daisy.'

'Oh, have you? I've never noticed it. But then
we don't meet very often, do we?'

Daisy laughed. She was nicely dressed, in what
one would call a suitable manner. Yes, she was
certainly nice-looking, attractive, though she had
not Jonquil's natural charm, or Zara's animation
and brilliance. Now they must try books.

'Have you read anything interesting lately?'

Daisy laughed nervously, it wasn't quite her
ground.

'Well, I don't get an awful lot of time for
reading, you know. I generally feel a bit tired at
night when I get home, and then I go out quite a
lot. Dances and parties. Do you dance at all,
Louie?'

Now Daisy had really caught her out. She had got the better of her. Did she dance? She remembered going to a dance when she was fifteen. It had been a fancy dress dance in some seaside town where they had had rooms and she had gone as a pierrette. Good Lord! she must have been mad. She had danced all the evening with a man who happened to partner her dressed as a pierrot. She had liked him because he reminded her in a very distant way of Tim. The same gentle manner. It was during the war then, and he was home on leave. She wondered where he was now, or if he had gone back and been killed. They had been most friendly, and had sat on the stairs talking about books.

'No, I don't go out very much, Daisy.'

Daisy looked rather sorry for her. 'I should have thought Tim would have danced very well.'

She was quite startled, she had never thought of dancing with Tim. This was very backward of her. She must make amends at once.

'Oh yes, he does dance, very well' said with the inflection of one who knows. Daisy laughed and shook her finger at her.

'Ah! there, I knew you danced. I hear the tango's coming in again. I rather like the French tango, don't you?'

Take a deep breath and dive. 'Yes, I do! It's very graceful I think.'

She seemed to be being rather successful. Daisy was giving her opinion on various steps.

'I think a man ought to be able to dance. Well, I enjoy dancing for dancing's sake, I do like a good partner.'

'My dear Evelyn, my life, nowadays, consists in doing such little things,' Edie was saying on the sofa.

'Well, girls certainly have a great deal more freedom than they had even a few years ago,' said Aunt Elise to Lulu. 'The war's made a great difference.'

Lulu was nodding her head, she had only heard the part about the war.

'It has indeed, to all of us.'

'Who do you like on the films, Louie? Or, have you got a stage hero?' Daisy pushed another cigarette into the pale blue holder. But the door was opening while she was wildly trying to remember the name of somebody who would do; Tim came in with Uncle Heston, William, and Uncle Philip. He leant over her chair in such a way that Daisy's thirst for a knowledge of her romantic leanings was immediately appeased. Daisy sat up in her chair and almost drank it in. The next best thing to being made love to by a desirable young man was to see somebody else being made love to by him. This was no doubt the secret of success for the film hero and the matinée idol. She felt that at that moment they were both performing an act of kindness to Daisy. But now Aunt Elise was holding him to that violin-solo and he was going to fetch his fiddle, which was upstairs in his room.

'Must be wonderful to play as well as Tim does,' said Daisy.

'Such a touch, such a tone,' said Aunt Elise.

Aunt Gainy was opening the piano, and she got up to help her. Together they swung back the lid,

the end of it rested near the old photograph of
Byng. Now Uncle Philip had taken the chair next
to Daisy, and she would be able to sit somewhere
in peace. She went to the ottoman behind which
Max was crouching under a tall stand with a
palm on it. Aunt Margaret was sitting quite near
with her arms folded, looking at everybody as if
she was the audience and everyone else round the
fire was the play. Tim had come back with his
fiddle and everyone was trying to get themselves
set into an attitude of attention except William,
who was talking in a loud voice to Uncle Philip.
Uncle Heston had seated himself on the sofa
between her mother and Edie. Edie was looking
distressed because he had got on the wrong side
of her, and she could not hear a word he said.

'Give us a little Beethoven, Tim.'

'Oh, Aunt Margaret, after sherry?'

He knew very well that no one wanted
Beethoven.

'Well, I like old Beethoven. That's my idea of
music.'

She changed the position of her feet because she
was nervous after having made such a statement.

'Oh, something emotional, Tim,' said Daisy.
'I do love emotional things.'

'Exactly how emotional would you like me to
be, Daisy?'

Daisy blushed. But one felt she would have
been quite content to look at his legs through the
most intellectual music and would have pronounced
it wonderful afterwards. William looked bored
and frightened. He instinctively felt that something highbrow was about to happen; and his

mind as well as his body was set forever against anything highbrow and complicated. He believed that life was a very simple affair, and that it was only exaggerated types of people who made it otherwise, and that exaggerated types ought not to be allowed to exist. He would never have believed it if one had told him that he himself was an exaggerated type. Tim had chosen something very simple, with a melody that would not be likely to tax anybody's imagination; but it was something very good and true that had come down through several centuries as a folk song. It expressed rather a melancholy than a great passion. It was the moan of the soil crying out against both its primitivism and its decay. As if the soil were crying into an age that it had foreseen for a long time.

If only William could have realized, it was all the things that he was not, crying aloud to him. And now and again through the main theme, would run a rude, jolly little tune like a cheerful slap on the face during a country dance. One could see faces glowing red under large straw hats in the light of the flares on the green. Tim played it as he played everything, with a careful, finished workmanship. He not only had a real natural gift for the fiddle, but he had been taught as a little boy by one of the once greatest among European violinists. Bidaud was now an old man, living on a small income which somebody had made him years ago. But he had known Anita Teresa and Uncle Bryan in Paris in their worst days of poverty, and had picked Tim out when he was quite a small boy. His two dark, badly-furnished rooms had been to

Tim like a security which was heaven, the first security he had ever known as a child. At least at Bidaud's there had always been something to eat, even if it was only bread and cheese, and there had always been music and a beautiful violin to practise on. Now it was drawing to a close. It ended with a final slap on the face, and closely on the heels of it, the melancholy theme came in rounding up the dance.

Everybody murmured something. Uncle Philip said: 'Very pretty'. Daisy said it was gorgeous. Aunt Gainy said: 'How funny I don't know that one, Tim. Yet I used to play a lot of those things at one time.'

'I think it has been forgotten now. They are not thought so much of as they used to be. But it was one of Bidaud's great pieces. He always used to give it as an encore.'

Edie said it had just that olden-time feeling that she liked.

'Do you think you could give us just one more?' said Aunt Elise.

This time he played a little French modern piece. Very sad, very grave, very austere. Full of silver tones. But there was something almost stark about it, and the patterns it made were very thin; they were like lace hanging on to a delicate old frame. Now and again something strange came and shook the frame and a shudder went over it; perhaps it was a ghost, or perhaps it was only the wind. Everything in it spoke of memories and departure. It was a poem in one colour only. He had played it to her before, and she had liked it. But this time, perhaps because of so many people

being there, perhaps because of something in
Daisy's silly conversation which had upset her, it
seemed to her absolutely tragic. It made one feel
that one would hang on to anything in the world to
prevent the frame falling to pieces. But the strange
thing about it was that the frame did not fall to
pieces. It made her feel intensely melancholy. The
sense of heightened depression, almost bordering
on despair, which she had known the night of the
accident at Bengartens when she had come home
in the fog, and he had opened the door to her, came
over her again in a wave, and all she wanted was
that everybody should go away so that she would
not have to be polite or talk to anyone for the rest
of the evening. Everybody clapped, and her
mother said 'Bravo' from the sofa. Though, of
course, they had not liked it as much as the other
one.

'But dear, it didn't seem to have a tune in it,'
said Edie.

Tim laughed. Now Aunt Gainy was being
asked to play something.

'Oh, but I really don't know anything nowadays.'

But Tim was hunting for some music for her in
the music stand behind, and had found a leather-
bound volume.

'Now, I heard you practising this the other day.'

He opened it for her at a certain page. Aunt
Gainy laughed. It was Schumann, and something
that she remembered hearing when she was a
little girl and had sat on the floor by Lulu's chair.
Tim was coming over to the ottoman. Now he was
sitting down holding her fingers close to her side

so that no one else should see. But Daisy had seen.
She was watching them as if she were in the theatre
watching the hero making love to the heroine.
Aunt Gainy had begun the Schumann. Aunt Margaret sat with her arms still folded. Lulu was
leaning back in her chair with that long look in her
eyes. Was she remembering Gainy as a pretty
young girl in a white dress with flowers on her
shoulder, or was she remembering still further
back? Uncle Heston was looking at Ulysses, who
had turned his back on the room as if he hoped by
so doing that he could imagine that nobody but
himself and perhaps Lulu were there. William
was staring at Daisy's right ear, which was the only
one he could see, as she had turned herself round
in her chair so that she could watch their romance.
Aunt Elise, beside her, had a sentimental smile on
her face. Edie looked attentive and leant forward
holding her ear apparatus, and her mother sat back
on the sofa and stared into the fire.

She let her hand lie in Tim's. He was cajoling
out of her hand what was the matter with her.

'I am afraid, and sad. That beautiful little
French skeleton piece you played has made me
feel like this.'

His thumb impertinently pressed her palm. His
fingers curled round her hand: strong wiry fingers
that always seemed to have a steady flow of energy
in them. William's looked limp things beside them.

'But I am not going to let you be afraid and sad,
I tell you I have the power of playing this fear and
sadness out of you.'—Blue nights and lights across
the square between black branches, and permission to ride the tricycle.—'Thank you very much.

I hate that Daisy.' 'She's a minx, don't take any notice of her; fancy letting her upset you.' 'Tim, I mightn't have liked you so much if you hadn't been a musician.' What dreadful things one does say, probably one hasn't really a very nice character. But then few people ever own up to what they really do feel. 'Ah, but I am, and you know you can't do without a musician in your life. You must have someone to play to you. You must have music, music. As for that tocsin, I can undo that stupid thing's work in less than ten minutes. Give me a quarter of an hour and I will make you forget you've ever heard it. Besides, you know I never make mistakes.' 'No, no, thank God one has found someone who never makes mistakes and yet remains a human being. How do you do it?' 'I have a great deal of natural talent.'—A charming smile: insidious devil. What does he mean?—'You too, let me tell you, you have a lot of natural talent.' 'Oh, that's flattery.' 'Not at all. Those hands.' 'What's the matter with them?' 'There's nothing the matter with them.' 'Supposing I had bitten my nails?' 'Ah, but you never would, you wouldn't have liked the taste of them.' 'But it's only a nervous habit. One probably doesn't taste them.' 'But *you* would have. You would have been curious to know what they tasted like, and then— horrible! No thanks. Besides, you know you've always liked your fingers since I admired them. One day I'll tell you that you are beautiful, and you'll believe me.' 'No. I shouldn't even for five minutes ever believe I was beautiful.' 'Well, listen to Aunt Gainy's Schumann.' 'It's not Schumann, and it's not Aunt Gainy. And yet, perhaps it is

Aunt Gainy. And yet something gets through, doesn't it? Imperfectly. But it does. If only she hadn't given up practising she mightn't have played so badly.'

'But now it's pale green twilight music. Evening on mountains full of dew. The Blue Mountains one knew as a child. Purple peaks going up into the sky. How splendid they looked coming into the harbour over the sparkling water. They really looked immense. The island lay before one, shaded in green and blue pencil. And there's Long Mountain coming down to the sea, dwindling away just before it gets to the sea—the great, green arm of a lazy giant. What a bustle at the wharves. Masts and funnels rise. Brown and black people in red, yellow, and white clothes, and coolie women with coloured handkerchiefs round their heads. Niggers laughing, shouting, rushing about with things on trolleys. Now we're lying in bed under the mosquito net, looking into the white moonlight and seeing the clouds over the mountains. Just one bank of clouds so that one can't see the top, mminng—mminng, murmurs the mosquito. But it can't get in. But oh, the cockroaches. I do hope there isn't a cockroach in my bed. "Rebeccah, is there a cockroach in my bed?" "No, Missy Louie, noa cockroach." "Please tuck the mosquito net in, Rebeccah." Now we're riding up the hills on a pony. A small pony for a small girl, says Byng. Smell of flowers, lovely mountain smells, heavy-leafed plants fat with rain. How large and near and blue the mountains loomed. Oh, mountains, I love you—throwing out one's arms.—If only I was big enough to

hug you, mountains. But now the mountains have
vanished. Wine-coloured days are falling into
eternity as they used to do when one sat by Lulu's
knee with *Trilby* on one's lap.

'Ah, you weren't there then, Tim.' 'No, I was
being a hungry little boy in Paris.' 'Poor little Tim,
I'm so sorry you were hungry.' 'Oh, that's over
now; besides I had fiddle lessons that made up for
it. But what dents of hate you put into your hair-
brushes when you knew I was coming, didn't
you?' 'Well, I hated boys, and I didn't know
you'd been hungry.' 'You thought I would be
like William over there, didn't you? You thought
I would break your dolls. . . .'

Aunt Gainy had finished the Schumann.

'Very pretty, very pretty indeed,' Uncle Heston
was saying.

'Oh, sweet dear, sweet!' said Edie.

Tim went over to the piano to discuss it with
Aunt Gainy.

OUTSIDE there was a March sky. The four
o'clock tocsin was clanging and they were coming
down the stairs. Not so far to go nowadays.
If one listened carefully enough, one noticed that
there was a pause between the strokes, hardly dis-
tinguishable at first, but just enough to give the
sounds time to run clear of one another. Now
there was no Jonquil. She had never come
back after Christmas. She had disappeared;
and it had not been possible to get near
Williams to ask about her. Nor did Williams
any longer come to the Patisserie. She had

sometimes seen her vanishing round a door, or
far away among a crowd of people, but that was all;
it was as if Bengartens never having approved of
either herself or Jonquil, did not intend that she
should have any information about her. So Jonquil's casual good-bye from the platform on the
night of the accident had really been good-bye.
Perhaps her mother had wanted her at home, or
perhaps she had just not bothered to come back.
Williams, who had always been a better disciple of
speed than either of them, had probably left by
now, as she had not seen even what looked like her
for a long time.

And now it was the end of her own time at
Bengartens; she had finished her course, although
she had not managed to get into the highest-speed
room. She was leaving the draughty, noisy place,
the singing of the machines and the crowds on the
stairs. Now they were all new people in the crowds,
one hardly ever recognized a face anywhere. It
was astonishing how quickly they changed. Very
few people took the whole course. Most of them
came to learn quickly, and they learnt quickly and
went. And yet there were the same kind of people
on the stairs. The same kind of conversation went
on around one. And one could tell new students
by the fact that they could only hear with difficulty if anyone spoke to them against the clanging
of the bell, or sometimes someone would mildly
express a dislike of being pushed. But no one
knew the secret which she knew about the lift,
though since the accident notices had been put up
on every landing requesting students not to stampede out of the classrooms when the bell rang. She

had missed Jonquil in the speed rooms; she had had to plod along by herself without the cheerful conversation and the delightful figure in the green dress.

Now she was on the ground floor, and was going in to see the secretary and give up her student's card of admission. The commissionaire said Mr. Piverton could see her. A rather grey room, a high window facing a side street. Mr. Piverton sat at a large desk. He did not look up, and she sat down on the chair on the other side. He wore a stiff collar with a black tie. He was writing and his hands looked cold, although there was a fire in the room. There actually was a fire before which Mr. Piverton, arriving early in the morning, could warm his hands. Round the room files were arranged in alphabetical order. Over the mantelpiece was a map of England, and on the mantelpiece stood a row of shorthand text books.

'Ah, Miss—er——'

She gave him her student's card.

'Miss Burnett.'

He sat back in his chair.

'Your course has come to an end. Been here some time, haven't you? And what is your speed?'

But he was reading the particulars on her card.

'Oh, well, you can easily work that up, can't you? I hope you have enjoyed the course? I see you took languages too.'

He spoke in the same careful way in which everyone spoke at Bengartens, almost separating some of their words, and pausing before each one.

'Yes, thank you, I enjoyed it very much.'

Mr. Piverton scraped his chin with one finger.

'And you have, of course, obtained your certificates?'

He rubbed his cold hands together. Well, that was really all. She smiled and rose. Did one shake hands with Mr. Piverton, and did Mr. Piverton shake hands with one? He seemed for a moment to be wondering the same thing himself. But evidently he didn't, and one didn't. She was only one out of many hundreds. Now a girl was bringing in a cup of tea for him, and she went.

Well, good-bye, Bengartens. That was all it was necessary to say. Perhaps it was too much to say. But since it did not seem to know what to say, one would tell it that on departure one says: good-bye. She got her clothes from the old woman and went out. A cold, grey building against a cold, grey sky. Should one turn back and say something else? But on the whole, why should one treat it as a personality? The tocsin might clang for ever, but she would not be there to hear it. The only thing she would wish to remember about Bengartens was a spring flower in a green dress. And even the spring flower had gone; probably it considered Bengartens too arid a place to be in now that the spring was really coming. She went down long, cold streets. The wind was like some brigand lying wait round every corner to knife one. Black branches in the gardens in the squares, here and there a tree budding. She was going to hospitality and the civilized hour, the hour which all her life she had tried to maintain a little longer. Such a short hour between day and night. An hour which should not be spent in restaurants among crowds of people, teacups rattling on trays, spoons jingling, waiters passing in and out among tables and a popular orchestral selection being played in a gallery above one's head; so that one's thoughts were made muddy, conversation was blurred, even personality seemed to become less real in the glare of electric light from lamps over-head.   Faces, voices, thoughts, everything was harsh and strained. Just as she had always as a little girl tried to make Aunt Gainy's music last longer, and to encourage Mary to go on talking in the kitchen, so she still tried to lengthen and spin it out. And for the first time in her life she moved in a flexible society, an intimate personal circle where people understood without a great deal of pressure being brought to bear on them; perhaps without even an expressed wish. One could sit back on the divan, and Tim would go on playing while Bernard accompanied him, or they would try over new things together while the hands of the clock went round from five to eight, and the transition period from day to night had been passed painlessly over.

It was as if one had drunk some magic liquor, which gradually becoming assimilated, produced an intoxication of the spirit. One's whole self seemed to be set free, one seemed to be able to feel accurately with every part of one's body; because it was to some extent impossible to be entirely oneself among a crowd of people, one all the time felt around one the pressure of their thoughts and feelings, one was involved in their humanity. And when they had been practising or trying over things for three or four hours, Bernard would turn round on the music stool and smile at her: 'Now,

you'll have to stay to supper.' He understood. He
knew that she wanted to keep that state of power
and richness just a little longer with her, and that
feeling of being at ease with people which was so
rare, of knowing that they were really one's
friends, that one might relax one's tension of mind
with them and not regret it afterwards. Tim would
look at her over Bernard's head, and his mouth
seemed to be made in a neat line. That sense of
security which he had found as a little boy in
Bidaud's rooms she had found in their flat. He
had meant her to find it. He had given it to her.
It was as if he were standing behind her life very
quietly, dangerously quiet. Then there would come
the dark journey back to Wickhampstead. He
would always see her off. Sometimes they both
came. The train would slide out under the huge
vaulted roof of the station and the journey would
seem less desolating, even less dark, because he
was there behind her in London, the person who
made no mistakes. He knew that he made no
mistakes. Just as he was conscious of his own gift,
he was conscious of having power in his hands.
What a wonderful thing it must be to be aware of
one's own power. To have that sense of certainty
in one's blood—I am, I can—even with set-backs
and despairs, and nerves that let one down, and left
one open to the sometimes intentionally brutal
excursions of other people into one's most delicate
reserves. To have through everything an aristocratic consciousness of the ability to achieve.

And now she was going to Mark's. Mark had
only lately joined the circle. She had at first been
afraid of meeting her; but then she was always

afraid of meeting new people. But it had been rude of her not to trust Bernard in the matter of a favourite sister. Tim had scolded her. 'How long are you going to have this fear of people? It's ridiculous.' In the hall, putting her into her coat one night going home. The next day when she had come into the room and Mark had got up to shake hands, she knew at once that there was nothing to be frightened of. Mark would not disturb the circle though she would certainly bring her own flavour to it. She was a long slender person with extraordinarily nerved movements. First impressions were strange things. When one first met a person did one then, and only then, get the real impression of their personality? Gradually, as one got to know them, they changed. The first impression was replaced by the impression caused by familiarity. They became set for one inside a frame. The vital feature of character or mind which had struck one at first, seemed to be submerged under a cloud of facts which one had come to know about them.

She had reached Mark's door, the last door in a row of houses. *M. Bocarro* on a small brass plate under the bell. Mark opened the door to her.

'Do you mind going into the kitchen for a few minutes, my dear? I'm not quite ready yet.'

She went through the hall, into the kitchen which faced the little yard at the back, as the studio windows did, and one could see the plane tree in the yard. The branches did not begin to grow till quite high up in the trunk, then they grew out and up. There was a little moss growing on the wall, and at the very end of the yard behind

the tree someone had once tried to make a rockery.
A few dark green shoots of some fern still strug-
gled up the earth by the wall. Over the stove was
one of Mark's drawings of Bernard. Her work
was very vigorous and vivid. She seemed to have
put all her own vitality into the pose. But it was
Bernard's face, contemplative and kind.

'Renée's staying to tea,' said Mark, looking
round the door, and going away again.

She made tea for them. Renée was standing by
the mantelpiece when she came in. Her black hair
was plastered back over her head; her skin was
very dark, and she had coloured blood in her. She
had been a model from childhood. Her eyes were
large and black; there was very little expression in
them. And yet there was something in them that
reminded one in a strange and unexpected way of
a faithful dog. The features were large but handsome; they were the features of a handsome half-
caste. They shook hands, and Renée sat down. She
was wearing a long string of red beads. Against
her black frock they looked like little red berries.

'Miles and I saw Pietre's picture of Vokara the
other day, Mark. It's awful.'

'Is it?' said Mark, amused.

'Oh yes. I'm sure Pietre's always tight, nowadays, when he's painting. But what a strange-
looking woman she is.—I saw her for the first
time the other night, when Miles and I were
coming out of Grimaud's. She was getting out of
a taxi with that new man of hers; I've forgotten his
name. She was beautifully dressed.'

'Thank you so much for making the tea,' said
Mark, smiling, as if in an aside.

'Miles says he thinks Pietre's work's gone to pieces since Flora left him.'

'Does he? I haven't seen Pietre lately.' Mark poured out the tea, standing by the table.

'I can't think why she did leave him. Whatever could she have seen in Lichfield? He's so thin, that man.'

'Don't you like him because he's thin?'

'I don't trust him. I know he used to beat Maria. She never told anyone, but she used to look dreadful sometimes. Everyone round at Allin's says he used to beat her; and then, you know, he killed her. He left her starving in the flat when she was ill, and went away for the week-end with some other woman; and when he came back, she was dead. Nobody knew she was there. I didn't know, of course, or I would have gone round to her. It was an awful shock.'

'Yes, I remember. That was sad. But I think Maria's better out of it; life wouldn't have improved for her.'

Renée swung her beads. 'No, she never had any luck with her men.' She looked down at her red shoes. 'Poor Maria, she used to be my best friend.'

There was only a very slight sing-song in Renée's voice; it had been adulterated by intonations picked up from many other people.

'Have you seen Rachel lately, Mark?'

'No, I don't think I have since I came back from Paris.'

'You know she's left Paul; or Paul left her. I can't think what women see in Paul. He's so effiminate-looking, isn't he?'

'I like Paul. He always seems to me the only one in Allin's crowd who's got anything like a mind.'

'Oh, but Mark, he's not in Allin's crowd! Not since that row he had with Allin over Nita.'

'I didn't know Allin bothered to row with Nita's lovers.'

Renée laughed. 'No, he doesn't as a rule. But for some reason Paul upset him. They had a fight in the hall one night, after a party. I wasn't there, but I heard about it. Nita looked over the bannisters, and had bets on who would win.'

'Who did win?' Mark was mildly curious.

'Oh, Paul did, because Allin was very drunk and as weak as a baby; but he gave Paul one or two nasty bruises. The next day the landlord gave Allin notice, because they'd broken several things in the hall and had gone through a glass door, or Allin put his elbow through it or something.'

'How creditable of Paul to have roused Allin to the pitch of action; it must have caused a sensation in the camp.'

Renée giggled and lit a cigarette. 'Oh, yes, it was talked about for days.'

'I hear Rachel's painting again.'

'Yes, so Miles says. He met her the other day in the street.'

'On the whole I think there's a lot to be said for Paul, Renée. If he roused Allin to action and started Rachel painting again.'

'He's so dissipated, Mark.' She stared again at her shoes.

Mark laughed. 'Compared with whom?'

Renée shrugged her shoulders. 'Oh well, it's life, isn't it?'

'Is it?'

Renée looked through the smoke she had just blown across the room.

'Everyone says you're a puritan, Mark.'

'Everyone is, as usual, wrong.'

Renée got up through her smoke. She put her hands on her hips and turned round in front of the long mirror on one side of the wall.

'I must be going. Thank you for giving me tea.'

'Don't you go and have your eyebrows plucked before I've finished my picture.'

'Oh, Mark, as if I would do such a thing.

'There's no knowing what you mightn't do now you're in love.'

Renée put on her things, grinning. Mark's saying that she was in love had pleased her. She kept her eyes half shut as she fastened her fur.

'Oh, it's a wonderful thing, isn't it, Mark?'

'Sometimes.'

'Good-bye,' said Renée.

Mark went out with Renée to the door, and she was alone in the room. The grey day was turning into evening. She knelt on the window-seat and looked out of the studio windows at the paved yard and the black trunk of the plane tree. She opened the middle pane. The air still smelt of winter. A motor lorry rattled by on the other side of the wall into a mews. On the other side of the mews, tall houses were staring at each other.

But somewhere along the river the beeches stood holding their branches rather stiffly and waiting for spring. Underneath them the spittle of rain was on their years' old thickness of leaves. The high main road came over the hill with a wall on one side preventing one from seeing the river. Then the wall ended in the gates of some private residence, and the whole valley came into view. Fields slanting down on the hill, and at the bottom of them the grey-toned river with the poplars; grey day over the Berkshire countryside. Perhaps a shivering, white light over the brown, ploughed earth. To the left, still some distance away, rolled the downs, but before one got to them Leathley lay in its hollow with the uphill village street, the cottages and old Mrs. Bortley's Georgian house, and the squat little *Beadle and Cup* at the top. Now we turn sharply to the right and continue up the main road. We pass the thatched farmhouse roof which is very old, and the Rabelaisian willow hanging over the bank. We come to the cross roads. The top road goes over the downs; the lower road travels towards the river. The corner of Barbican's garden has come into view. The trees are like a thin veil. They are drawn in the grey air in a light brown crayon. All except the ilex which is covered with its bottle-green leaves and stands by the house. Everything is very quiet, but there are some birds singing in the garden. We don't go in by the front entrance, that is for strangers; we take the lower road, and now we go up the steps planked with wood,—Barty made them herself. We knock twice, loudly, on the wooden paling. Wonderful, expectant feeling. Why has this place always seemed so wonderful? A place of dreams that one found in one's childhood. In the drawing-room the small table is laid with the tea-things. The fire in the bricked-in fireplace— Barty made that too; she likes making things—

throws strange yellow gestures about the room, lights up the old prints of the two capitals on either side of the fireplace. Carlos gets up and stretches. Ethel rises, but not at once; only when it is really no longer polite of her to remain sitting. Carlos comes round to say 'how do you do' because his mistress is being concerned about our welfare. How far have we walked? Are we cold or tired? His mistress is standing behind us with her hands on our shoulders; a very light, a very kind touch.

'Louie, have some more tea, my dear,' said Mark.

It was Mark's hands upon her shoulders.

'I'm so sorry, I didn't know you were far away.'

Mark smiled. In the middle of her mouth was a little droop, as if one had rouged it in for effect; but on either side the line of the lips went straight like a pencil line.

'Only fifty miles away.'

'Only fifty? I'm afraid that talk about all those people was rather boring, but I wouldn't let her talk to me to-day, and she's been wanting to get it off her chest all the afternoon.' She sat down by the stove where Renée had been sitting, and watched Mark pouring out tea again. The sleek brown hair fell just as it was required to fall, on either side of the head from the middle parting. The fine, neatly-placed ears were visible. She was all fine, neatly-placed; made in little points, rounded here and there. Yet she was a tall woman with long legs and a long back; her lithe, thin body, her features, her hands that were slender yet had broad palms—all seemed to be full of a sparkling, brilliant life. One felt that her body must be sensitive to the smallest wave of nervous feeling. She gave one an extraordinary sense of vividness. One felt that nature must have been in a complicated and hesitant state when it had made her, and had produced in her a mingling of elements, an extravagant pastiche, as if it had wanted to mock its own more ordinary aspects. As if life had said: 'You can't!'; and it had replied: 'I can!' It had combined a great delicacy that was feminine, with a vigorous and active temperament. And in the delicate, pointed and rounded lines of her face there were also two elements. There was, on the one hand, a certain hard brilliance that made one remember Zara; and on the other, something that the underlip portrayed. A melancholy drooping; a suggestion, and a suggestion only, of a profound scepticism that had sprung from a sensitive and tender nature which had been wounded very early in life, but by reason of its own vigour had to some extent recovered.

Mark was handing her her cup, and now she sat on the floor, drew her knees up and put her hands round them.

'So you've left the Robots' kindergarten?'

'Yes.'

But she didn't want to talk about it, she wanted to get Mark to talk about herself.

'Do you talk while you're working, or does it disturb you?'

'Oh no, up to a point I do. I never used to be able to when I was younger: I used to sit up tight; feet drawn together. Back straight. Biting my

lips.   Holding on for grim death, and hoping to
God my model wouldn't talk or want to talk.
Painting used to terrify me.'   She was rocking
herself slightly. 'Now I don't care! No, that's not
quite true. But it isn't the same thing. I'm not
frightened any more. Perhaps one worked better
when one was. One never knows. That sketch of
Myrtle up there I did when I was twenty-one. Of
course I hadn't began to paint then; I was doing
black and white. It was some years later that I
began to do straight painting. For years I fought
against colour.' She laughed. 'It was rather like
fighting a passion one is determined not to give in
to, out of sheer pig-headed principle. Of course
Berne had known for years. I can remember the day
we were in father's instrument room unpacking
something that had arrived for him—we always used
to do all the unpacking of his things for him—I remember feeling that I wanted to knock somebody
over the head that morning. Berne looked at me over
the packing-case and said: "Do you know what's the
matter with you? You want to paint." I didn't say
a word; I threw my cigarette into the fireplace, and
ran. Nobody but Berne could have said it to me,
and he knew that. He and I always did everything
together. Even before the war, when Spindles was
there. Of course Spindles was a few years younger
than us. He was such a nice, jolly child; a most
charming little fellow; I don't think he ever quite
grew up.   But it was Berne and I who ran the
family. We always did. I only remember Mother
very indistinctly. She died when we were small
children. She was a Frenchwoman; which accounts
for Addie and me having been called Adrienne and

Marcelle.' She paused. She seemed to be looking into the redness behind the glass door in the stove. 'I think it was the happiest time when we were all at home. There was a very close family tie between us.' She looked down at her hands. 'After father died, life seemed to go to pieces. Spindles had been killed—Berne and I couldn't face the idea of living in the house again. We'd all got on so well; cared for each other so much. It seemed impossible to believe that Father wouldn't be always there, pottering round in his instrument room.' She bent her head a little. 'Sometimes when I go there on Sundays, it still seems impossible. So we kept it on with Addie in it; she didn't feel as we did about it. Addie's, perhaps, the one member of the family who isn't quite like the rest of us; and she likes living in a big house where she can give musical parties; and likes us much better when she doesn't see us too often.' She stretched her fingers out and looked at the palms of her hands. 'Perhaps it was sentimental of us not to sell the house; but we couldn't. Although neither of us felt we could live in it again for any length of time; we felt we still wanted to have it there. It was something to do with Father—do you know what I mean?—it has a place-value for us. One says to oneself: "There I have been happy." We had our childhood there. We all worked at what we wanted to do, and grew up together there. Berne and I picked up the pieces life had left us and put them back into the house, and Addie keeps them for us although she doesn't know it.' She smiled. The slender lips broke their line. 'I often wonder if it isn't a disadvantage having been very happy when one was very young. If it doesn't spoil the rest of life for one. Of course one wasn't always happy there, and one didn't always live at home. The thing that knocked my life up most happened when Father was still alive. But it was different. Then one could go back; and there they all were. Father with his instruments, looking so pleased and proud over a new treasure; Spindles so cheerful and charming, patting one's arm. And Bernard, sane, civilized old darling that he is, understanding it all, knowing what one was going through. Even Addie in her simple, puzzled way —because she always found Berne and me hopelessly complicated—doing her best to cheer one up. And the house knew it too. That once-having-been-happy feeling closed round one and shut out the thing that had hurt one.' She leant back, her fingers locked together over the knees. 'I'm thirty-five. I feel that the best part of my life is over. Of course there's always work. One has that. But apart from that I don't expect anything better out of life.'

So that was it. That was the melancholy drooping of the underlip. She had a curious feeling as they sat there opposite one another; as she looked at Mark sitting on the floor, and at the brown hair that fell so neatly on either side of the middle parting: that the pattern of life repeated itself over and over again; in situations, in people, in nervous moments. The same combinations crossed and recrossed in one's life many times. Mark got up slowly, and one saw how very long those limbs were; but how very controlled were their movements. She drew the curtains across the

long, wide windows. It was getting dark now, and
a gust of rainy wind swept over the plane tree.
She looked back over her shoulder as if she had
just remembered something amusing. 'Do you
remember when you were a child swallowing a
boiled sweet whole? Didn't it hurt horribly? One
cried and hit oneself in the chest to make it go
down, but it seemed to stick there for hours. And
now I seem to remember that it was always the
same kind of sweet. It was an acid drop.'

Mark was sitting down again, knocking the
tobacco into the end of her cigarette.

'A long time ago I swallowed an acid drop, and
it's never quite dissolved.'

She was laughing at herself. Her eyes laughed,
but the droop in the middle of the mouth was very
pronounced.

Yes. She also remembered swallowing acid
drops that had taken a long time to melt; and how
frightened one had been, wondering if perhaps,
they wouldn't melt at all. And sometimes they had
been of the square and not the round variety and
had hurt more than ever. But she was not thinking
of different kinds of acid drops. Mark was
sending powder-grey smoke out from between her
lips, and the smoke was like a veil between them,
hiding those rather deeply-set grey-green eyes;
though really, one didn't know what colour they
were. But it was not Mark she was seeing. The
smoke was taking her away to a summer evening
sky over a row of lime trees. The expectant,
tearful look of the sky just before the sun is going
to set after a wonderful day. A beautiful, mobile
image sitting very near her. The light came

through the lime trees and entered the fair hair, making it look golden, which it was not; and she saw the image, not in a navy-blue frock with two little strips of green braid holding a belt over its narrow hips, but in soft ethereal clothes. Green, blue, and gold. What was that about an old farmhouse and a sharp, spicy smell of apples? Yes, that was it. And a room with beams in the ceiling where she used to wake in the morning. One could imagine her waking in the morning, a flush on those high cheek-bones, looking very beautiful. Well, nothing became beauty so well as black.

Those people who said that one could not experience real emotions when one was very young, were, as Mark had said to Renée, as usual, wrong. There was a clarity, a roundness, a luminosity about early emotions, that later on, tinctured and muddied by a growing experience, one did not get. When one had realized that the world for the most part was made up, not of pleasant but of reasonably unpleasant people, then one had arrived at a point when one was able to accept them as they were. But the time of first perceptions was over. That wonderful thing that one had felt waiting for one outside the gate of Linden. What was it? A shadow, a dream, an illusion that one would be chasing all one's life? But even dreams were built upon a background of reality. They might be made of spider's web, but the spider had to make his web. Was it perhaps, a certain reality that had its habitation in oneself that had waited for one outside the gate? That feeling of richness and expectation; that creative life that had seemed to emanate from the smell of winter, from the smell of spring; that had been behind one in summer and again in front of one in autumn; that look in the sky that even when one saw it from the middle of the city, made one think of the sea; that feeling that came out of trees and grass so strongly that it seemed there must be a personality there; she now knew what it was. It was the personality of creative life. She had taken all this time to find it out. She had once been so misguided as to think it existed only in the past. It was in the past, the present, and the future. It existed through all time and projected itself into eternity. It was the thing that said: I'm damned if I'll die—the challenge thrown in the face of destruction. She felt drunk with her own discovery. And now she would have to go home because Lulu was in bed again with another chill, and she was anxious about her.

'You look as if you'd just found out something that pleased you very much,' said Mark.

She got up, and Mark stood up too; and she put her hands into Mark's. She felt she must touch her. She must share this thing with her, although she said nothing at all about it. It had been raining, but now there were only little gusts of wind moving the branches in the square. The streets were wide, black and shining, with yellow lamplight on them; and in a spring-blue sky, was the moon. Mark stood and watched her go down the pavement to the corner. Then she waved, and Mark went in.

Her body felt luminous, smooth, not particularly important. Perhaps she had shed it. She seemed

to float down the street, carrying her attaché case.
She took a ticket for the tube. She saw the hands
of the clock; but immediately forgot the time. She
went down the lift, and looked at the programme
of the Alhambra without taking it in. It might
have been in Chinese. Now she was walking down
stone passages with a man in a bowler hat, a stout
elderly woman, a child with a brown paper parcel,
a thin man in a mackintosh with red and yellow
spots on his tie. They waited in a warm, dry
atmosphere; being underground was like being in
another world. There was a neat little roaring
noise, and she followed the men, the stout elderly
woman and the child into the train. She sat down
under an advertisement for Scotch whisky, and
suddenly realized what was the matter with her,
and why she had floated down the street. She
began to tremble. The man next-door rustled his
paper and coughed. A child was sitting opposite
with his face tied up. Above him hung an advertisement for wedding rings. She opened her case
and took out the only available paper she had, her
shorthand note-book. She had nearly finished it,
too. Underneath the last speed test there was a
space. The point of the squat little yellow pencil
needed sharpening. But it didn't matter:

  Your heart shall live forever—
There was a neat, dry sound of doors being
drawn back. 'Holborn!' shouted the man at the
door.

  Your heart shall live forever—
That came from the Psalms. She remembered
thinking how beautiful it was, how she would
like to use it one day.

Like the flower that does not fade.
And if of my extravagance an hour
Of you shall live:——though all else should
evade——

'Covent Garden!' shouted the man at the door.

My touch, my understanding, and my power——
I shall not mind:

The dry, neat, humming noise ran evenly between the current of thought and feeling.

I shall retrace and wear
The minute's fragrance that you left behind——

So it had come down to a minute now?—But hush.
. . . Leicester Square. . . . What did one do at Piccadilly? One got out and changed. Why changed? Because one was going to Waterloo.

Oh, I'll be proud: I'll wear my single strength;
Its breadth shall be eternity's bright length.

Ah. . . . Put it away. For God's sake put it away.
. . . She was walking up the stairs. She was sitting in another train. The train moved. She took out the notebook and looked at the lines. Then she put it back, shut the case, got up, and went out with a lot of other people of whose presence she was only vaguely aware. They went up into a huge cold place, carried there by some means of transport of which she was not conscious. But she was conscious suddenly that it was a damp night. She felt sick, lost, exhausted beyond words, and wanted to cry.

V

SHE sat in the window on the other side of the dressing-table. It was a soft, early April day. She could see the two poplars on either side of the gate; a faint gold veil hung over them. Lulu lay in her large bed, her hand under her chin on the pillow. It was the second attack of influenza and now she was recovering; but she was still very weak. The past was in Lulu's eyes; memories of years long before she was born, long before even her mother was born, were in those veiled, austere eyes.

'I feel much better to-day. I don't want you to put off your visit to-morrow, my dear.' Lulu was looking at her anxiously from the pillow.

'I shall see how you are to-morrow.'

'Margaret is here, and Gainy will be in the morning. Margaret will sit with me in the afternoon. I want you to go to-morrow. I'm afraid I've been a great deal of trouble lately, and no one hates being ill more than I do.'

She went and sat by the bed for a moment. 'Of course you haven't been any trouble, only you mustn't get up too soon and have another relapse, Lulu.'

'No, that was a mistake last time. Do you know I haven't been to Mass for a month?'

Lulu was feeling for her rosary under the pillow, finding it, she drew it towards her. She got up and went back to the window. The birds were singing in the garden; Lulu's birds too, were beginning to look up inside the bird-house, as if they felt that spring must be coming outside the glass panes. But there was a tearful, crystal, rainy feeling about the way the birds were singing in the garden; they went from tree to tree, fluttered among the branches, and then would unexpectedly start up with their tuneless songs. Sitting back again in the chair by the window, she imagined the earth stretching herself after the long, wet winter; a tremendous gipsy woman putting up, slowly, her great arms. Her breasts moved as she stretched. The rings jangled in her ears, and a sly smile, not altogether without malice, went over her broad mouth. In the evenings one imagined her sitting down squat on the ground, that smile still on her lips, smoking her clay pipe, waiting.

She looked across the room. Lulu's eyes were closed, but they opened again and smiled at her. Lulu was saying her rosary. But she wondered if the tearful sounds the birds were making in the garden, and the soft, spotted spring light which was on everything, even on the pictures on the walls, reminded Lulu less of the Sorrowful Mysteries of the rosary than of her own life; because her mind was nowadays continually going back to her early childhood. She liked to talk about it. She remembered it so much better than things that had happened in between. It was curious, she said, but she did not remember the births of some of her children. Many of the things in her life had tumbled into a Lethe from which she could not rescue them. During the last few days she had been talking about her life a good deal, and some

of her natural reserve seemed to have given way.
She liked one to sit by her with one's hand on the
bed while she talked. She talked too about things
in one's own childhood which she remembered,
but which one had almost forgotten. They seemed
to be once more back on the old ground of intimacy
which they had had when she was a child; when
she had felt that Lulu belonged to her in a special
way, that there was a kinship between them which
she had never felt for any other member of the
family before Tim came.

The eyes were shut again. The face was very
pale. How small and frail she looked in the big
bed. To think that she had had thirteen children,
and had been a beautiful and imperious woman.
But beauty was still in her face. The strange part
of it was that one saw it more now that she was in
bed, and that there was not even the slightest tinge
of carmine on her cheeks. And now in her old age
she had turned to the gentle love that neither of her
husbands had given her. She knew that this had
been the reason of Lulu's conversion to the Church;
though there was also Catholic Highland blood in
her family, and she always said that her conversion
was only a return to it.

In the drawing-room, there was a portrait of
Lulu with her beautiful, young Victorian mamma.
Lulu, a little girl of seven years old, stood against
the mild-eyed lady, her spotlessly white muslin
dress slipping a little off her rounded child's
shoulders: two ringlets on either side. And the
mild-eyed lady's hair was parted in the middle, sleek
and black, drawn gently over the head. She sat in
her chair, a statuesque yet fragile figure in a

lemoncoloured dress; her fingers over Lulu's, which
were in her lap. There was, too, a portrait of Lulu's
Aunt Letty, her mother's sister, handsome, very
like Lulu's mother, but with fair hair and a much
harder face. Perhaps Lulu was thinking about her
mother. Remembering those long, white fingers
with their rings, the emerald ring upon the third
finger; perhaps she recalled the soft, scented smell
of the lace on her mother's dress, her mother
bending to kiss her. Those cool, smooth lips; for
the first kiss that one remembers in one's life, is a
woman's.

Her parents' house in Madras had been a long
white building reached by an avenue of palms.
There was a photograph of it over the mantelpiece.
Green jalousies over the windows, the hot noon,
the smell of heat rising from the ground; the kind,
canny, enigmatical face of her ayah bent over her
giving her water to drink because she was thirsty.
Tall trees flashed in the garden in the heat, or hung
down in the evening, cool and heavy. The carriage came round, and her father and mother went
out. She remembered the sweet, aromatic smell of
her father's cigars, and the dogs barking on the
lawn and her father telling them to be quiet, calling
to his servant, in Hindustani, to send them to the
stables. Then there was a pause in memory. The
next thing she remembered was going on to a ship
with her father and her mother and ayah; going up
the gangway holding on to her mother's hand.
The water flashing round the ship, the crowds of
people, the heat, the glare, the noise of embarka-
tion. On the voyage home to England, both her
parents had died of malaria. She recollected going

into the cabin and seeing the tall, lovely young Mamma lying in her bunk, asleep. The lace on her nightgown hung limply over her breast, the rings had been taken off her fingers. She was very pale; she was like a yellow tea-rose. A burial service was held on deck, and the two coffins were placed side by side with the Union Jack over them. When she had begun to realize that in those two wooden boxes, dear, darling Mamma and dear Papa were lying, she had wanted to scream and beg someone to let them out. Instead she had buried her face in ayah's clothes, and they had gone down to the saloon, leaving the two wooden boxes and the people standing and kneeling on the deck. The young Victorian Mamma, the sweet smell of her clothes, the rustling of her silk skirts had disappeared; and with her Papa and his cigars; and at that time it had seemed quite logical that they should have gone together.

She did not remember going with ayah to her aunt's house in England, but she remembered the first impression of Aunt Letty, and it was probably very like the portrait downstairs. She had a large family of her own without her sister's child being left upon her, even though Lulu had money of her own. Lulu was sent almost at once to an expensive establishment for young ladies, near Brighton. She said she remembered her life at school very well. They had been half starved, but the tuition had been thorough. They were grounded in the classics, in history, and in literature. They learnt languages as well as the polite accomplishments which every young lady was supposed to know. She had somehow managed to survive the starvation; though many of the pupils either did not return to school or died from neglect. She remembered, vividly, going for walks with her dearest friend in the crocodile, planning the day on which they would both run away to London. The friend had died early in Lulu's life, in childbirth. When she was sixteen she did not go back, she was naturally clever and had been commended for her aptitude for learning, but Aunt Letty had other plans. She had found her a husband. Looking back at this period of her life, Lulu could not understand how it had all happened. If it had been out of a desire to please Aunt Letty that she had let her own strong character be so completely overpowered. But within six months of leaving school, she was married to a good-looking young Irish dandy who had just succeeded to his father's title. She was quite ignorant of men. She had never shared her cousin's interest in them. She was too intelligent to behave in the manner of other young women when in the presence of men. She was also quite unaware of her beauty and attractions. 'He is a most desirable young man, he has property in Ireland, and you are not badly off yourself. A woman has to get married. I hope you will be happy,' said Aunt Letty; and that was all. After the briefest, slightest of courtships, when Grandpa Mallord only once kissed her cheek, though he always paid great attention to her hand, she became a married woman; and here began the ever-widening valley between the past and the present. Oh, Grandpa Mallord, may you sleep soundly, may you be forgiven.

Her mother had gone away for a week, Aunt

Gainy was up in town shopping; Aunt Margaret
was probably taking her daily walk; Uncle Heston
was staying with cousins in the West Country;
Uncle Philip was asleep in his room, and she did
not know where Uncle Tony was. No one ever
saw him nowadays, he went in and out of the
house like a ghost. They were alone. The house
was quiet. An atmosphere of melancholy ease
about it; like a person who sighs in a moment of
relaxation after a strain. She also wanted to sigh
and lean back in her chair. During the last three
weeks she had woken up every night, in the
middle of the night, in the early hours of morning, had sat up listening for the sound of Lulu's
breathing next door. Sometimes had got up and
had come into the room, and Lulu would be
asleep. She would go back, get into bed,
lie there straight on her back, thinking, wondering how much she could will out of life so
that Lulu should not die. She hated the word
almost as much as Lulu did nowadays. Then she
would suddenly turn over and cry; stretched out
in blackness, in loneliness, lying on straight lines
of darkness. Gradually a grey light would begin
to move about in the room, a clock would strike
somewhere, and then the birds would begin their
tearful, crystal twitterings.

'Louie dear, I think the nightlight's going out
under Our Lady over there.'

She got up at once. Lulu was looking anxiously
over at the altar on the left-hand side of the wardrobe. The light was flickering. She renewed the
wick in the oil, and put the blue shade back over
it. It burnt up again. The favourite Virgin

still looked down with her hands extended.

'Thank you, my dear. I think I shall doze now till tea-time.'

She went back to the chair. Lulu's little head lay on the pillow, and the eyes were shut again. Some way off the trams swung down the hill into Wickhampstead. They always reminded her of Mexican Gate, and washing in cold water in the dormitory.

THE air was dangerously soft. The day seemed to be smiling a tricky, uncertain smile at them. As they passed down the lane from the station a bird in a little flowering tree trilled, a perfectly fluted trill, and then two long notes. They stopped to listen. As if it were conscious of them standing there on purpose to listen to it, it fluttered the branch and went on to another tree. Now they were going over the white stone bridge. She left Tim's arm, and stepped back to lean over and look at the lock. The river was swollen. It had over-flowed the boat-house landing stage, and was no doubt several feet high behind the closed doors of the boat-house. The island in the middle of the river under the bridge was covered. Trees were growing out of the water, and old, brown willow trunks showed dark and large beneath. The water rushed over the weir, bubbling and frothing. The lock-keeper was in his garden, bending down with a pipe in his mouth and his shirt-sleeves rolled up.

'Come on,' said Tim, touching her arm.

They went on, passing the Weir Inn sign. Now they began to climb the hill, they passed Leathley

Church and saw in the distance the row of trees on one side of the churchyard where some of her old and numerous friends among the adopted dead lay. The strong, sweet smell of the river hung in the air like a heavy scented flower. All the trees were coming out, and against the tricky blue of the sky, large white clouds looking like traditional angel's wings were travelling at a slower pace than usual. They passed Mrs. Bortley's house. One wing was evidently devoted to the servants' quarters, and the curtains were quite different from the rest of the house. Some of the windows were open, and inside, the furniture in this wing seemed to be all white-painted wood against very hideous wall-paper. Over one of the beds there hung a text decorated in bright colours. Perhaps *Consider the lilies of the field, they toil not, neither do they spin*, for young housemaids who rose every morning at six, to scrub, sweep and dust bric-à-brac. Or *Rest in the Lord*—a consoling reflection after a hard day's work. Mrs. Bortley was getting very old. They had seen her once in the autumn still driving her high pony trap, regardless of increasing motor traffic. Still the same hard-brimmed beaver hats, as if she were ready for the hunting field. The look of the 'county' sat upon the scrubbed doorstep seen through the iron gates. It was said in the village that a dissolute younger son, whose brother had been killed in the war, was waiting for her money; but he did not live with her. Probably she sat down to dinner in lonely state every night, with the pompous old butler, whose chest reminded one of a fat pigeon, in attendance; and the two pekingese dogs beside her. Poor lonely, narrow, old Mrs. Bortley. The vicar might change; but she remained Low Church for ever.

A woman with a cross-eye was looking at them out of a window in the policeman's cottage. Tim had already seen it, and was making the sign of the cross first on her forehead, then on his own. He swung his stick. It was years since they had walked up the hill together. It reminded her of being a little girl, of being half in love with him. He never had allowed her to be in love with him. Perhaps he knew her too well, or he was too clever to make mistakes. Whatever it was, she was glad he had not allowed her to be in love with him. She much preferred walking up the hill with her hand on his arm; keeping their light, flexible relationship between them. They had got to the top of the hill. They had passed the *Cup and Beadle*, the doctor's house, and the laughing willow. The cross roads were in sight. She trembled, and her heart began to beat quickly. Barbican's gate was open. The ilex looked at them; all the trees looked at them. The garden looked, and the house looked at them with its melancholy eyes. Overhead, the angel's wings seemed to be dipped behind the trees. Tim put an ungloved finger on the bell, and took hold of her arm as if he thought she might run away. The door was opened by a nervous maid. They went into the drawing room. Ethel was not there. Carlos got up as Barty rose, for he always did everything she did. Barty was so pleased. There was a flush on both her cheeks.

'My dear,' said Barty, holding both her hands. Then she turned to Tim. 'It's so nice of you to have come all this way to see me. You can't think how I appreciate it. Ethel will be down in a minute; she's had a headache this afternoon.'

Ah, how considerate of Ethel to have had a headache; though one knew exactly why she had one. It would not have occurred to her that she would have been most powerful if she had been there to receive them. Barty was looking, at that moment, better than she had ever seen her look. She looked many years younger; much more like the portrait over the cabinet. There was a smoothness, a mobility about her face, as if for a moment she had shaken off the years that were between herself and the person on the wall.

'But I thought you were never coming.'

'We wanted to come before.' Tim spoke as he always did when he was nervous or agitated, as if he were a foreigner.

'But our grandmother has been ill, and of course Louie has been anxious.'

'I am extremely sorry, but I hope she's better now?'

'She is better; but Louie has been nursing her,' he said, before she could speak. Barty's eyes were very soft as she looked across the room.

'Not entirely,' she said, correcting Tim. 'My aunts have been there, and my mother most of the time, but of course we have all been anxious.'

'I think the greater part of it has fallen on you,' he said, in a very urbane manner which he assumed when he was going to be insistent about something. Barty looked at her again; then the door opened, and the situation became entirely diplomatic. Ethel came in busying over the tea-tray. The nervous maid came in after her, nearly dropping something in her nervousness. Tim was introduced. Ethel's thin figure was encased in a tight-fitting black frock that looked as if it had once been a Paris model. She wore a long chain of little white glass beads which fell below her waist, and she had long earrings in her ears. Her hair was taken tightly over her head, and coiled into two little plaited buns on either side. She was slightly made up. Even Barty seemed surprised at her appearance. Ethel was extremely cordial.

'You look thinner, Miss Burnett.'

'She's been nursing her grandmother.'

'Oh, dear, nothing serious, I hope?'

She remembered that Ethel had once been a hospital nurse. It was exactly the business-like, unsympathetic tone one might have expected from a person who had been a nurse. They sat down. She knew that Barty wanted to pour out the tea. She saw her looking at the teapot. And Ethel knew too; she flittered round and simpered like a girl of sixteen. She was so long over it, arranging things here and things there, ringing the bell for something she pretended had been forgotten, that at last Barty had to ask her whether she was going to perform the office at all; and that was exactly what she wanted. She made a noise that was like a miniature shriek of joy, and almost ran to the chair.

'One or two lumps?'

The same comedy over the sugar which always used to take place before. Tim, who was talking to Barty about dogs, pretended that he thought she was asking him, and said:

'Yes, please.'

Ethel laughed and turned again towards her, tongs poised in the air.

'Miss Burnett?'

Tim looked over at her.

'If it will save you any trouble, we both take the same amount of sugar in our tea. Two lumps, please.' It was said with a smile. Ethel tittered.

'And are you alike in all your tastes?' It was the first time she had spoken to him since they had been introduced. It was as if she had been trying to ignore him.

'Yes, it's quite remarkable, but we have a number of tastes in common.' He spoke as if it were a fact that he had been considering for some time.

'For instance, we nearly always like and dislike the same people.'

It was said with the greatest goodwill, even with a suggestion of innocence, of youthfulness of outlook, which meant that he was going to be dangerous. Barty looked amused.

'What an ideal arrangement.'

Ethel dropped the sugar into the cups rather heavily. By her tone she seemed to be inferring that they would perhaps marry, that they might be even engaged. Tim took her up at once.

'Yes, isn't it?'

More and more innocent; but now he turned back to Barty, changing his fresh, young, innocent manner to a graver, courteous, older one.

'But, of course, it's an accident when that happens, isn't it?'

'A very happy accident. One that is unfortunately, too rare.'

Barty reached for a cigarette, and Tim lit a match for her. A voice came from behind the tea-table.

'Barty, don't have another just now.'

Barty hesitated, and she saw that this was going to be too much for Tim. He pretended to blow out the match, but did not seem to be successful, and in a minute Barty had changed her mind.

'Don't blow it out. Do you know, Ethel, I think I'm going to be disobedient to-day, just for once.'

She looked sideways at Ethel, and there was a certain light in her eyes that reminded one of that hansom she had driven down the Strand.

'It's such a recreation to be disobedient some-times, isn't it?' Tim was saying, as if they were both being disobedient together, and he was taking some of the responsibility off her shoulders. Barty laughed.

Some of Ethel's cordiality had gone, and they seemed to be quite a long time getting their tea; though Tim got up and did all the things that he, as a man, was supposed to do. He talked almost exclusively to Barty while he stroked Carlos's head and plaited the hair that fell over the sentimental eyes. Ethel glanced restlessly about, pretended to eat a scone, and talked about the weather and about London, which she said she missed. Sitting there beside Ethel, and looking at her dressed in the tight frock which showed, beneath its black brocade, the thin locality of her pigeon-breasted chest, it suddenly seemed to her almost indecorous that such a very thin person should have any chest at all. After tea they lit up again, and Ethel smoked too, although she did not seem really to enjoy it. Tim said he wanted to see the garden, as he had heard so much about it; and Barty, turning to her, started asking her about Lulu. They were still talking about Lulu's illness when she saw that Tim was gradually beguiling Ethel towards the French windows. Then they were left alone. Tim and Ethel were walking on the gravel outside.

'Do you know, I think Ethel was right. You're getting thin.'

'Oh no, Barty, really I'm not.'

Barty came over and sat by her on a low chair.

'You musn't do too much and get ill.'

Then she seemed to pull herself away from the subject. She spoke about Tim. How charming she thought him. And she looked away into space through the fireplace, through the prints, as if she were looking into another world.

'Yes, Tim has nearly everything, I think.' And she hated herself for the spasm of jealousy which shot through her because Barty had praised him. It was the first time she had ever been jealous of him in her life.

'I think you have a very nice friendship.'

Barty spoke slowly. Then she smiled and became embarrassed, as if she felt she had said too much and yet wanted to say more. They sat there; and there was silence in the room. Time was pinned by the hind leg under a weight of thoughts. She looked at the brown hair with the chestnut streaks in it, and thought how neatly and well it was done round the head, and how it suited her. One couldn't have imagined it done otherwise.

'I wish you would both come and stay with me, I believe I should grow young again.—'

Then she went on to say that the tulips were rather good this year.

'Come and see them. I had some lovely hyacinths, but I'm afraid they're over now.'

Barty had remembered that she liked hyacinths. Smoke that they were both making, went out into the middle of the room. The fire was quiet. The tea-things, the old prints, and they themselves were static. A dog was running down an old street in Dublin. An old woman with a shawl over her head was turning a corner of the street, and in the distance horses were coming. And to think that the dog would always be running down that street, the old woman always just about to turn the corner, the high-stepping horses always coming in the distance, bringing some lady's carriage into town. Carlos lay pretending to sleep. The plait that Tim had made, fell down the middle of his head, brushing his nose, but he did not mind.

'Don't you want to see your old friend, the garden?' said Barty, smiling and putting a hand on her arm: and they got up. Tim was making Ethel take him round the greenhouse, and asking her questions about the habitat of various plants, which she was unable to answer.

THE sky was a deep blue. So deep that one felt eternity must be rolling back behind it. The angel's wings were folded and put away. The tricky smile of day had gone, and the air had a heavy, rainy softness about it reminiscent of evening on mountains, as they drove down Leathley Hill. She sat in front with Barty. Behind, Tim was talking to Ethel and making her answer him. He was talking about the village, about Combesmere, about old residents, the churchyard, the graves. She wondered why he seemed to be so insistent on graves and towards what the subject was tending. Barty's hat was annoying her.

'Why not take it off?'

'I'm afraid Ethel will disapprove if I do. I'm not allowed to go out without my hat or gloves,' she whispered, 'and I very seldom do go out except in the car nowadays.'

Then she took it off and put it between them. Ethel did not notice. She was in the middle of telling Tim a story; before she came to the crisis of the story she laughed, a shrill wavering noise. It was one of her experiences when she was a nurse in a big hospital. A patient she had been nursing—a man—had died. He was taken overnight to the mortuary. In the morning she had to go to the mortuary, and the first thing she saw was the man sitting bolt upright, with his eyes open, staring at her as if he were accusing her of something. For the moment she thought that he wasn't dead, and it had given her a fright. But he was dead. It was merely a contraction of the muscles that had caused him to sit up like that. She laughed again, and Tim made a polite sound. Now they were flying through the soft, dark air. Ethel leant forward.

'Barty, you're driving *much* too fast down this hill.'

'Now, Mrs. Hildermore,' Tim said, in his most innocent and playful voice, 'you know you really oughn't to speak to the man at the wheel. If we had an accident, I should have to hold you responsible for distracting Miss Berringer's attention.'

'But hills are so dangerous and Barty's such a fast driver.'

'Nonsense, Ethel, and there isn't a crossroad anywhere here, and we've got to climb again on the other side of the bridge.'

But Tim was talking again behind, and there was peace. The river bubbled over the weir; ghostly-white water in the blue darkness, the noise mingling with the light, regular throbbing of the car as they went over the bridge.

'Come down again soon if you can spare the time; come and spend a week-end. I'm getting so horribly old, my dear.'

'You're not old. You don't look old.'

'Well, I'll tell you how old I am. I'm fifty-two.'

That wasn't old. Some people were old at fifteen. Age was a state of mind.

'My heart isn't old. At least I don't think it is.' She laughed. 'But sometimes the world feels very heavy in my bones, and there are so many things that I think I'd like to do. And all I do is a little woodcarving, a little gardening, and sometimes I read a book, and occasionally—but Ethel musn't hear this because I'm supposed to be a reformed character nowadays—I back a horse for old time's sake. I sometimes think that life seems to be getting narrower. Perhaps it does as one gets older.' They were slowing down. They had arrived at the station.

They walked up and down the platform; the train was not due for a few minutes. The blue in the sky looked breathless, suspended.

'Barty, *where* is your hat?' said Ethel.

'Oh dear, I've left it in the car. Isn't that naughty of me?' Barty offered them both a cigarette, standing between them with a hand on both their shoulders.

'I feel I should like to kiss you both good-bye.'

Ethel looked astonished, then she giggled.

'Please do,' said Tim.

'No, I'm not going to allow myself the privilege of an elderly woman.'

The train was coming round the rocky bend.

'Come again,' said Barty holding her hand.

She kissed Barty's cheek, and shook the skinny hand of Ethel. Tim was saying good-bye. Quite unobtrusively, with his back to the train, he bowed over Barty's fingers. They were in the carriage and he was shutting the door. Barty waved her gloves and called good-bye to them. Her voice was clear, but sounded far away. They were moving. She saw the faintly chestnut head lowered, a slight drooping of the shoulders, and Ethel leading the way out of the station. Still some few hundred yards away she saw the headlights of the car burning like two large cat's eyes.

Tim pulled her down into her seat. The trees in the fields were dark and heavy. On the other side of the river, a dark line of woods began to climb a hill, famous woods, she knew them from picnics in the past. Black reeds stood up like spears out of the water. Willows dipped down into shadows, bowing over banks as if they were hypnotized and drawn down by the water; but the poplars held themselves straight, a long line of them. They were not like the voluptuous willows,

they refused to be wooed; the river would never
get them to dip their long bodies in it. Tim was
leaning back, alone in his own world, looking at
the sky. The train moved quickly now. Soon it
had passed the big junction and was on its way to
London. The dreamy country of the upper
Thames seemed to drift away back into the night
under banks and bridges, only the sky with the
stars was left to them.

IT was a quarter past eleven when they walked up
the chestnut avenue. It was dark, for there were
very few lamp-posts. This part of Wickhampstead
still wore its almost country air, like a little old lost
village just too far out for the town to have yet embraced it. But Linden was a blaze of light. Lights
streamed from every room in front of the house.
They went up the steps. The door was immediately opened for them by Mary. She was holding
her blouse together at her neck. She said nothing.
She looked as if she had been in bed and had
hurriedly got up and put on her clothes. The
green eyes blinked and would not look at her. The
peppery hair was twisted in a bun behind the head.
She wondered why Mary should be opening the
door to them at this time of the night. Suddenly,
swift, black apprehension came over her. Mary
seemed a long time shutting the door after them,
but she did not wait. She heard Tim asking about
something; but she was halfway up the stairs, the
slippery bannisters under her fingers. Lulu's door
was open. Aunt Margaret, Uncle Philip, and Aunt
Gainy were in the room. Old Dr. Meikle was

bending over the bed. Aunt Gainy shook her head at her; she looked distracted. Uncle Philip seemed stupified. Aunt Margaret stood staring at the head of the bed. She caught hold of Meikle's sleeve.

'Your grandmother died half an hour ago—in a fainting fit, came on quite suddenly.'

He moved aside. Lulu was lying propped up very high, her head back, her lips slightly parted, and blue. She was the colour of ivory. Here and there, veins were showing. The ringed hands were stretched out on either side of her as if they were trying to hold on to something. Gainy was crying. She put her hand over Lulu's hand stretched on the sheet, the fingers wide apart. It was cold. —Please remember me to Miss Berringer, my dear, and tell her I hope we shall meet again one day—

'Isn't it dreadful, dreadful, Louie?' said Aunt Margaret.

'Her heart was never very strong,' said Meikle, to Tim behind; 'she was considerably better when I came yesterday. She wanted to do too much. Too active, you know. Never ought to have got up to-day even for five minutes.'

'She insisted on getting up for a few minutes after lunch; she wanted to sit in the sun, by the window. It was only for a few minutes,' Aunt Gainy said.

Meikle and Uncle Philip went out of the room. The lights blazed. She looked down at the pattern on the blue quilt. How many deaths did one die before one died in reality? To go away somewhere into a quiet, dark place; to sit down alone, and to say to oneself—Lulu is dead, Lulu is dead.—A black sea was rolling in among rocks. It was moonlight; she was sitting on the rocks counting shells. What a strange occupation. Someone was holding her hand, and she was going down the stairs with them. Over the stairs there were two huge pictures of Queen Victoria holding a court; first, in the early, and secondly, in the latter part of her reign. She had known them all her life, but now they looked quite new and strange. Her mind was dislocated and divided. A new part of her mind which had not seen them, now saw them—the white dresses of the débutantes, the little ribbons round their wrists, their bouquets, were all quite new to her. Somebody was speaking on the telephone, it was Meikle. In the urn-like looking vase on the hall table, there were three duck's feathers. They must have been there for years.

She sat down in the dining-room. She was very weak and small and insignificant, sitting there. Why were there so many oil-paintings on the wall? Too many!

'Is it true? Is she dead?'

The old scepticism of childhood that had never quite believed in what the grown-ups said, that had always suspected the adult world of being liars who enforced their rule by a terrorism of lies against which her soul revolted.

'I am afraid so,' said Tim.

An arm encased in a black sleeve was near her. He put her fingers, or perhaps she put them herself, round a very cold glass. Life had narrowed down to a very fine point. She wore it like a peaked cap on the forehead. It pressed further and further into her brain, and now it seemed to be gathered into a little knot. She took Tim's fingers and held them to the knot in her head. She remembered what it was. Lulu was dead.

THERE seemed to be a feeling in the family that women should not go to funerals. Uncle Heston opposed her going. Even Uncle Tony said: 'It will be much better for you to stay at home with Gainy and Margaret, Louie.'

Her mother stood up in her mourning on the other side of the table.

'Well, I suppose no one's going to forbid me to follow my own mother to the grave, and I don't see why Louie shouldn't come with me. Even we women have to die, Heston.'

'Well, that, of course, settles the matter. I was merely thinking of it from the point of view of Louie being a young girl.'

'Louie's been a young girl for the last three weeks, while mother has been ill.'

'Please let us say no more about it. By all means let her come. By the time she is my age, she will have had quite enough of these sad occasions not to want to attend any more.'

'You're insufferable, Heston.'

He put up his hand. 'Please, please, Evelyn. This is hardly the time for a private quarrel. She is your daughter: you say she may come, and that's an end of it.'

One almost had to have permission to exist if one was a woman in Uncle Heston's world. Tim smiled at her from the window. They all stood

rather stiffly round the table. Uncle Wilfred and
Uncle Ken were standing by the mantelpiece. All
the males of the family had come up for the
funeral; Aunt Elise was the only woman who had
accompanied her husband, but she was not going
to the funeral herself. She was staying behind with
Aunt Gainy and Aunt Margaret. Only two
strong-minded women among Lulu's nearest relations were going to see her put into the grave.
Edie was meeting them at the cemetery.

She left them talking, and went into the
drawing-room. The light-coloured oak coffin had
been brought down and set in the middle of the
room. Aunt Margaret was standing by it, looking
at it. There were lines under her eyes as if she had
not slept for several nights.

'Isn't it strange, Louie? I can't believe it, can
you?' She drew back. 'But it's beautiful wood.
Oak, you know.'

Everything was the same in the room, the swing-
basket where Lulu kept her knitting wools was in
its place beside her chair by the fireplace. A piece
of knitting, unfinished, had been hastily put into it,
and the needles were sticking out of the basket.
The strange, narrow box looked incongruous in
the middle of the floor. It was incongruous to
think that it contained the body of the woman she
had loved more than she had ever loved or could
ever love her mother. The box did not seem to
bear any definite relation to her. She had seen
Lulu lying in her shroud, a hand folded over each
arm, and the pale ivory complexion that looked as
if it were made of paper. The door was opening.
The black and gold screen had been folded up and

put away; one could see immediately who was coming in. It was Tim. The hall door was being opened. Uncle Heston was talking. Men were wiping their feet on the doormat. Four men in black coats marched through the hall. They solemnly laid their top-hats on the stand. They came into the drawing-room, and she went out with Tim and Aunt Margaret. Aunt Gainy was upstairs with Aunt Elise.

Ulysses was sitting on the writing-desk in the smoking room, watching everything that went on outside the window. She waited there, looking at the yellow light on the black trappings outside the gate. The whole thing was unreal. It had nothing to do with Lulu. Funerals, one felt, were designed with an eye to the enjoyment of the living; the person was only a puppet carried in a long box. There was a marching movement in the hall. The men were carrying Lulu out over her own threshold. She saw Aunt Margaret drawing back in the darker part by the door leading to the kitchen, hanging about restlessly, to see the last of Lulu, but not wishing to be there, as if she wished to be invisible.

'Come along, Louie. You and I will have to go in the carriage next to Heston,' her mother was saying.

Ulysses turned round at the sound of the voice, and then pressed nearer to the window. The coffin was being taken down the path; perhaps he had realised something. Now her mother was buttoning her gloves. What a fiercely dogmatic woman she was ... but also extremely sentimental. She had a superficial masculinity about her, perhaps not altogether superficial, yet a deplorable weakness of character in some ways.

She followed the plump, black back down the stairs. Aunt Margaret still wavered in the hall, a hand over each arm. She would have liked to come with them, but the bulk of male opinion in the family was too strong. Also she thought that perhaps she ought to stay with Gainy. She felt a kind of anger over the possessiveness, the arrogance of the uncles. After all, what superiority had they? Only the fact that they were men. Fair, ineffectual, though quite pleasant, Wilfred; misanthropic Uncle Ken; pompous old Uncle Heston; Uncle Tony, looking rather old, though he was younger than the others, with a slight stoop about his shoulders. There was something less aggressive about him. She had always liked him. He had a certain flexibility; was not quite so impressed by his manhood as the rest. And Uncle Philip in an old, black coat which had not been in use for years. temporarily shaken out of his habit of life. He too, had had some other distinction in his time.

The flowers were being arranged over the coffin. Among them, Barty's wreath, the most striking of all, made of brilliant little red roses packed tightly together, their faces cheek to cheek. And Barty had written on a tiny card, underneath, in her symmetrical handwriting: *Sincere remembrances*. Strange words. Not words one wrote to the dead, but to the living. They were almost like an act of exquisite courtesy that was bold enough to pass over the state of death, and to reinstate in its place, one of living remembrance. Both the wreath and the words seemed to her the one

streak of blood against a background of what was
like a spiritual anæmia of only half-conceived
emotions. Tim was helping them in. He had often
reminded her of a fine etching. Uncle Bryan must
have been different from the others. He had been,
of course. Had drawn away from them. Married
a Spanish jeweller's daughter, and lived in poverty
in Paris. And out of it they had produced this
difference—a person with fine eyebrows and
beautiful hands. Something too, that had a resistance to life finer than anything they knew of.
Now they were settled in the carriage and Tim
left them. He had to go with the uncles. They
were moving. She saw Aunt Elise's face for a
second in the middle window of Lulu's room,
those, pert dark eyes always on the look-out. Then
the gate was shut. They went slowly, and at first,
jerkily, down the avenue. A brilliant sun shone
down on them—a black line of horses and
carriages crawling up the road between heavy
trees.

Her mother held her handkerchief in her hand,
resting it on her knee. It was a marvellous day. But
it seemed to her as if there was a deathliness in its
beauty. Behind the sunlight, the soft air almost
like summer, the light and shadow in the trees, she
felt something, suspected something, but did not
know what it was. Her mother cried a little. Now
they were going over the tram-lines. People
stopped in the street to look at them. She felt
ashamed, suffocated. She had always said that
there were certain occasions in life when a crowd
of people should never be there; and here she was
acting against her own code of what was right and

decent. She was conforming to the spectacle of death: to an impresario in a silk hat. They were over the tram-lines now and in a quieter road. Only little villas on one side, and on the other a field behind iron railings.—*Remember, man, that thou art dust, and unto dust shalt thou return.*— Contrary to what was ordinarily meant by the words, they did not make one think of the shamefulness of the poor human body going back into decay, while the superior soul went on to another life. But of the kindness of the sane earth to whom at length one returned. She sat back and thought of nothing, and yet of everything. She noticed the familiar road, the turnings, the crossings, the place where they branched off and came into the countrified part outside Wickhampstead, where there was actually an old farmhouse. In the distance now they could see the cemetery gates. She was very tired; and physical disability of any kind always brought about a feeling of dislocation in her mind. She became submerged under the physical. A heaviness, a stupor, and at the back of her eyes a dull, indistinct ache. The jerking of the carriage, the sound of the horses on the road, seemed to be inside her head.

They had come to the gates. They stopped for a moment, and then went on again. As they turned in she could see the hearse round the bend. They kept on with the swinging, jerking movement up the drive. On either side stretched graves. Graves white and grey, and old, brown stones beginning to sink in; and lying back from the path, with their sedate cross and their verse upon the last step, Laetitia and Marian were still sleeping with the

grass growing over them—1880 and 1881. Now,
as the verse said, they were in the garden of all
time. How did they find time? A moment of
folly, or an infinity packed into a sharp hour? Or
the whole stretched out and very near, so that it
could be looked at with microscopic clearness;
every blade of grass, the markings of every leaf,
chiselled-looking trees, the edge of clouds, the
shaking out of evening on to the sky that immediately became full of the promise of every wonder?
No one to say: You're wasting time, my dear. One
would be in a position to reply: Time now belongs
to me. Now that I am no longer dying every moment, I can afford to waste it. The grave of the
sisters smiled. They had stopped, they were
getting out of the carriages. Tim had come round
to their carriage to help them out. In a tired,
half-hysteria of her mind, she felt she must hang
on to him in her life. She must not let him go.
He represented the sharp image, the reality, the
needle-point of things. She had dropped her
black gloves, he picked them up and carried
them for her. Her mother hurried on in front of
them. The coffin was being carried to the side of
the grave.

They all stood round and the priest blessed it
and read the last prayers over it, and the consign-
ment of the body to dust. Then the men lowered
it into the grave, and it disappeared into the earth.
Somebody was crying. Several people had their
handkerchiefs out. The uncles went forward and
looked into the grave. Someone threw in a bunch
of white violets. Tim took her arm, and they also
went and looked at it; the walls of earth sheltering

the light oak box a long way down. There was a
pause, and the family drew away, talking to each
other. She recognized Edie among them. A stout,
round person in an old-fashioned coat and a black
hat came out from behind two rows of people. It
was Mary. She shook her head at them. She
knelt on one knee with an old black rosary in her
fingers while the tears wriggled down her cheeks
from the green eyes. She made the sign of the
cross over the grave and then rising slowly, her
old knees stiff, came over to them and put a hand
over each of theirs.

"Twill be meself that'll be goin' next, an' plase
to God Almighty I'll not be lavin' any to mourn
me, avourneen.'

She left them at once. She had to go back and
see to the lunch for the family and friends. She was
not supposed to have come at all, according to
instructions which she had ignored. She had told
Uncle Heston the day before in the dining-room
when he had sent for her, that she considered her
term of office to be ended and that she would have
no master after melady, whom she had served for
fifty-five years of her life. Indeed, since she had
first learnt to make a pancake, and when he, himself, was not ten years old. He had looked uncomfortable at the suggestion of his age, had told
her that her services would not be forgotten, and
that he now remembered that she had known his
father. 'Me services? 'Tis no reward I'd be
wantin' for me services; while melady lived they
were hers. An' as for Sir Bryan, I knew him well.'
He had looked still more uncomfortable then, as if
he had expected that some unwelcome information

might be coming. But she had been quick to see
what he was thinking. 'Sir Bryan was a foine man
for all his vagaries,' she had said, firmly, in the
doorway, rebuking him for thinking that she
would have said a word against her father. There
had been something in her tone that seemed to
imply that she did not consider him to be the fine
man his father had been.

And now Uncle Heston was making a sign to
her mother and to the uncles, and they went back
to the carriages. The long, weary drive back to
Linden was in front of them, and Edie was with
them now, dressed in neat mourning. Her pretty
little plump face and waving grey hair under a
black hat. She was leaning forward.

'But, dear. So sudden—so terribly sudden.'

Her mother sighed. Edie continued to prod
her mother's knee with two fingers.

'I can hardly believe it—only the other day it
seems I was seeing her. Tell me, dear, were you
there when it happened?'

The question was asked with a certain diffident
curiosity. She dreaded that shortly she would be
drawn into a discussion.

'Louie was. She came in half an hour afterwards.'

Edie was turning to her, eager, sympathetic,
wanting to worm out of her silence something that
would give her a conclusive picture of Lulu dying,
and dead. Edie was used to funerals; she had
attended so many during the last ten years.

'Dear, was she conscious right up to the end?'
The fingers in the silk glove were now prodding
her knee.

'She knew nothing. She died in a fainting fit,' she said brutally.

The jerking and swinging motion of the carriage was once more going on inside her head. Little pin-pricks of pain gathered in groups and talked about things among themselves. She took no part in their conversation, although some of it was about her. She lay in a coma in an inner room in her brain, while the voices talked outside.

'Dear, how dreadful,' Edie was saying to her mother. 'And yet, perhaps merciful for her. She did dread death so, didn't she?'

They were drawing into Wickhampstead, leaving the country part behind them.

SHE wondered if it was imagination or if everyone really was rather merry, in a subdued way of course, a decent way, as befitting people who had just buried someone who was dear to them. Three decanters were being constantly passed round the table. Uncle Heston had asked her mother to sit at the head of the table, Lulu's old place, and she had done so with a certain importance in her bearing. Aunt Margaret and Edie were sitting together, and Edie was satisfying her curiosity about Lulu. Aunt Gainy was between Aunt Elise and herself, looking very frail. There was something widowed about her appearance in the new mourning with a touch of white at her wrists. The uncles were talking among themselves. Strip most people of veneer and assumed feelings, and how much capacity for reality had they underneath? It seemed that it needed a certain intensity of character to be able to suffer. She remembered one of the few occasions, years ago, when Daisy had spent part of her holidays at Linden. She had been very upset over something. She remembered that coquettish schoolgirl air of Daisy, saying: 'You know, Louie, you take life too seriously.' At the time, in her child's way, she had minded; had felt crushed by the air of light flippancy and the easy patronage of someone two years older than herself. Her mother was leaning forward.

'Why don't you go and lie down, Louie? Take some aspirin.'

'Yes, I think I will.'

'Have you got a headache, Louie?' Aunt Elise, gently solicitous.

She rose, hoping the uncles would not notice. Tim's quick look arrested her at the door. Then she went out into the quiet hall, up the stairs, solid, red-carpeted; the barren first-landing with Lulu's door still open. She shut it, and went into her own small room. She threw up the window at the bottom and pulled down the blind. Smells of blossom came in from outside. She had accused them in her mind of not being capable of reality, and yet, at the moment, she did not feel anything properly herself. A blanket of pain was over her. She felt disagreeably unreal. Lying down, stretched out and wide awake, she heard a bee outside the window. A gate banged; Mary's voice came form the kitchen below; then silence. Outside, the April day was warm and scented, nearing Easter. . . .

A wandering dream just on the surface of the mind, of going upstairs, many, many stairs. At the

top of them she saw the sun setting, and a group of
old dove-grey houses were flushed with an expectant sunburn. They looked young again, in the
hey-day of their youth, when love had been so
delightful.

She turned. What could she do? What should
she do? Those valuable accomplishments learnt at
Bengartens. Her mother's money must not be
wasted. On Mondays, Tuesdays, Wednesdays,
Thursdays, and Fridays, most of the year round, she
would not see the sun set. But on Saturdays and
Sundays, providing it didn't rain, she would.
Fancy thinking of that! *We* would never have
thought if it. No, *you* wouldn't, would you? But
then, do you ever think enough? Laughter. She
was furiously angry. She sat up and stared at the
person in the wardrobe mirror, the strange opponent mocking her in her own person—Don't dare
laugh at me! What do you know of any consequence—you head without a face?

She lay down again. The curse of an imaginative
temperament was that it lived nearly always in
anticipation, in the monstrous jungle of the future.
It arrived there, panting and exhausted, worn out
already by a feverish experience. One should not
project oneself into the future. Someone knocked.
Then opened the door and came in. It was Tim.
He drew the chair from the dressing-table and
sat down by her. He leant forward facing her,
and she saw the straight parting on the side of his
head.

'Come and stay with Mark for a little, or go
down to Barty till things are settled here.'

'What things?'

'Money, and all the other affairs. Perhaps it isn't the time to speak of it now, but if I have anything from father's portion of the estate, it's going to belong to you.'

'Don't be silly, Tim. You want everything you have for yourself, music's a most expensive profession.'

He smiled at her like a father. Anything she might say would be merely amusing. He had already made up his mind. Vistas of peace opened. A blue pond, dark trees hanging over it, with the fine network of their leaves. How wicked of her. Lulu was only just buried, and here she was thinking of these things.

'You've never been able to get that rather primitive little boy who broke your doll out of your head.'

'I never think of him in connection with you.'

'No, but he's there.'

Silence. Flowering garden outside. Sweet smell of blossom. Peace. Easter sun, and Lulu lying in her grave, a hand over each arm; dear, dear Lulu. Somehow the bands drawn tightly round the mind, collapsed. There was a breathing space, created by his coming in and sitting down in front of her. What was wisdom? Something maternal. Things apprehended without knowledge or observation. A hand, kind as a woman's.

'What are they doing downstairs?'

'Just finished lunch, hanging around, talking.'

'When d'you go back to Paris?'

'In June.'

The elms were very green now in the grove. On the lawn, all the daisies had gone under the

mowing-machine. Aunt Elise, Aunt Gainy, and
her mother were finishing the sorting out of Lulu's
letters and possessions. The pictures in Lulu's
room had been taken down. The ornaments were
grouped together in one place, the silver in another. And on the altars the statues, prayer-books
and candlesticks were arranged. Lulu always so
hating the idea of death, had made no will, and her
private possessions were to be divided up among
the family. When one went into the big room
and saw the stripped bed and the tables and chairs
out of their places, it made one think of someone
going to start a shop who had just taken over the
premises from the last tenant. The last tenant had
perhaps cleared out unexpectedly, and his possessions were to be sold by auction. So they were
grouped together in little lots round the room. It
was unfriendly, cold-blooded; she went in there as
little as possible. Aunt Margaret walked in and
out of it like a ghost re-visiting scenes that were
dear to it, but took no part in discussions, made
no suggestions, and generally refused everything
that was offered her. Linden was to be sold by
auction. Uncle Heston had no desire to live in
such an out-of-the-way place as Wickhampstead,
especially now that it was becoming almost
suburban. He had a small property of his own in
the West Country. Each member of the family
now had his or her portion of the remains of
Lulu's fortune. Nobody either wished or could
have afforded to keep up the house and the garden.
She was glad that none of them would go on living
there. Linden would go out of her life, except in
memory. She would not be there to hear the

tramp, tramp, of the city people, which would come
in time, down the chestnut avenue. Meanwhile
the elm grove looked at her. Whenever she went
out or saw it from a window, the starry-eyed trees
seemed to be looking at her, they were like the last
outpost of youth in a world that death had put out
of action.—'Remember us, remember us, remember us.'—As if she could ever forget them.... But
they were like children. They twined themselves
round the heart, insistent, till they had drawn from
one: 'Don't, don't, please; will you break my heart?'

The attitude of the family towards her was
rather like the attitude of a court towards the
favourite of a lately deceased king. Lulu's death
had given everyone a new importance. They were
all planning and talking about their own lives and
themselves, and what they would do after the
house had been sold. It was quite natural. When
Lulu had been alive there had always been a
currying for her favour, a jealousy among them,
especially those who had married into the family;
Aunt Elise particularly. Those sharp, black eyes,
that insidious smile, were now more evident than
ever, and she was very kind; so kind that it was
wonderful that she did not begin to suspect her
own kindness. Usually, her mother and Aunt Elise
did not work well in harness; they were both
people with managing dispositions. But whether
through some stroke of finesse on the part of Aunt
Elise, or some bargain they had made, equally
satisfactory to both of them, they seemed to
get on excellently in the business of sorting-out
and dividing. Aunt Margaret withdrew from all
decisions, and Aunt Gainy, who had always relied

so much on Lulu, stayed in her state of widow-
hood, agreeing with most of their ideas. When she
found it more than she could bear upstairs, she
took refuge with Mary in the kitchen. Together
they would sip tea, and sigh over the good old
days, and Mary would say how she was really
looking forward to laying down her bones, and how
the old life would never come again. There was a
sort of consolation in doing this. The gentle
stimulation of the tea and the soothing inflections
of that old voice, and the surroundings, always
associated in her mind with peace, a haven where
people could not get at one, helped out the
days.

Now she had come into her mother's room, the
room that had never been called anything else but
'the spare room.' Her mother was standing by the
fireplace with her hands behind her back.

'Well, my dear, what are you going to do?'

A long catechism of inquiry was going to
follow. A cardboard box full of waste paper
thrown out from among Lulu's things, was
between them. She went towards the window and
stood there, her face turned to the room, but her
body sideways so that she could see, without
appearing rude, into the garden, and watch the
grove. It recalled times in her childhood when she
had had awkward interviews, and that feeling of
always wriggling away from the lust for power,
quite unconscious, that her mother had always
wanted over her, as well as an appeal for an affection which she could never give.

'You don't want to live with me, do you?'—Sad;
making one feel pity.

'At least, I don't think you do.' Her mother changed her position.

'And nowadays, I really think it's better for young people to live their own lives. Carve out their own careers.'

That sounded generous and broad-minded; on the other hand a certain shifting of responsibility.

'If Byng had lived, of course, it would have been different.' Byng's ghost was looking at them from the frame in the middle of the mantelpiece. Up to now she had said nothing, had contributed in no way towards a solution of what was to happen to her. Somehow it began to be unimportant; as if the issue of the one-sided discussion had already been settled.

'I don't know what I'm going to do, I shall think it over.'

Her mother was again changing her position, sighing as she did so. She felt suddenly emotionally tired, sterile.

'I hear Tim wishes to make a settlement of whatever comes to him from mother's estate on you.'

So here they were down on the groundwork; sooner or later one always came down to it.

'Very generous of him. Of course, Heston may not allow him to do so.' Her mother paused. 'And supposing he marries? One has to think of that.'

She was shocked, startled. It was just like her to suggest such a thing.

'I don't want him to do it. I've told him so already.'

'Perhaps *you'll* marry him?'

A moment of swift, immediate reaction. 'There

are other things in the world besides marriage, Mother.'

'Oh, I quite agree with you, my dear. I hold no brief for marriage. I was only making a suggestion. He must be very much in love with you if he wants to do this for you, that's all.'

'Tim's not in love with me.' How could they be expected to understand? The real barrier between them was the unfathomable depths of the commonplace mind, something which turned everything it touched, even the kingdom of heaven itself, into sawdust.

Her mother laughed. 'There may be two opinions about that, but all I can say is that he must be quite unlike other men.'

She moved her foot from the fender. 'I don't believe most men care about a woman's brains.'

All the passionate bitterness of disappointment was in her voice. The disappointment of someone who had found the inside lining of romance to be made of cotton. She wanted to go. To escape this conflict of being sorry for both of them, for her mother, and for Byng, gently ironical on the mantelpiece behind the blonde head. Behind this kind of life from which she had come—the suave, elegant exteriors, the charming form, the speech, the easy, ready-made social idioms, the charming but vacant whole, was a tragedy; small, pitiable, a skeleton hidden in a decently narrow cupboard of the soul. And had Byng been nothing more than that? A delightful thing to look at and to listen to? 'Come on, Babbams, let's take a day out of life.' Surely, there had been something else there. Some hankering after something real, more real than the life it knew. 'You're my last love, Babbams.' Ah, there one stopped to think what that had meant. 'The love of one's vision'—that was unusual. People of Byng's type didn't talk about the love of their vision. They might think about it, but they did not talk about it. It wasn't done.

'You and Aunt Gainy are going to have a house together, and have Max for the holidays?'

She was determined that they should get back to a place of safety.

'Yes. We shall have to live very quietly, of course. You'll come and stay with us sometimes, Louie?'

'Of course, Mother.'

It was already accepted that she would not live with them.

'It seems so queer us all splitting up like this. But I suppose it had to come. Mother couldn't have lived for ever.'

She sat down on the sofa. The light-coloured hair was still full of colour. The very pleasant pink and white complexion was still attractive, and especially suited to her mourning. The eyes were still very blue. She sat with her feet on the fender, knees a little apart. An unfeminine pose. The strong hands and muscular arms that could play a game or manage a horse as well as any man, better than many. There was a generous, dogmatic fear-lessness in her whole attitude. The capable left hand was clenched on her knee, a good hand on a horse's mouth. It was this side to her mother she had always liked, a certain good, executive, masculine quality. The side in which she could see quite clearly those unrealized temperamental talents and gifts; which, because her mother had grown up and lived all her life in a society which acting always by rote could never pause to try and understand, had been wasted; or at least, utilized only in their least productive sense, and as remained in keeping with the known and sanctioned, purely womanly virtues.

HER trunks were ready, strapped and standing against the wall in the passage. She went back into her room to see that she had left nothing. She did not go into Lulu's room. That was finished. She would keep those memories intact; not to be destroyed or overlaid by impressions of dust sheet, and walls showing the marks on the wallpaper where pictures had hung for years. Still a faint aroma of lavender there; Lulu's spirit laid in lavender; the days when the room had been friendly, rich with associations. A tall figure in black with a high neckband was waiting for her in the darker part of the passage by the top story stairs.

'Tell me all about it. Where are you going to live? Do you like this Miss Bocarro? Is she a nice person? Is the place on the ground floor? If it is, take care you're not burgled.'

'It's quite safe, really, and what are you going to do?'

Aunt Margaret put her head on one side and laughed a little. 'Oh, I shall have some small place of my own, I hope; some very small place.'

She stopped and looked down at her foot, which she was tapping on the floor.

'I can't believe she's gone.' There was a break in her voice, and she began to whisper. 'Isn't it strange? Death is so strange. It's a great mystery. To think that we shall all go that way, Louie. And mother always hated growing old so; couldn't bear anyone to talk about it, could she? I hope you'll get on. I always said you had it in you.'

She paused again, a hand over each elbow. 'I should like to have been an artist myself. I used to draw once, but I wasn't good enough, you know. So much competition and that sort of thing—'

Now she was peering through the half-light in the passage. Directly behind her back her own drawings were hanging in their old frames, but probably she did not even know they were there. She was drawing back, hesitating, finding it awkward to say something.

'If you're ever in need of anything—well, you can always write to me, you know. I think it makes a great difference when people believe in you, don't you?' And she began to laugh in a half falsetto to pass off her embarrassment.

She pressed the hand that drew back shyly, and then returned to shake hers in a hearty manner. The black figure turned and went up the stairs to the top storey. She would not go up herself. She could not say good-bye to Pomoroyal. She went in to Aunt Gainy. Aunt Elise was also there, standing by the dressing-table. She said good-bye to her first.

'I hope you'll have every success in your new life,' said the suave voice.

But she was not deceived by the tigerish quality of that smile, or the voice.

'We'll be seeing you again, Louie,' said Aunt Gainy.

They kissed. Smiling, easy heartlessness. She was already dismissed. Pretty little Aunt Gainy with the lines on her forehead. She kissed her again in a sudden wave of affection, remembering Lulu. Aunt Gainy was puzzled, but she responded; her cheek smelling faintly of powder.

Aunt Elise stood looking on. They were going through old trinkets of Lulu's. There was nothing so desolating as the atmosphere of boxes and packing. The room was full of things. Different when the boxes were packed, the room vacated. Something surgical and clean about that. But that moment when things were laid out on beds and chairs, cupboard doors opened, drawers in disorder, had always seemed to her heart-breaking. It was a leave-over feeling from her childhood, the feeling of never having a home, of always rushing after Byng on foreign stations; in the midst of which Linden had seemed something wonderfully solid and immovable. Now there was only Mary. Mary was waiting for her in the kitchen. She felt the tears behind her eyes, but they were already in Mary's.

'I'm takin' your little cushion back to old Ireland with me, Biddy. Yes, I am that. An' in the evenin's I'll be sittin' with it behind me back, thinkin' of ye, avourneen.' Mary held her arms. 'Perhaps when you've the toime you'll be thinkin' of old Mary?—Well, just ye remember and say to yeself when ye think of her: Och, she was a great and pretty fighter in her toime, was old Mary

Mullins; many's the pitched battle Oi've seen her have under me own oyes.'

She was a little drunk, also she was trying to pass off the occasion for them both.

'Yes, 'tis tipsy I am. Oi've a drop taken, an' at my age too.'

The tears were on the old burnt apple cheeks. The time had come when she would really be laying down her bones, and the old spirit was still there, unresigned, and fortified by rum.

The trunks were being strapped on the taxi. Her mother had come downstairs to see her off. The poplars stood tall by the gate. Ulysses was looking out of the dining-room window; so he sat and watched everybody go, living or dead, in his huge Persian coat, growing older and older, no more resigned than Mary. She kissed her mother. For a second perhaps, they both shared the same feeling. They were both sorry. Aunt Margaret waved from a window. She stood in the middle of the path, and looked back at the garden, and the front of Linden covered with Virginia creeper. The house smiled. The garden lay back with its long lawns, indolent, with an immaculate, clean-shaven look; long moving shadows of trees here and there. A lifetime, a world of memories seemed to be moving in those shadows, something that would never come again. She got into the taxi. . . . Good-bye, Linden. . . . Sweet, dear Linden. . . . In the distance across the lawn she saw the elms standing in their marching line, now in a darker green. Summer. . . . Remember us, remember us. . . . The gate closed. They drove down between the heavy chestnuts.

VI

OUTSIDE the windows in the paved yard the plane tree stood wearing all its leaves. It dispersed its shadows on the wall behind it, and on the grey stone beneath. When a little wind now and then moved over its tall head stretching up into the air, a shiver would go over the branches, and one saw between patterns of leaves the architecture of the tree. Dust and noise came in through the windows flung wide open, but also the smell of early summer coming to the city. Damp warmth in the air, and at night sometimes, the thrill of dust lying under a shower of rain.

She was alone in the studio, Mark was out. But the place was always invested with that personality. Something reminiscent of a garden with a lavender walk, and at the end of it—two fields distant—a pale sea coming in; cold northern blue mingling with the mist of lavender, making a background for it. At the same time there was nothing effete or declining about it. Somewhere behind bushes covered with white blooms, was a noise, a curious, scintillating noise; as if someone with great sleight of hand, was busy circulating hundreds of little glass balls for their own amusement in the air. Yet, an activity so rapid and light, like a fairy juggling with hundreds and thousands—a fountain, stirring the fringe of lavender, throwing the scent further afield into the garden. It was the same

with both Bernard and Mark. When one shut
the door of Bernard's flat, or it was shut after
one, one had entered into another world, and left
outside a restless, eddying stream; had come into a
walnut-smelling, richly stocked world of books and
older arts. One felt, too, that it was quite definitely
meant to be so. It had always made a contrast
which she had wickedly enjoyed when she had
come to it from Bengartens. It was so strong, so
violent, and at the same time so exquisite. And
Bernard knew. He said nothing, but he knew.
Sometimes when she looked at him, square-
shouldered and much shorter than Mark, studied
his urbane back while he sat at the piano accom-
panying Tim, or improvising on his own, she
wondered why he had taken the trouble to put up
this barricade so well made, between himself and
the world. Both he and Mark had drawn just a
little away from the time in which they lived. Not
that they despised it, but that they preferred to
remain a little austere, apart from it. Without
living in any atmosphere of the past, they took
from the past what they liked, and built it into
their lives; it came naturally to them to do so. Even
if one had tea with Bernard it seemed different.
An intimate conversation about nothing over a cup
of buff-coloured liquid, but the conversation was
not perhaps really intimate. It was Bernard's manner, giving everything an added significance that
made one feel one knew him extremely well, had
been friends with him for years.

She got up and went out through the side door
into the yard, and stood under the plane tree. She
had a letter from Barty in her pocket. She was

wondering about it; asking the tree. The tree looked at her with its hundreds of little green eyes. 'You will find out,' it said, speaking through her own mouth. The shadow on the wall drooped. It was like an arm inside a voluminous sleeve whose folds trailing on the ground, passed through the angle where the wall met the ground, with the ease of a ghost. The worst of it was that she took such a long time to find out what she ought to do about things. Hesitated; went from one corner to another. Not like those people who made up their minds at once, and held to them for all eternity. Not that one thought that a bull-terrier mind was particularly desirable.

The plane tree said nothing further. Perhaps because its growth was also slow and it was not greatly troubled by it, or over-anxious that it should be so. A van bumped into the mews on the other side of the wall, its brakes shrieking as it was pulled up. For over a fortnight Barty had not been well. She wrote about it cheerfully, but she was annoyed that she did not get any better. There was an undercurrent, too, very slight but distressed, in this last letter. A suggestion of something not being quite right. A half allusion to a fear of being really ill and of not getting better, which now worried her. She had been painting the gate herself. She liked doing odd jobs—just as she had made those neat steps planked with wood. And when it was finished she did not feel very well. That was all; something quite ordinary. She had had the letter four days and had answered it. Twice since, she had been on the point of getting a few things together and

going down to Leathley. But she had decided that
she was a fool. That she had not got over Lulu's
death and was over-anxious about things. It would
all be perfectly right and simple. Barty would get
over the slight indisposition, and she would go
down and spend three weeks of the summer with
her later on, when Tim had gone back to Paris
and Bidaud. She looked up through the plane tree.
Standing under it, it made a sunshade, torn here
and there, and letting the sun in through little
holes. In a way it was a symbol of the grove, a part
of the heart of all trees; it was a great luxury to
have it there.

Someone was calling from the windows. She
turned and saw Mark; her hat pulled off, and
waving something white in her hand. Mark
leaned out of the window. It was a letter. The
postmark was Leathley, and the handwriting that
small hand now familiar to her; and now, somehow always associated with *Sincere remembrances*.
She tore the thin envelope, splitting it almost in
half, though usually she opened letters carefully,
hating to see them too much destroyed. It was a
note written in pencil, from bed.

*'If you aren't very busy, I wonder if you would
come down for a few days. I feel very low in spirits,
and don't seem to get any better.'*

She looked again at the date, then at the postmark. It was three days old.

'What's the matter?' said Mark, coming
to the window; knowing with immediate in-
tuition.

'It was written three days ago.' She handed
Mark the envelope.

'Are you sure? When one isn't well, one sometimes forgets the date.'

Mark being very kind, framed in the window.
But Monday was plainly written across the top of
the sheet, though the handwriting was not as
steady as usual, and the signature trailed away.
The yard, the windows thrown open to admit the
summer air, even the plane tree, and Mark standing
there in her grey clothes, with compassionate
eyes, and the envelope in her hand, seemed to swim
round her. 'She is going to die, she is going to die,'
they all said, without speaking the words. 'Why
don't you trust to your own instincts? Your
instincts are always right.'

She went in through the side door to the long,
narrow room which was hers, next to Mark's.
Opened the wardrobe, and carefully got out her
coat. Gloves from the top drawer. A scarf. Things
usually worn. Mark was packing some things for
her into a small case, very quiet and methodical
too. Used to this sudden going off to see a friend
who might be dying. She went to the telephone
and rang up Tim. Bernard answered her, reassuring, balanced, from his world. The next
minute Tim spoke to her. He would meet her, he
would be there. It was natural to send for him, to
tell him where she was going. Quite ordinary
for him to meet her at the station. They found
a taxi-cab roaming round in the square with
the large old trees in the middle and the Adam
houses standing around it.

'It'll be all right,' said Mark, shutting the door.
She leaned out and caught hold of Mark's fingers.

'I'll come back, Mark.'

Mark nodded and smiled at her. Then she seemed to withdraw into the doorway, over-shadowing her. A tall, slender woman in light-grey clothes, waving her hand, merging back into shadows. Why had she said 'I'll come back' like that? What did it mean? It was irrelevant. The cab swung round, like a beetle used to turning itself rapidly, and they cut through a side street. They passed a clock at the top of a grey stone building, an impersonal clock which said a quarter past four. A quarter past four in the afternoon, and the smell of dust and petrol. Noise of trams and motorhorns. Black hands on a white disc, that meant a quarter past the hour, and Barty dying in Leathley; the sun shining on the water, shadows of trees moving in a looking-glass, people in white flannels punting, a gramophone. They passed another clock where the quarter was being struck. Time went slowly now because one watched it. Not even five minutes had gone. For Barty to have said that she was feeling very low in spirits meant that she had come to the ebb of her energy. In spite of her natural manners she was a person of a reserved, in-kept nature. Even from the little she knew of her, the short visits, and from letters, she knew this.

They had turned down another side street and now had cut into a crowded thoroughfare. They were being held up, packed tightly with traffic wedging them in on either side. The reek of petrol rose, mingling with smells from the street. There was a cheerful, stolid quietness about all the wait-ing machines; they were used to these necessitated pauses. Engines hummed, sometimes horns were blown, but otherwise they stood quietly humming away in the long minutes. Beside their patience her own impatience was the fever of a burning soul wanting to leap out of the cab window, to be a thousand times quicker than any fifty-horse-power machine. They seemed disgracefully slow things. Now they crept up. Jerked. Stopped. Then some barrier seemed to be swept away. An arm moved in the air. Everyone pushed forward, the snub-nosed taxi leading the way. They went on. Twenty-past. Twenty-five past. Half past. They were nearly there. That was better. If one kept the rhythm with time, it did what one wanted. Memories of Bengartens—Who's putting the rhythm out there?—Of course, one had to get used to the rhythm. Not fight against it. It was a technique, that was all. Not fight for the survival of person-ality, as she had always done. Part of her slowness perhaps, fear; and a certain aristocratic dislike of being classed with a clockwork toy capable of doing a certain number of little tricks when wound up, then getting run down and re-tiring.

They were going down under the vaulted roof of the station. No. One did not believe it. Refused to accept it. One might bow to Miss Swangstee's ruler, but one would maintain through the keeping of the rhythm the right of free will. She was walking across the station, passing quays of plat-forms, when she saw Tim coming towards her from behind a printed notice of the trains. The first fast train from town went in fifty minutes. He took her arm and they went into the restaurant with the red plush chairs. She told him about

Barty's letter. He leant back listening, then forward, smiling at her under fine eyebrows, out of Bernard's world.

'I'm so sorry. I was afraid of this ever since the day we went down there. I thought she didn't look strong—something transparent about her face—and then there's Ethel.'

'What do you mean?'

'Well, how unpleasant it was when she came into the room that day.' The waiter brought their tea. 'It's pretty clear, I think, she's made use of Barty all these years, and Barty's very kind. It fitted in after Ethel had been nursing her mother for so long, that she should stay on and do the housekeeping.'

She poured out the weak tea correctly, but mechanically.

'And then do you remember that night when we drove to the station—that story about finding the dead man sitting up in the mortuary? She enjoyed telling that story. She went through with the greatest pleasure every sensation she had felt at the time. The staring eyes, the naked body sitting bolt upright as if it were accusing her of killing it, and then: "but it was only a contraction of the muscles." In other words: "I was only *pretending* to frighten you".'

He pushed the plate of bread and butter towards her, and began talking about a Danish sculptor he and Bernard had met the day before. But the analysis of Ethel was burning in her mind. He had dramatised Ethel. Produced her as the parasite sitting around for years, sprinkling her little grey powder in the air. An avaricious woman. One saw it in hands and eyes—the things that betrayed nearly everybody. But she had always passed over Ethel as an obnoxious theme. She did not want to think about her. Barty in her own setting was big enough to obliterate Ethel. Ethel was mediocre, and now Tim had produced her in one or two strokes, probably on purpose. He paid the bill, and they got up and went on to the platform for her train. It was not yet in. People were standing there waiting for it, reading their papers. In spite of the warm day she felt cold. He put his fingers round her arm.

'Don't be frightened. You're taking life with you.'

'I can't make her live if she's going to die.'

He looked at her deeply, significantly, as he had done before on a few occasions which she remembered.

'For us—there is no defeat.'

Quietly. And that military phrase came out of Bernard's walnut-smelling world. The whole thing had been given another meaning. A journey to the end of the world. He smiled at her. The train was coming in. Porters were shouting. They waited till it was emptied of a few stray passengers, then he found her a seat.

'Don't get tired. If you want me, you'll send for me, won't you?'

'Yes.'

A woman with a shopping basket got in. He stepped out and shut the door, standing smiling outside.

'I won't go out, in case you want me to come down.'

Then he said good-bye as if she were going off on
a casual, even amusing visit and that was all. The
train moved. She saw his back down the platform,
wondering if he would look back, but he did not.
He would not, of course.

She sat in her corner; the woman with the
shopping basket opened an evening paper.
Headings in black capitals stared out at her.
Actress in Society Divorce Case. Famous Jockey Hurt.
A long, leading article on the tendency towards
decadence in modern life. She looked at the sub-
divisions, but they were not interesting. They were
what people had been saying for hundreds of years
and might still be saying in a hundred years' time.
They recalled an article in a book Bernard had of
extracts from current journalism towards the end
of the nineteenth century. An article written in the
'eighties. Women had just begun to ride bicycles;
and the rector of a fashionable diocese wrote
deploring the emergence of women into public
life in an article entitled, in all ecclesiastical gravity:
The Age of Knickerbockers. It dealt with the increasing number of women who rode daily into the
city on bicycles, where they worked in offices.
From which the outraged clergyman deduced the
decay of the race. She wondered what expression
of humourless wrath he would have applied to this
age. After all, everybody wore knickerbockers.
They were an article of the most decent attire. To
have attacked them had shown a lamentable lack
of insight in a member of the Church of England.

A quarter of an hour had gone. They raced past
factories, dumping yards. Gradually they left the
environs of industry behind them, and long fields

with trees and hedges in full leaf were on either side. Old horses grazing. Young horses who buck-jumped as the train passed, and snorted, galloping to a far corner. Then, while she was thinking of other things, the beginning of the river country came into sight. Corn growing up green on either side. Light playing among leaves. Simple things she had seen many times before. And now they came nearer and nearer to the lovely pastoral country in its decorous half-tones. Lightly shaking poplars, smooth lawns without a crease. They passed an old river resort, and spun over the bridge with the river beneath them. She began to recognise familiar signs. Hills on either side of the valley. Dark woods that looked as if they were dreaming histories. Villages and farm-steads. Here and there a country house standing in its estate. There were a few boats on the river; people coaxed out by this sudden warmth of early summer. White flannels, coloured dresses, reflected in the water. She was alone in the carriage; the woman had got out without her being very much aware of it some stations back. The train was drawing into Leathley, and she was disturbed, frightened by this look of summer in the face of something that so much resembled death. There was a car outside the station. Sanderson, whom they had known for years and who owned a garage in Leathley. He said Miss Berringer was very ill. It had all been quite sudden.

Now they were going over the white stone bridge, and a punt was outside the lock waiting to go in. A steam roller was coming over the bridge. They were obliged to stop and wait for it.

There was a gramophone in the middle of the punt between the two young men, and out of it a tenor voice singing: '*O Shenandoah, I love your daughter, A-way you rolling river*'. Clear and strange over the water. The young men looked pleased and eager. Then something very like mourning: "*Tis seven long years since last I see thee, A-way you rolling river*'. The steam roller was beginning to pass them, and the voice faded behind a grinding noise. It passed, and now the lock gates were opening. The punt was going in. One of the young men had a boat-hook in his hand. '*A-way I'm bound to go, Cross the wide Missouri,*' called the melancholy tenor voice, fading into a roar of water.

They went on. The ilex was standing by the house. It was always the first thing one noticed. The gate was open. She paid the fare and then asked Sanderson for his telephone number and what hour of the day or night would find him. He said someone was always there. She did not know why she did it, or why she told him that she might want him within the next few hours of the evening. But she was not surprised about it. Dimpy opened the door. His pink and white, rather worn face, looked concerned.

'I'm sorry to say that Miss Barty is not expected to live, Miss.' There was real anxiety in his voice as he shut the door after her. She had known that all along. It was nothing new. Nor was it surprising to be met by a note of defeat on the doorstep. He told her that Mrs. Mandarin, Barty's cousin, and Lady Curvy, her cousin by marriage were already in the house. He had come down with Lionel the day before. Ethel had sent for them. Lionel was lying down in the study. She left him and went upstairs. She knocked on Barty's door. It was opened almost at once by a very young woman whose rather vacant face was crowned by a white cap. From the big double-windowed room, she could see the garden, the beginning of evening on the flower-beds. Barty lay on her back. The sheet drawn under her chin, very neatly, without a crease, as if the nurse had arranged it, and she had not troubled to move. The young nurse asked her to sit down, and they seemed to be alone; but she knew that the nurse was somewhere in the room, moving about in those clothes that reminded one of clean sheets and hospital wards. Barty was awake. Her eyes seemed to be burning out of her face.

'My dear, how kind of you to have come.' Her voice was just above a whisper. 'I shan't ever get up from this bed.'

She turned her head, and again the eyes gave that burning impression. There was a slight blueness about the skin.

'Some sort of poison; d'you know I can hardly move my hand?'

The drawing-in of one side of her mouth was very pronounced. She felt wounded by the sight of this helplessness so honestly expressed.

'I didn't get your letter till to-day, or I would have come before.'

Barty shook her head, very slightly. Even the head seemed heavy. She began to think very quickly. Time would go, and the nurse would come round and tactfully suggest that the conversation must be brought to a close. The room was cool, quiet. A feeling of whiteness about it, as if it were preparing itself for death. She leant forward on the chair.

'You will get well. You'll promise me?'

'My dear—I don't think I shall ever get well.'

No self-pity in her voice, only resignation, the resignation of someone who was tired. But the eyes still burnt out of the face. Life was ebbing, but something in the eyes remained of an energy that still wanted to live, that was still strongly alive, and would fight up to the last moment for its existence.

'You must get well. You shall.'

A child in her was speaking, and yet a strong, fantastic child.

'My dear child—'

Barty smiled. Her mouth was twisted, but it was a smile. Even Barty had said it. The nurse came to the bed and touched her. She got up. At the door Barty called her back, her voice going off into a dry whisper.

'Yes, Barty?'

'Get Ethel to make you comfortable.'

'And you'll remember?'

The eyes smiled but no sound came, though the lips moved, and the nurse hastened to her holding a glass for her to drink. She shut the door. On the landing she saw what she had not noticed before, coming up quickly in her need to be there at once. Carlos was lying by the windows. Motionless, stretched out, looking at nothing, concentrated in one melancholy act only. He saw her, recognized her, but could not move. His misery was human and real, but it was a profound misery, faithful and uncomprehending—the terrible faithfulness of animals.

The smell of scented cigarettes came over the landing from a half-open door on the other side, and women's voices, subdued, murmuring. Someone was coming upstairs. The tall figure of Ethel with the Doctor behind her. Dr. Morley, the comfortable, rather degenerate country practitioner. She remembered him from childhood, though in those days he had been thinner; not so many rich patients perhaps. They shook hands.

He whispered to her: 'Very bad, I'm afraid. Woolington Davis coming down from town.'

'I don't know where you're going to sleep, Miss Burnett,' said Ethel, 'if you're staying the night, but we'll see about that afterwards.'

They passed on into the room. She went slowly downstairs, reciting to herself in her head: *At the corner of Wood Street when daylight appears, At the corner of Wood Street when daylight appears,*—it seemed to give a new meaning to the lines. She remembered getting up in class and having to recite it in the fourth form. Zara sitting next to her. Her black hair tied behind her back in a bow, just beginning to be brilliantined with that odourless brilliantine that she used to the end of their time at school. In those days over a period she had been plump, a little Rubenesque, before she began to fine down into an early maturity. *Poor Susan has passed by the spot, and has heard In the silence of morning the song of a bird.* There it was lovely and true—in the silence of morning. Dawn. Waking up, and feeling happy. How rare. . . . But in a line of poetry one could be happy. She was in the hall.

Light-coloured table with cards in a brass tray.
*Mr. and Mrs. Henry Gossett, at home, Thursdays.
Clive House, Langthorne.* The next village to
Leathley.

She would have to get drunk. When she was
drunk she was as brave as a lion. Usually a rather
timid disposition. The fact had often filled her
with annoyance. She was easy to bully. Zara had
had to stand up for her in the old days over her
appearance. She was the easy prey of dictatorial and
hectoring personalities. She would get drunk, get
into a temper, and get these people out of the
house. Ethel must go; and the others whom she
had not met.   *Oft, in the stilly night, Ere slumber's
chain has bound me, Fond memory brings the light
Of other days around me.* Poetry always came to her.
Quantities of it from everywhere in times of great
anxiety. The counter-rhythm perhaps. Bearing one
up. Keeping one's mind swinging properly into
place. Difficult juggling and some acrobatic feats
were accompanied by a sort of music.

*I feel like one Who treads alone Some banquet hall
deserted, Whose lights are fled, Whose garlands dead,
And all but he departed.* She too would be alone
with trees, earth and river.

She walked through the drawing-room, opened
the windows and went into the garden. Roses were
dying on their stems. Barty had not been there to
cut them. She leant against a pine tree. A beech
was growing beside it, and at the top the two met
like brothers and twined their leaves together. She
was thinking: If some universal power came to one
and asked one to make a choice, what would one
say? One would of course ask for the gift of life.

A slow smile from the universal power. Devil. It stood there tormenting one, withholding life. She rocked herself against the tree talking to the devil, who smiled. Could one pray to absent friends? Then, kind friends; kind, civilized friends, stretch out your hands in spirit over the distance. Think of me in an hour of nightmare. If it was true that one could communicate with the dead, one must be able to have some expression in thought with the absent living in certain moments. She put her face against the tree. She was really powerless. What could she do that would be of any use? It was madness, and yet life was full of madness. She began to feel calmer. The tree smelt of resin. Something round and rich, a feeling of power entered her body, perhaps from the trees. She began to pray to them. She stood in front of the pine and made an act of volition. Aah, aàh, aah, came over the tops of the trees, a little wind setting in with the evening like a sigh of relief from a person who had been in agony.

She went in. Dimpy was standing in the hall reading a telegram from a relation who had not been able to get there. She drew him into the dining-room and shut the door after them. The table was laid for dinner. She would make a friend of little, quiet-voiced Dimpy. He had been with Barty's family for twenty-five years.

'Dimpy—will you help me about something? If you thought that by doing a certain thing we could save Miss Berringer's life, would you help me to do it?'

They stood by the sideboard looking at each other.

'I will do anything that could possibly be done for her, Miss.'

But looking at him she realized that he had not much imagination, and that she must keep away from imagination, from anything that would sound like magic. His nature was that of a kindly defeatist. He had not been cut out with any idea of a great resistance to life. He had remained as he was. Very kind and considerate and faithful, and a little sad. Any ideas she had must appear to come from the dictates of that sober fool—common sense.

'Will you help me to get everyone out of the house, so that we can keep the house perfectly quiet? There are too many people in the house, Dimpy.'

He paused. 'Yes, I think I see what you mean, Miss. As a matter of fact, I said all the time that Sir Lionel should not have come. He's no use on these occasions. It was different when her ladyship was alive; he was younger then. I will do anything I can.'

He had never wanted to come. He had been torn between the loyalty to Barty and the anxiety of taking an invalid into a house of sickness. She was going to seal the compact so lightly made. The wines for table were kept in the corner cupboard. She poured him out a brandy.

'Thank you, Miss, but I never touch spirituous liquors,' he said simply. 'I should like a glass of sherry, if I may.'

There was sherry too. Very good old sherry, One bottle yet unopened. He drew the cork for her. She drank the brandy, and he had his sherry.

Behind them the dinner table with the white d'oyleys and the glass, was growing dimmer. When his glass was empty she filled it up again and then her own. He looked diffidently at it, then drank it off. Magic was not so impossible after a few glasses of old sherry. They stayed there by the sideboard, talking in low voices; and still Ethel and Morley were upstairs.

'Supposing Mrs. Hildermore should come, Miss?'

She waved Ethel away. She asked him if he liked Ethel. On ordinary occasions one did not ask these questions; but the occasion was not ordinary. She was prepared to sacrifice every unwritten code in the world for what she wanted. Dimpy was not yet quite regardless of discretion; but after a few minutes he spoke his mind. He had never thought it was quite the thing for her to have become Miss Barty's housekeeper. Miss Barty had such a young heart. She ought to have had cheerful company around her. And Mrs. Hildermore—he had no doubt she meant well, but it had never seemed to him that she had a cheerful disposition—

'Not a happy disposition, I should say.'

He never did care much about her when she was nursing Lady Berringer in her last illness.

'But I did notice one thing, Miss. It seemed to me'—his voice was lowered—'and it's a dreadful thing to say about a person—but it seemed to me she was happiest when there was a death in the house.'

At the time he had thought it was his imagination, and he hoped it was. But he had since wondered if it wasn't true; if she wasn't, perhaps, missing the hospital work. It was said in all seriousness; no hint of irony in his gentle, sympathetic voice. She looked at him gravely, as he looked at her, and agreed with him. The scene had become unreal. It had been growing unreal for many minutes. She wanted to burst out laughing, not with amusement, but to break the spell. He stood there before her, his fingers round the glass now empty, with a tiny golden stain at the bottom of it, and she noticed everything about him. His soft, felt slippers, his coat, rather shabby but very carefully pressed, his new black tie, his watch-chain and the buttons on his waistcoat. She saw where his baldness began and where it ended, and that he was not bald in the middle of his head. Ethel and Morley were coming downstairs; and they waited, and then went out. She met Ethel in the hall.

'I don't know where you're going to sleep.'

She did not even add her usual Miss Burnett.

'Everything's upside down, and the rooms are occupied. Of course, Miss Berringer's relations come first.'

Not Barty's, but Miss Berringer's relations. She had been relegated to the rank of strangers, outsiders. She begged her not to worry about it, she would not require to sleep. Ethel went upstairs, saying something about a cold supper in a few minutes. Time had ceased to be. She had lived whole years. Years in which sleeping and eating and changing clothes played no part. She did not particularly feel that there was a future of these things in front of her. She had become

riveted somewhere in the middle of time. She was
not sure whether it was yesterday or to-day she had
got Barty's letter and had come down from London. She washed her hands because she always
washed her hands before eating, and Ethel had
said they were going to have cold supper. The
idea of cold supper bore no definite relation to her
in particular. She associated the words with something instituted in the past. Cold suppers on Sundays at Linden and the pleasant decorative effect of
a bowl of salad, reminding one it would be good always to eat those things whose colours pleased one.

Mrs. Mandarin sat at the head of the table, her
nearly white hair done prettily over her head and,
one suspected, kept in its neatness by some invisible contrivance. She was at least ten or twelve
years older than Barty; the daughter of an elder
sister of Barty's mother. She had been a very
pretty woman. The prettiness of those du Maurier
drawings. Always so fascinating because they
were associated very definitely with a certain kind
of romance. Polite and polished. Perhaps of the
drawing-room, in which one would have suffered
from an equally polite ennui, interspersed with
little French chansons. And yet something there
that always delighted one, remembering what one
had felt about it as a child. She was very much
powdered, wore rings and bangles, and was a
little made up. She had bowed quite graciously
across the table when Ethel had introduced her to
them with a nod. 'Mrs. Mandarin, Lady Curvy,
Miss Burnett.'

Lady Curvy had made a stiff movement of the head, without a smile. She was nearer Barty's own age than her sister-in-law. A tall woman with extremely spatulate fingers and very hard-looking hands, devoid of jewellery except for her wedding ring. Her hair, cut to her ears and straight, was turning grey; brown eyes that seemed to have no clarity about them, and skin that seemed to have no colour. She was well dressed and very well informed; with a perpetual discontent on her face suggesting neurosis of some ordinary kind, probably due to an unsatisfactory and unsatisfying marriage, by which she had had four children, all now growing up. She was the daughter of a rich brewer who had been knighted; and had married, very much to Mrs. Mandarin's disgust, into her family over twenty-five years ago. For twenty-five years they had disliked each other; Lady Curvy always wooing Mrs. Mandarin, and Mrs. Mandarin refusing to be wooed. A hypochondriacal and very narrow woman herself, Mrs. Mandarin resented intensely her brother's marriage. She received Lady Curvy because she was his wife, but she never let her think for a moment that she looked upon her as a sister. She sat at the head of the table, upholding all the social severity in which she believed, in a stiff, silk coat over a silk dress, with an old lace scarf round her neck. For she had caught a summer cold, and with her, a cold easily turned into bronchitis.

In ten minutes she had discovered that Lady Curvy was far more of a social snob than her sister-in-law, and that she was graduating through Anglo-Catholicism. She spoke of Father this, and

Father that; of certain people as having Catholic minds, and of how Catholic certain present-day writers were. She saw what was very plain to see, and what Mrs. Mandarin, sitting listening to her sister-in-law with a sardonic smile on her little pointed face must also have seen, that Lady Curvy was drawing nearer and nearer to a time when she would call herself not Catholic but Roman Catholic. She watched Mrs. Mandarin's thin little mouth gently delineated with a touch of red, and gave her whole admiration to the proud, conservative Protestantism of the old lady, who sat there despising this new-fangled neurosis of the mind, and put it down unhesitatingly to the democratic influence of beer. But she decided that the old lady was wrong. Lady Curvy's religious tendencies were the result of a marriage that had been a failure, and of a desire to achieve a distinction which had not come off. Sentimental idealism was in that hard, discontented face, now turning towards the shadowy confessional; and because of that idealism, a certain emotional starvation which was looking towards the body of a tangible God. Her own real Catholic blood, nowadays tempered by an open minded atheism of which Lulu could never know, felt for Lady Curvy's conversion an inborn scepticism and disapproval. She turned towards the wholesome Protestant scorn with relief. The old lady would die a proud disciple of the Reformed Church, and hating her sister-in-law to the end. Lady Curvy was temperamentally—had life and certain gratified ambitions not diverted her from it—a Nonconformist. She did not know that she was looking, not for a pagan purity of form, but for a genuine, rousing, sensationalism. Now she was talking about her daughter who was at Newnham; and her other daughter who was to be presented next year.

All the time Mrs. Mandarin smiled. She said she could personally remember Barty's presentation. How sweet she had looked. . . . But Barty never could be bothered with ornate, feminine clothes, and directly it was all over she had run away in a hansom to a friend's house where she took them off. She related it with a certain flippancy, as if inferring that neither of Lady Curvy's daughters would ever have the courage or perhaps even the right to fly in the face of established conventions. Ethel sat at the other end of the table, unhappy all through the conversation. She was afraid of both of them, though she had a great respect for Mrs. Mandarin. After the story about this second escapade of Barty's in a hansom, the conversation began to be more general. It was an irritated, polite conversation, in which there were from time to time pauses when one felt that very little would break the superficial good-humour of it. Pauses made by three people who all disliked and distrusted each other, but who were brought together forcibly by a common interest.

She sat back in her chair with her feeling of timelessness. Seeing them in an entirely objective light, not as in relation to herself, and yet feeling that she had a definite relation to them. Like a stranger sitting at a dinner table who has, in an inner waistcoat pocket, something that controls the destinies of all those present. She belonged to a secret society of her own, in the interests of which she, a stranger, was going to send these people sitting with her at the table from the house. The thing was so certain that she was not very much interested in it, she was more interested in looking at Mrs. Mandarin's smile, and watching Lady Curvy's face, and Ethel's nervous manner in front of them, and building up, behind them, their histories. It was strange to think that Ethel was a mother. Though often the most unlikely people were mothers. She was seeing Ethel being married to a patient she had nursed in hospital, and three months after, the husband deserting; and then the advent of the little pale-faced boy who was at a preparatory school, and for whose education Barty had made herself responsible. There was nothing maternal about Ethel. She had also heard her say once that she disliked children. The long, thin neck and bony shoulders gave one a comfortless impression.

Now she was peeping down Lady Curvy's life. Wondering what sort of a mother Lady Curvy made, and what domestic harmony there was in her house. Seeing Father This and That coming to lunch with her; and the intimate conversation afterwards over coffee. The unfolding of religious ideas, the tracing of religious thought, along with the commending of the coffee, and Lady Curvy pleased, telling him where it came from. A charming man, thought Lady Curvy, wondering if she had Wednesday free. Now she was looking back at Mrs. Mandarin as a very pretty woman. Gay, trivial, perhaps a flirt in a perfectly correct way. Going to race-meetings with her husband. Holding her skirt up behind her, or wherever it was held

when she was young. A gay hat at some strange
angle on her head, over a pile of wonderfully
crimped and curled hair. And then one was
reminded of Barty. Perhaps Barty's horse was
running that day. What excitement. . . . Mrs.
Mandarin always indulgent towards Barty. Rather
attracted by her cousin's daring and masculine
temperament, and genuinely liking her too. 'Oh,
my *deah*, you simply *must* put something on Barty's horse.' The third race. Mrs. Mandarin was
childless, now perhaps a rather lonely old lady,
with a photograph of Mr. Mandarin as a young
man over the dressing-table, and Mr. Mandarin
ten years in his grave.

'If you will excuse me,' said Ethel rising, 'the
nurse must have her dinner.'

'What time is Woolington Davis expected?'
asked Mrs. Mandarin.

'He should be here quite soon, Mrs. Mandarin.
It's nearly half-past nine now.'

Ethel was one of those people who never
addressed anyone without saying their name. She
said it in an assertive way, as if she expected that
they might question her right to the use of it at
all. They were alone, without Ethel. Mrs. Mandarin sighed and pulled the lace scarf tighter round
her neck. She said the summer evenings were
nearly always chilly; Lady Curvy said she always
found the Thames valley so damp, even in summer.
She was sure it wasn't healthy for Barty to live in
it. Mrs. Mandarin said she didn't think that—
one suspected that she always politely contradicted
her sister-in-law, on principle. Barty had always
liked the Thames valley. It was natural, since she

had been born in it, spent so much of her childhood, except when they went abroad, by the river. She herself was very fond of it too. Lady Curvy said she preferred the East coast.

'So flat, and so unsympathetic!'

'Oh, Norfolk's delightful! You don't know Norfolk, Alice?'

'I don't. And I can't say that I want to,' said Mrs. Mandarin.

'Well, I've taken a bungalow there these last two summers for the children, and they love it. I'm sure you'd change your mind if you came and spent a fortnight with us, Alice.'

'Oh, thank you very much, but I never pay visits nowadays, except on special occasions like the present. It doesn't suit me to move about now.'

When Mrs. Mandarin said that, a screen was suddenly removed in her mind. Why, she wondered, were they here, either of them? They had come to see Barty die. Possibly. But they had also come to see that Barty did not alter her will before she died, in favour of Ethel. Ethel had sent for them because her subconscious, professional instinct was to summon relatives to the bedside of the dying. She probably hoped for the best with regard to Barty's will. The picture of Mrs. Mandarin as a pretty woman backing Barty's horse, and later as a childless and lonely widow, was blurred for a moment by another picture of self-interest not quite so picturesque. Of Lady Curvy, she could have believed it. There were in those hands profoundly practical business instincts which would not have allowed her to stay away on any occasion which she thought would benefit her financially. If she had been frightened into acknowledging it, she would have excused herself by saying that she was representing her family. She turned again to Mrs. Mandarin, the sardonic smile at Lady Curvy's Catholic tastes, the crisp voice, and pieced together her objective view with a sense of relief. She felt sure that, as Barty's first cousin who had known her quite intimately all her life, she knew what Lady Curvy did not know. That Barty's money was tied up in family concerns and went back through them to Lionel. Whatever private fortune she had would be far too insignificant for her sister-in-law to have bothered her head about. She felt quite sure that this was so, and that Lady Curvy did not know it. Somehow it exonerated Mrs. Mandarin and reinstated her. It strengthened her position, gave her a poise which perhaps she did not altogether deserve. It was going to be her sardonic little joke against Lady Curvy.

Lionel was not well enough to have dined with them, and Dimpy was with him. At last they were leaving the table. Neither of them had spoken a word to her. Mrs. Mandarin had been polite, but Lady Curvy distant. It added to her position of spectator, and fitted in with her feeling of timelessness—a ghost. Now they went upstairs together, Mrs. Mandarin first. She went into the drawing-room and sat in shadow. The garden was dark, evening had set in without her noticing it.

Two white searchlights were piercing the trees, showing them up in a frightened whiteness. A long, purring noise; then the ripping of a silk cloth from top to bottom. The door was opened.

Dimpy was taking someone upstairs. Two people. She heard Morley's voice, and another. Suave, rather high. She went to the doorway and stood in its darkness looking out into the hall. A door opened. Then there was silence all over the house. A pulse was beating in the silence. Dimpy came downstairs, lightly touching the banisters like a ballerina, something mincing about it. He said it was Mr. Woolington Davis. Dr. Morley had arrived with him, had met his car coming up. He lingered in the hall, listening like herself. She walked about the room in her solitary madness. The arena made by Ethel for Barty to die in must be broken. The spectators sent away. The impresario of the occasion disposed of. Someone was reading aloud: '*When the lamp is shattered, The light in the dust lies dead, When the cloud is scattered, The rainbow's glory is shed*'. They read it as if they enjoyed reading it, as if they enjoyed the arrangement of those words. Yet quietly, with no dramatic effect. Sitting down and leaning forward, with the book on their knee: '*As music and splendour Survive not the lamp and the lute, The heart's echoes render, No song when the spirit is mute*'. But she liked herself so much that lyric which broke forth with: *I dream'd that as I wandered by the way, Bare winter suddenly was changed to spring*. . . .

'They're coming, Miss,' said Dimpy looking in.

Then he went. Why were they coming? Such a short visit.—*Abandon hope all ye who enter here*, —The two men passed the door. Went into the dining-room and shut themselves in with a swift, important closing of the door behind them. Huge anger, like the nightmare images that were too big to hold, was filling her mind. They must and should go.

'Dimpy, prevent them from seeing him. They must not see him. Have they seen him?'

'No, Miss, but Mrs. Mandarin is asking about it. What shall I say?'

'Say he says the house must be kept absolutely quiet. Tell them that. Tell them their rooms will be wanted.'

He was hesitating in the darkness in front of her. 'And Mrs. Hildermore, what shall I say if she asks me?'

But what did Ethel matter? She could not see why she should be told anything. He seemed to understand then, and left her still pacing the darkness, feeling that something was now taking solid shape in her mind, had passed the stage of being impossible and grotesque, had begun to come into being by an act of will. And now she was going to disturb the consultation, break through their heavy silence. Going out of the door she saw Morley pass through the hall and rush upstairs as if he had forgotten something. The professional figure of Mr. Woolington Davis was standing by the table.

'Is there any hope of saving Miss Berringer's life?'

He looked at her. 'I'm afraid none whatever. If I had been called in earlier, it would have been a different matter.'

He took her for a relation. He was clean-shaven, getting stout. The case was very complicated. At the best of times, the patient was delicate.

'But is there nothing, nothing to be done?'

'Nothing that will make any radical difference. We can give her morphia. Death will come quite easily.'

'When, do you think?'

'I should say within the next twenty-four hours.'

'But isn't there something that can be done? Something even experimental?'

He looked surprised, severe. 'One doesn't always make experiments on dying persons, you know.'

'Surely when it's a case of saving life?' She was over-stepping the margin allowed to her as a layman. He was annoyed. He became a truculent little man, fussy, with an influential tone of voice.

'There is nothing to be done. I should have been consulted several days ago. The case has been wrongly nursed from the beginning.'

So she had got something out of his annoyance, broken through that ice-block of medical etiquette. Someone had made a mistake. He tapped on the table, he had already dismissed her.

'Couldn't you give some sort of injections? Something that would work against this particular kind of poison?'

She did not really know what she was talking about. Some recollections of an article in a medical paper on the treatment of certain poisons which had interested her. He looked at her again, surprised, forced to acknowledge her as a person in the room with him who had made a suggestion, perhaps not of great importance, but a suggestion.

'We could give certain very special injections, but there is always grave risk and responsibility attached to them. Especially in a case like this.'

But the tone of the great man in his voice was lessened. They were now in the operating theatre, coming down to actualities.

'What relation are you to Miss Berringer?'

'Her first cousin.'

There would be no time now to verify her statements. One part of her mind was upstairs searching for Morley and seeing Dimpy in the exercising of tact. He was asking if there were any other relations in the house. She was telling him that there was nobody but Miss Berringer's only brother, who was not in a condition to be consulted as he was himself recovering from an illness. An invalid. He thought he had heard that. There was a silence in which she noticed that the corner cupboard had been left half open. The key still in it under the coloured glass knob. Ethel thinking of other things had not seen it.

In the event of a new decision on the case, was she in a position to take any grave responsibility upon her? he was asking in clipped phrases. Looking at her as if he could discover in her something that would give him some clue to her birth, status, the number of years she had been in the world.

'Yes,' softly, from a long way off.

He was going upstairs to have another look at Barty. Perhaps to lock himself in again with Morley. She remained standing on the other side of the table in a still terror, seeing Mrs. Mandarin perhaps waiting for him on the landing, Ethel denying this kinship which she had taken upon her. But he turned round and asked for something. The telephone. Perhaps she could make some provision for his chauffeur and car. The ripping of that silk cloth at the door.

'Certainly.'

She was the mistress of the house. Somehow she saw herself in perspective, in a long gown with a bunch of keys. The days of passive wives who had the vapours on the least provocation. Poor wives. Life had been difficult enough for them, they might be allowed their vapours. The days when the dominant personalities in books had nearly always been men—Becky Sharp, after all, regarded as a monster, an adventuress. She left him sitting down to the telephone. Morley was coming downstairs; he went past her into the dining-room. She stayed in the hall, feeling stupid, not bothering to wonder what they were talking about. She was not going to think about Lady Curvy and Mrs. Mandarin now. They had died. She had taken on their function and dismissed them. But there were still Ethel and Morley. And as she thought of Morley, he came out of the dining-room, took his hat down, and smiled at her.

'Well, he's changed his mind about the case. Very glad. Yes, I'm going. Nothing more for me to do at present. Good-night.'

She was seeing him out; professional, courteous, both of them. Closing the door after him. He'd changed his mind. She had one more card to play. Carlos was still lying on the landing by the windows. He at least was an incorruptible personality, a dog.

There was a deeply-shaded lamp in the room. Ethel and the night nurse were whispering by the window. So there was a night nurse. When it came to the point, Ethel perhaps had not liked the idea of being on duty when Barty died. She was tired, or the responsibility was too great, even after all her years of experience in this sphere particularly hers. A little behind the bed was a table with a white cloth, glass bottles and tumblers, cups, other things. Everything in a state of great order. A clean, experienced-looking table. Barty was asleep. She seemed hardly to breathe. A yellow look was on the skin. For a moment she felt suspended in terror at what she was attempting. Death seemed too near to be able to hold it off any longer. The yellow snake was crawling up, growing nearer and nearer, mounting up under the heart. But there was to be no looking back. No fear or suggestion of defeat. Life must go back into those veins. The scales must drop off and wither.

'May I speak to you? Something rather urgent; downstairs.'

Ethel was surprised and at once set on the defensive by a note of authority, but she came. She went down with Ethel following. She was wondering which would be the best place for the interview; Mr. Davis was in the dining-room, the drawing-room had too many happy associations for her, she could not use that room. Lionel had the study. The only place was the kitchen at the end of the hall passage, if the cook had gone to bed. It was of course the proper place for their interview. It was not the kitchen of childhood, friendly with Mary, a place of privilege; but a hard, cold place, suggesting Ethel as housekeeper.

'I'm very tired at this distressing time. Couldn't

you wait till later, Miss Burnett? Surely nothing you can have to say can be important at this time? And why in here? There are other rooms in the house, I suppose?'

She was nervous. She anticipated something, and was trying to smile it off. But she had been caught off her guard and was not quite so assertive as usual. They both sat down on hard kitchen chairs at the table. Then she talked. Laying out what she had to say like a lawyer, a little arid and bare, but with everything in its place. Read from a paper in her head which she was seeing for the first time. Ethel would have go. She was going to ask her to leave the house that night. It might sound odd from a stranger.

'Very odd indeed,' said Ethel

But she was going to be quite frank about it. As Miss Berringer's friend, she considered it most negligent of her to have left things till so late. She had been talking to Mr. Davis, and that was also his opinion. Up to that moment Ethel had shown scorn for her youth and inexperience; inferring by looks and smiles all sorts of reasons for her interference. But at the mention of Mr. Davis she became serious, as if she could hardly have believed her capable of it. Her feeling of respect for the doctor's opinion rooted in her from years back. But suddenly, with a flash of triumph, as if she had had him in her pocket, she brought Dr. Morley out.

'It is the business of the doctor attending a case to call in a second opinion, Miss Burnett.' Superior years of knowledge, at least on this subject.

'But I think one can always ask for one; you should have known that it was necessary.'

Ethel was furious. How dare she, who knew nothing about it, make such accusations? She was an upstart. She had known it from the first day she had set eyes on her. They both stood up; but she saw that Ethel was wondering how much Lady Curvy and Mrs. Mandarin had to do with it. That there might really be some truth in the matter of asking her to go. She heard herself telling Ethel that as Miss Berringer's friend she was going to make herself responsible for certain of her interests while she was ill. In those interests she was asking her to go. She was no longer needed in the nursing. That if she remained in the house with this bulk of opinion against her, things would certainly be very unpleasant for her.

'You are not in a position to turn me out of the house, whatever your private views on my nursing may be. I am in Miss Berringer's employment. *She* is the only person who can do such a thing.'

So at last she had got it out of her. She had acknowledged herself to be a servant. But Ethel was not finished.

'I have been Miss Berringer's housekeeper and friend for nearly eight years.'

She walked past to the door. 'You can't send me away, and I am not going.'

She saw two people standing on either side of the kitchen table. One of them said:

'You *are* going, to-night.'

'I think you'd better be careful what you say, Miss Burnett.'

'If you don't go, Mrs. Hildermore—'

'You're threatening me.'

'I'm telling you what I shall do.'

She saw a hand that she knew very well by sight—she had often washed it—curl up as if it were going to plant a blow somewhere on an opponent's body. She said to the person: 'Take care. Better not hit her. Trouble if you do.' But looking at it she knew that the hand belonged to someone whose forefathers had rallied rebellions in mountainous countries, and had been sent to prison or to the scaffold for them, or shot in the open street. Turbulent devils with the courage of the devil who had died fighting and cursing, and calling in the same breath on God and their children to avenge them. She was very surprised to see it in this person. She had looked at the person often before, and had always thought it rather weak and inoffensive. Not really fitted to the struggle for existence. Too sensitive and delicate to get the better of the struggle. Far more likely that it would go under, crushed. Had been sorry for it, even nervous about it, felt maternal towards it, and advised it for the sake of its own happiness to keep quiet, not to risk occasions of combat for which it was unequal. But standing there looking on, she felt interested to know what would happen.

The person she knew went round the table and caught hold of the other person's wrist and held her against the door. The other person stared in amazement, both frightened and angry. Again she warned the person she knew, while she stood on the other side of the room looking on. 'Don't hit her, it will be fatal if you do,' she said. She saw that the person with her back to the door and her wrist imprisoned would be cowed for the moment if she was struck, but that she would be unpleasant afterwards, and would do whatever injury she could. Suddenly an extraordinary stream of language poured out of the mouth of the person she knew.

'Don't stand here wasting my time. What have you been doing all these years? Sitting down and making life as unpleasant as you could for everyone. Waiting for what you could get out of it. Haven't you? Do you know what you are? You're nothing better than a scavenger. And where you ought to be, is in a dustbin.'

If she had still not been afraid that the situation might at any moment become more serious by the use of that fist, she could have laughed. All the hate in that voice had only produced a single word of abuse; but had produced it in the mad heat of violence. The other person broke down; probably frightened. She said she had done everything for the best; that this on top of everything was too much. But the person she knew was not impressed by the sight of tears. If anything, they seemed to infuriate her even more. It appeared to her, as an onlooker more or less without bias, though she had of course a leaning towards the side of the person she knew, that the encounter ought to terminate, and she accordingly advised her friend: 'Take her upstairs and make her pack her things.'

Her friend took the advice. Holding the other woman still by the wrist and now with a hand on her shoulder as if she thought she might escape her, they went out.

'I hope you will regret this Miss Burnett,' said Ethel.

Sanderson was standing outside waiting with a car. It was the only defence she had made. She had stopped crying, and it was said in her usual voice which sounded odd with her face swollen with emotion. An object perhaps of pity, for those who felt it. Sanderson said that if they were going to catch that midnight from the junction, they ought to be gone. She did not think it necessary to answer Ethel. She nodded to Sanderson standing there in his driver's coat watching them, and closed the door with Ethel still standing on the step before it. Dimpy was coming out of the study where Lionel was sleeping on an improvised bed.

'They went, Miss. Lady Curvy took Mrs. Mandarin in her car. They were rather annoyed at first. I think they felt it a great nuisance moving out at this time of night. But I told them they could stay at the hotel, and could come and see Miss Barty to-morrow. I think I smoothed matters over.'

'Yes, Dimpy, I'm sure you did, and now?'

THE darkness was soft and spongy, with a certain amount of elasticity in it. If touched, it rebounded gently, comfortable walls of it against which she was leaning. Although she was in darkness and not there when it happened, she remembered seeing Dimpy open the door to someone whom Mr. Davis had sent for, and was for some reason surprised that the person admitted should be a woman. But then it was probably a nurse. Stories of childhood went through her head, and now and then she was back at school. Now she was going into chapel with Zara and Zara was constantly tripping up in her veil behind, and being angry when she did so. She wondered why Zara was wearing such a long veil. They went into the benches, and fat old Father Murray was giving them religious instruction. He always made a great show of language, and after a while one gave up trying to understand what he was trying to say, which he was embroidering with such erroneous ideas of oratory. At last she was astounded to hear him say the simple words: 'Who made you?' to a child in front in the lower school. 'The devil, Father,' said the child at once, and sat down. The whole chapel rose and looked at it, and the child began to cry. Father Murray took no notice of it and was now launching forth on the horrors of Hell, painting the torments of the damned. 'I don't believe it,' she said to Zara, angrily. 'It's extremely wrong of him to talk like this to us, it isn't true.' And now there was the story of the little boy who died in mortal sin, and who, when the priest was preparing to say a mass for the repose of his soul, appeared to him in the sacristy, wreath-ed in flames, telling him it was useless. 'It's very wicked of him to tell them this,' she said again to Zara. But Zara was asleep and holding her veil up under her chin as if it was the sheet and she was in bed.

She woke and pressed the spongy walls around her, fascinated to feel them fall away and rebound. They stirred thoughts of food. Sponge cakes dipped in wine. Bouncing jellies. Coloured creams, layer upon layer. Ambrosial apricots the size of cherries, Chinese. She lay back with some-one's arm round her. She was sitting in a restaurant in Soho with Tim. His arm was round the back of her chair. He was talking about Vienna, where he was going to make his first public appearance next year under Bidaud's management, saying that of course she was coming. She must come; she must be there. The thought of going with him reminded her that she would see Zara, and of course Zara would come to hear Tim play. They would have a reunion.

A very happy, clear feeling. A gentle ecstasy felt with the point of the soul. The soul must be an emanation of the body. Just like it in shape and lineaments, but without the heaviness of the body, the tiresome disabilities of the flesh. She wished to see her soul. There was a long mirror in the room, and she went to it. Stood in front of it. And very slowly she saw her soul emerge out of the flesh. Smiling; more so. A truer edition of her-self. A light, intensely delicate thing. But it was moving from her, she tried to catch it and bring it back; begged it not to go without her, not to leave her. But it was floating above her head; and looking down at herself in the glass she saw that her body was covered with dark blue marks that had settled in patches, here and there. It was very much disfigured. She went closer to the glass and tried to make out her face. It was gone. She was horrified, and wondered what had happened. If she had met with some accident. Had fallen from a height, or had been knocked down in the street.

Very gradually it came to her, although she fought against believing it. As if to allay her horror at the discovery, her soul was standing behind, holding itself out like a coat waiting to receive her, and she slipped into it.

SHE started up from the chesterfield and went into the hall. She stood there trying to remember what had happened. She and Dimpy had made beds together upstairs, and had prepared a room for Mr. Davis when he should want it. Then he had said: 'What about you, Miss? Aren't you going to lie down for a while?' She had said no, but that she would go and sit in the drawing-room for a few minutes, and that was all. She had sat down for a few minutes, or perhaps a few hours, and then the dream about being dead. It was still strong upon her, the memory of the thing she had seen in the glass, so that she was afraid to go back into the drawing-room. She sat down on the stairs. The lights were still on in the hall, and above on the landing; but there was silence all over the house. People all hidden away behind closed doors, discreetly silent. She was grateful to them for remaining there. The thought of seeing anybody was horrible to her. Especially the idea of seeing faces, human faces. If she shut her eyes, she saw thousands looking at her, and every one of them alike. Incredible to think that there was so little variety in the human countenance. She kept her eyes open, and then she only saw the hall. The table with the visiting cards in the tray. The soft strip of carpet down the middle of the polished

floor. The place for hats to hang. Carlos's lead
hanging from a peg; queer to think of Carlos on a
lead. She wondered what the time was. But it did
not seem to be important. She sat with her elbows
on her knees, her chin digging into the palm of one
hand, looking down at her feet. She wondered why
she was wearing black patent leather slippers. It
was years since she had worn such things. She did
not remember possessing any since the days of the
dancing-class at Mexican Gate. Miss Pullar with
short, fluffed-out hair and no chin, and her short,
fussy dress, standing in the middle of the room
while they all walked round her. And her pianist,
a woman in a black silk dress with a long neck and
glasses, constantly turning round while her fingers
still played on. 'Now, take your partners for a
waltz, please, girls,' reminding one of *Invitation
to the waltz*, making one giggle. Hailing Brenda
from over the room: 'Brenda, my dance, you
promised.' Brenda very much in demand, and
knowing it, flushed, coming over the floor to her
arms. Now they went decorously up the room
together. Zara dancing with Di Van Anderman,
Diamonds, they always called her. A tall, conceited
girl, with a good-looking, hard face, so hard
and set that one always felt it must be made of
stone. It had only one expression.

She got up and went into the dining-room,
aware now that she was not walking, but was
directed by some impetus inside her. She sat
down in the alcove off the room at a small table
on which there was an instrument, a toy in some
black metal. She sat staring at it vacantly. It had,
if one looked at it closely, a kind of face. A disc,

and set in the disc a small protruding horn. Another part of it hung by its side on a hook, attached to it by a cord. She remembered having used this toy before. It brought people's voices to one over the distance; it was a line of communication. Riding over space without any trouble, one said quite calmly, without thinking about it, 'Hello—' and was not surprised to hear someone a hundred, two hundred, or even three hundred miles off, return the greeting as if they were sitting beside one. Strange if one had been born into an age where such things had never been heard of, and would have been looked upon with suspicion, as some artifice of the devil perhaps, and the inventor promptly burned. How against anything that had appeared to be supernatural people had always been, and immediately wanted to destroy it. Terrified of the imagination. No magic. Burn the witches. . . . Crude, brutal people who could stand by and watch their fellows hanged, drawn and quartered. Lust. The dark ages. Theirs had been a cruel, lustful god, a god of death. And now, cruelty had gradually become more refined. Hidden, wrapped up, diverted, occasionally breaking out in wars, then going back again; but smouldering underneath. The death-lust still alive, waiting to be able to break out again and destroy something. And since one sets a thief to catch a thief, to go on guard before the death-lust, one must take a sword.

ONE man was playing to a crowded hall, and thousands of unseen people over the world were listening to him. A phrase was called out of an instrument by the beautiful tone of an artist. Then another and another and still another. Until a certain whole was being formed. A fine pattern of music was taking shape in the ether, transmitted and communicated to many minds. The accidents of time and place were conquered. Though was this perhaps altogether an advantage? But who was it she was thinking of? Who was it she wanted? She wanted Tim, and she could not remember his telephone number. It had got lost in her memory in a crowd of events, a lifetime of experiences. Tumbled. Perhaps sitting next door to a forgotten verse in a Shelley lyric, and on the other side an event in very early childhood. The day they took her comforter away. The desperate longing, the despair, the fits of crying for the departed friend. Leaning against the wooden railing of the verandah, the mid-day tropical sun streaming down. Teddy Bear sitting up against the railings in a white flannel collar, a mourner with her over the tragedy. She held him to her, feeling the tears run down over her mouth. 'Oh, my darling, darling, they shan't ever take *you* away.' · But it was Tim's telephone number she wanted. She sat there staring at the toy. But it could not give her the forgotten numerals, and yet the numerals were there. They were there waiting to be picked up. Because the future would contain them they must be somewhere waiting. 'I will remember.' She took hold of the instrument. And as she put her fingers round it, an insistent tingling sound began as if it were answering her. It was those forgotten numerals. They had mustered themselves

U

together and were coming over the ether to meet
her.

There was a blank space in which she was cut
off from everything. Then a murmuring started.
The sound heard in a shell. A bird's eye view of
some ocean washing in a long way off at the end
of the world. A door opened in the shell. The
ocean disappeared. Someone said: 'Thank you.'
to someone else, in a voice very well known. And
she spoke to the voice, which was eagerly saying
her name over the distance. It did not know that
it was speaking to a ghost, and she would not tell
it. For it was such a living voice. Coming from a
race of people who had real feelings, and showed
them. Like a warm wind full of its own enchant-
ment. He said he was coming.

And now she must go upstairs. She was still not
conscious of moving her body, but she knew it was
necessary to go up and make some enquiry. Now
she was standing outside Barty's door, tapping
softly. How long since she had been upstairs, how
long since she had become the mistress of the
house, and what fantastic happenings had taken
place? She was forgetting why they had taken
place, but remembering that it had been necessary
to remove certain things. A figure in a white
surgeon's coat opened the door. When he saw
who it was, he came out on to the landing. They
stood by the windows near Carlos still keeping his
watch. The cuffs were rolled back from the wrists,
giving him a workmanlike air. She liked him
better in his executive capacity. Action often
transformed people. To see people at leisure was
perhaps a test very few could stand. They were

better working: occupied, merging themselves into something constructive.

'Of course, it's early yet to say anything, but I think we shall be able to do something. I think it's just possible with very careful nursing afterwards. Of course, it's always touch and go in these cases. You looked tired, I should have a few hour's sleep.'

He was almost smiling, pleased.

'Then you think there is every hope of Miss Berringer's recovery?'

He became grave immediately, strictly professional. 'I shouldn't say every hope. I should most certainly say there was hope. Hope and hard work. Those things make the world.'

He was smiling again. Something fatherly. An elderly man-of-the-world air. Was he really being sententious about hope and hard work? Did he really think that those things alone made the world, and was it on those foundations only he had built his own career? No, she understood. Partly because he expected it.

'I am so glad. Of course now that *you* are here, one feels one has every hope.'

Lady Curvy or Mrs. Mandarin might have said it. He was most unprofessionally pleased.

'I must confess I never thought earlier in the evening we should do it.'

Still, it was easy for him to confess that after he had changed his mind. She felt for him a sturdy contempt, and went back to the rolled-up cuffs, trying to see again that executive side which had pleased her. Probably in his own line he was one of the highest authorities. But it did not matter.

*U

Flattery meant nothing. One flattered people one disliked, perhaps to hide one's dislike, or because one was sooner rid of them that way. She was grateful to the capacity in his wrists. Beside that which was of most importance, personal feeling about him did not matter.

Going downstairs again, as if she were not moving, but was being propelled by some act of will or purpose in herself, she turned on the light which lit the gate-posts from the hall. A single white star came into being as if by magic, showing the trees near the gate, and across the blackness of the road the light-coloured path leading up the bank to the gate of Combesmere. In the darkness it looked deceptive, exaggerated, only half-seen between the posts, making one think of a lonely mountain path at night.

A long way off, someone was knocking at a door; knocking insistently. Light, hollow taps. As if fearing to disturb the inmates of the house at such a late hour, but finding it an imperative necessity to get in. A young man, coming home late, had forgotten his latchkey. A cursed nuisance. He would have to wake his landlady. What the Hell did he go and do that for? Must have left it on the table this morning, waking up tired after last night's lateness; the worst of living the other side of the town. And then he nearly missed the last train to-night. Would have done, if it hadn't been for that old man who had seen him running. Mrs. Gore would be furious. Perhaps turn him out. But then you couldn't expect a man not to forget

his latchkey sometimes. He yawned on the doorstep. Stared down through the area. A cat was
prowling around, sniffing at the dustbins put out
overnight. Marvellous, Lois had been to-night.
She was lovely. It wasn't just his imagination
because he was in love. That lilt in her voice, the
way she held her head. Mrs. Gore was opening
the door a little. Then a little more. She was in a
flannel dressing-gown, her face reminding him
more than ever of a white distempered wall
through which the damp had penetrated. 'Oh,
it's *you*, Mr. Herbert!' pronounced as if it had
a double H; she was so particular always over those
aspirates—'What a *fright* you gave me!' In at
last. The misery of many stairs. Stumbling up,
nearly falling over a piece of torn oilcloth. The
furnished room at the top. The elderly look on the
lace curtains. 'And oh, curse it—' he had run out
of soap, and had forgotten to get any more.

A long way off, someone was knocking at a
door. She stirred, vaguely hurt. Discomforted by
that hammer that was beating, beating, on her
brain, trying to split up her brain. It was keeping
a rhythm too. One, one two. One, one two. But
she had forgotten—she had no brain now. She
had left it in her body. But still the nerves seemed
to be able to feel. Perhaps it was like that after
death for a little while. One still felt with one's
nerves, although they weren't there. She was no
longer afraid of her body lying in the room, somewhere on the floor. Life had become purely
abstract. It belonged to higher mathematics. And
she had never been able to understand mathematics. They had always frightened her. But nothing

now frightened her, because she had shed her body.

It was the physical that had always been so terrified of that unknown quantity, x. The physical that had always rebelled against x, refused to multiply it, and did not see why there should be any x at all. What business had x to come into perfectly harmless sums? It had been done to frighten one. Whenever she had seen that x appearing on the blackboard, she had been frightened and had withdrawn into herself. And those ridiculous propositions in Euclid. What were they about when one got to the end of them? Nothing at all. No doubt one could prove anything by pure reason, irrespective of its being right or wrong. A vicious circle. First you accumulated matter. Then you worked it out till it became less and less. Then there was nothing. The triumph of pure reason seemed to be that matter could be reduced to nothing at all. Yet matter triumphantly winked behind it, existed and flirted with it for all that. 'But dearest, it's quite easy,' said Zara, trying to explain. 'Then what do they want to make it so difficult for?' 'It's a mental exercise.' 'It's no use giving me those kind of mental exercises. My brain works slowly, I can't understand.' And she had laid her head down on the desk and cried because at fourteen she could not understand Euclid. 'Never mind, my poet,' said Zara, laughing, 'you will understand one day.' And now did she understand? She, who had herself become a mathematical abstraction? She was x, the unknown quantity, the horrid little figure that had sat on the blackboard and competed in unjust and elusive contest with other figures who had real values and those values only.

All the time, someone was knocking at a door. But the landlady had let the young man in. He had gone to bed. She had seen him pull the blind over the window. Now it became harder, more decisive, no longer afraid of waking the house, but determined to get in. She could hear the knocks saying: 'Open the door, open the door,' as they fell, one after another. The hammers were beating against lives wires in her, pulling them out, hurting them. She would have to go and open the door. But how could she, a mathematical abstraction, get up and open the door? By an act of volition.

She drew back something half-way up a wall. And the door opened. Her head was still full of the young man waiting outside and looking at the dustbins. A fresh, simple young man with a pink and white complexion. So that she was not prepared to see someone who did not in the least resemble him. She recognized the person, but had forgotten his name. But she remembered that she must not tell him that she was no longer a living person, because he was still living himself, even though he had about him an air of timelessness resembling a spirit. One could imagine him growing old and never changing.

'My dear, I thought I was never going to get in. Have you been asleep?'

'I don't know.'

He was in the hall, unfastening his coat. 'I knew it was all right, directly I saw the light at the gate. I knew if you'd remembered to put it on, she was all right.'

'Yes. She's all right. How did you come?' She must keep up this pretence of being a living person.

'Bernard borrowed somebody's car for me. My dear, is there somewhere where the man can sleep?'

She was once more the mistress of the house, having unlimited room at her disposal.

'There's probably a room upstairs. Ask him to come in.'

Now he was coming forward; perhaps going to touch her. And she drew back because, fond as she was of him, not even he must touch her soul. It was a thing no one must do.

'Don't touch me, Tim.'

'I'm not going to my dear; but you look very tired. I think you ought to lie down.'

'I'm not tired. I'm dead.'

He might as well know. He would have to know soon. He seemed to refuse to take it from her.

'It's the same thing, sometimes.'

She was comparing this personality in repose to the other upstairs, thinking that it would always stand the test. One did not need to see it performing to know what it could do. He was smiling at her.

'You don't really think you are dead?'

'I don't feel alive. I don't want to be touched. It hurts. Everything hurts. When you knocked it hurt horribly.'

'I'm so sorry, but I had to get in. You will trust me not to hurt you. You'll give me your hand.'

He held his hand out over the short distance between them, the right hand whose fingers she

had so often seen on the violin bow. Fingers she
had always thought strange for an executive artist.
But now because she was seeing with her mind,
she saw their exact moulding, the slight broaden-
ing towards the end, so slight that it was hardly
perceptible. He was arguing with her, gently, as
one might with a child.

'My knocking on the door hurt you. You're
afraid to let me touch you because you think it will
hurt. And yet you think you're dead.'

'It's my mind that feels hurt.'

'But your mind is in your body. In your head.'

Looking at her with head slightly bent, the hair
a little strayed from its parting where the wind had
blown it in an open car rushing down through the
night. She knew what he was doing. That critical
half-humorous and yet significant expression; he
was trying to make her believe she was not dead.
If necessary he would force her back into her
body. He was going to establish a contact between
her and himself. And she didn't want it. She
didn't want to go back into her body. She wanted
to go back to the place where she had come from
when she had heard him knocking. He was again
arguing with her about it. Gently; he would never
force anything.

'Let me touch you, or give me your hand.' The
hand was stretched out, waiting for hers. She must
make one more act of will, the last. She had already
willed her soul out of her body, and had recognized
in it a mathematical abstraction that had sat for years
upon the blackboard in the shape of a letter called
x, a hybrid figure. It was painful, but she did it
because she was too much weakened by a heavy

experience which hung behind her to make any resistance. The blood always seemed to flow warmly in his veins, his hands were never cold like hers in winter. He was drawing her nearer and nearer very slowly, forcing her back into the consciousness of her body. But there was no feeling or hurt. Some merciful anæsthetic had come over her. The pressure stopped. She was swung up into space, and a rocking movement began, sweeping her back over years to being a little girl swinging in a hammock, gently backwards and forwards in the white heat of the afternoon, and singing to a long green lizard, listening on the edge of the verandah. Everyone else was resting upstairs, while the sun blazed down, making the railings of the verandah feel as if they were burning, and even the trees had a glassy look. After a time, lying in the hammock always made her feel sick. She used to stay there just to see how long long she could bear it, singing to the lizard, who would listen by the half-hour, waiting there motionless, as if hypnotized.

Something lit up inside her brain, and she remembered over a whole range of experience. She had attempted to do something very difficult. She had willed something almost impossible to happen, and in the act had died. Now she was being forced back into her life. She was lying back in the spongy, comfortable darkness, back on a stratum of things half real, yet not real enough to matter too much. Somebody was asking questions; 'Is there a moon?'

'A moon? It's half-past five, my dear. The sun's rising.'

So the sun was rising over the downs, not very far away. Shutters were being opened. Who had shut them? She remembered she had shut them herself overnight. The air was coming in. Tim was pulling down the light-coloured blinds over the windows to prevent too much of the pale early light getting in. Objects in the room seemed to be trying to creep back into a darkness which had been taken from them, as if they resented the light. Full, thick fragrance of flowers was coming in through the windows. It was so strong that it seemed as if there must be thousands of flowers in the room. And she looked. And there were thousands. All white and heavy and fully blown, jostling each other. The sky was thick with them. They were like leaves being blown over a roof from a high tree in an autumn gale. They were all talking, shouting, calling to each other to get out of the way. At last it subsided. They fell to the ground with heavy and despairing noises, only their scent was left in the air. She knew it was a dream.

She woke up for a minute; felt herself lying on the chesterfield with cushions under her head, and something light over her, and heard Tim go out and shut the door after him. Then it was suddenly extremely quiet. So quiet that she felt that she must be outside all living noises. She began to walk down a road, a road she knew very well. High, flowering chestnuts stood on either side, and the day was full of an intensely bright light. She was very happy because she was going back to a place that she loved. Now she was walking beside old brown palings, touching them affectionately as she went. A steady, rounded happiness was running lightly in her which nothing could disturb. And so she caressed the palings with her hand, feeling love for them, as one does sometimes for things and persons who bear some relation to a person one loves. Behind the brown palings someone was waiting for her whom she had been expecting to meet for a long time. There was no mistake about it this time. They really were there.